George's Terms

Z is for Zombie Book 1

Catt Dahman

1
GEORGE

It stood to reason that after getting the good news that his three best friends were alive, were immune to the Red, and for safety moving to his home, he would run into some bad news. That was how the odds worked and why he wasn't a gambler. Anything good was expected to be balanced by a few bad things; take life with ups and downs.

"Don't say no…it's the end of the world," he hummed Skeeter Davis's song as he finished up in the kitchen, again missing having a woman around to do the more feminine jobs, but his wife had died a long time back. He wasn't even sure those were the correct words to the song, so he hummed through most of it. It sure as shit beat most of the music they played nowadays. At seventy, he was just too old for these big changes in the world.

Nothing about this had been positive; there had been one more bit of bad news after another since the virus, nicknamed Red, had swept the globe like some cruel hand of a death-god, wiping out towns, families, and maybe parts of the world with people suffering. Their life's fluids poured from every orifice, leaving them to suffer in fear and misery. Death was never pretty, but thankfully, most people never had to see the ugly parts and this Red virus had left no dignity.

George had quickly decided that even if his friends were ill, he'd nurse them as best he could and then make bigger decisions as events unfolded. No one was going to tell him to abandon his humanity and turn a cold cheek to people he cared for. He had done a lot of thinking.

His friends had come to his house because he had supplies that he kept as if he were an end-of-the-world survivalist. None of them had wives that were alive, and any children that they had, were not living in town. It had given him company, a peace of mind and comfort to have his three best friends with him. His home was in a cookie-cutter neighborhood with a neatly trimmed yard, rose bushes, and trees, all kept to HOA standards. The house had far more room than he and his wife had needed, but had been great for entertaining friends and family.

"Where you off to, George?"

Stepping onto his porch, head cocked sideways, he glanced at one of his oldest friends, Thurman, a still-strong, black man that he had hunted with the better part of his young and middle years, until he developed a distaste for the so-called sport. "I heard something. Did anyone else hear a scream?"

Benny crowded onto the porch with his border collie, Dallas. "You say you heard something?"

Dallas growled.

"Yes," Thurman and George responded, as they had a million times over when Benny had repeated things.

He straightened, "You want I should get the guns?"

"Not yet," George warned him. Since the news reports had begun, Benny had wanted to go into a fight with guns blazing. You can take the boy out of the Blue...

The high-pitched wail let loose again, sounding full of sorrow, fear, and raw anger. "That sounds like a kid," Thurman mumbled, taking a few steps down the porch.

"Yeah." Benny agreed.

From the backyard across the street, they heard screaming and saw people running frantically as they came into view from the side yard. A woman carried a little girl and set her down behind her as she faced towards whoever was chasing her.

"You don't think?" Benny asked.

"Maybe. You know what the news has been saying,"George told him.

Benny made a 'plltt' sound. "Those newscasters are crazy and panicking like everyone else, the hospitals are turning sick people away at gun point, this country is going to hell in a hand basket. Healthcare has gone to hell."

"When they're full, they're full," George said, "and don't go on about FEMA trailers again, or I'm liable to scream. There isn't enough medical staff to go around. We have way too many sick this time, and it isn't in one place."

"Not enough medical," Benny 'plltted' again.

"Now, Benny, they say that about half of the population is coming down with the Red; that's a lot of people," Thurman said. Maybe it was more than fifty percent of the population getting ill, maybe a quarter, but it was a lot.

George had spoken to his children and grandchildren, and they were sick. In a different world, and if he were another person, he could retain hope that they'd recover and he'd see them again. The hard reality was that Red was taking casualties, and if you got lucky, then okay, and if you didn't, well; it sucked, but it was the hand you were dealt. Stores were closing; hospitals were turning away people, the military was vanishing from the streets, and police and firemen were leaving their post. More and more businesses and services closed, the ill were too bad off to work, and just crawled into their beds where they stayed, only to get up again to struggle to the bathroom. Even truck drivers and rail service workers were unable to get food and supplies to the stores.

"Well, I believe it's bad and that many are catching it, sure, but I just don't think we're gonna get the rioting that Europe and other places have. We know better than to act that way."

"Los Angeles knows better? Detroit does?" George scoffed.

"Give me a hungry group of mamas with kids to feed, and I'll show you a riot beginning right fast," Thurman added.

Benny shook his head, "Well, I don't see how's we're going to start biting each other even if that thing is like rabies."

"They said it's like mad cow."

"Yeah, and you don't see cows biting each other," Benny pointed out. "That makes the brain stupid. Maybe rabies, but then I didn't see anyone foaming at the mouth."

They still watched the woman and child.

The woman shouted at whoever was coming after her to stay away. An older couple, a man in pajamas, and a teen boy, wearing his boxer shorts, covered in blood, stalked into his view. The older woman was covered with dark brown stains below the waist and down her legs. The older man was in jeans and a shirt. The woman, still in front of the little girl, picked up an ornamental rock and lobbed it, hitting the man solidly in the head.

"Ouch," Thurman said.

The man rocked back a bit from the hit but continued forward.

"You gotta be kidding; that was a Nolan Ryan pitch." Benny slapped the porch railing. "That gal can throw."

"They may not be foaming, but they look mad to me," George stated. "They did on television, too. Looked and acted like mad dogs."

"Hey, what's going on over there?" Thurman was in the yard now, watching, with his big voice like thunder in the quiet of the neighborhood.

All faces, long, turned to him. The little girl, in a light blue dress and hair platted in a long braid down her back, glanced at the men and pulled at the woman's arm, telling her to come on.

George felt familiar adrenaline wash over him; he was way too old for this, his joints aching on a good day; he was long-retired from the force, and he just wanted to be left alone with his friends to see how the new world would change. But he didn't hesitate. He stepped out to meet the woman and girl.

She would be pretty, if not for the exhaustion on her worn face. She had dark smudges beneath her eyes, blonde hair, and big blue eyes full of worry and fear, and a tall, trim figure. The little girl had to be her daughter, about five, cute face that had been contorted with terror.

" My daddy is trying to bite us," she wailed.

"Bite you?" Benny glared, "Why that's unacceptable."

"Master of understatements." George chuckled a little.

"So are Mr. and Mrs. Perez, and they were so *nice*." The girl wailed harder. That couple had just moved in.

"Get up on the porch." George motioned to them. "What are your names?"

"Gina. This is Katie." The woman did as he asked, watching behind   her.

"Why is Daddy playing like this? It isn't funny." Katie said, stomping her little foot in anger. She knew her father wasn't playing, but accepting that this was real was more than she could handle right then.

"Now, Gina…you and your Katie stay back there, and if they get past us, you get into the house and lock the door. Tink is in there, and he'll take care of you. I'm George, and those two are Thurman and Benny."

George was a bit flummoxed with having to introduce himself, but neighbors didn't get to know each other as in times past. They had lived there for months, maybe a full year and the Perez couple…all Perez had done was to give a nod here and there, a wave, but people didn't know their neighbors now. And this to George, was the real downfall of the country.

The four bloodied people were crossing the street, shambling closer.

"What the hell?" Thurman took a step back while brushing his nose with one hand. "Is that them stinking?"

"Good Lord, they smell terrible."

Their eyes were full of fury.

George moved over to where he and Tink had removed a small, dead, tree the day before, unfortunately putting away the tools, but leaving a few good-sized limbs. He wished for an axe and chainsaw, but wish in one hand and spit in the other, and see which one fills the fastest. He took one branch, handing Thurman a second one and said, "Benny, you may wanna take the ladies in now."

"You want to get off this property now." Thurman warned the approaching man who didn't seem to take notice. Up close, the smell was eye watering. The man's pajama top was red with dried blood, his legs inside the pants appeared to be caked with diarrhea, and his feet were filthy. He drooled and gurgled at them.

The older man was in worse shape: deep scratches along both arms, a huge chunk that looked bitten from his neck, and most of his lower jaw torn off in blackish, bloody tatters. He looked as if he should be dead from those wounds.

Standing by the older man, the woman in pajamas and barefoot, was covered in blood and thick, partially dried greenish feces; her mouth and face were awash in fresher blood.

The teen boy moaned, extending an arm with shattered bone jutting from the wrist; his knees looked like raw hamburger that leaked yellow, thick pus.

"Jeff, stop it," Gina demanded of the man. He didn't look at her, but moaned, eyes roaming vacantly and slightly clouded.

"Mommy, make him stop playing." Katie sobbed.

"Get gone." Thurman gestured with the limb, moving closer.

Jeff, the husband, lunged at Thurman, whose reflexes were just a little slowed by age. Mr. Perez had angled behind, snarling angrily and reaching for Thurman, and as the man sidestepped that threat, Mrs. Perez tripped him. He went down on his backside, painfully and with a grunt.

"Hey." George jabbed his branch at Jeff's midsection. Then, he stabbed at him harder.

The man hissed and moaned, and spit flew as he tried to get around the branch poking at him, to reach George.

Thurman tossed the old woman back but was struggling with the man, who snapped at his throat like a wild animal.

In a flash of black and white, Dallas bolted at the man, growling and snarling, knocking him to his back and biting at his arms.

"He's trying to bite my dog," Benny was yelling, moving on aching joints from debilitating arthritis. "Get away from my dog."

George was so distracted by Benny and Thurman's struggles that the teen boy almost got him. Going to his instinct and training, George didn't think, but pulled the limb back and let it swing against the boy's arm, almost enjoying the sound of crunching bones. He wished for his Glock in a spiteful moment.

Thurman got a good swing, and then before he could slam a second one, the branch was yanked away by Mr. Perez, as he and his wife fought over their spoils.

Benny piled in, yanking back on Mrs. Perez's arms and body, punching wildly but solidly as she struggled to pin him with her weight and get to his arms or throat.

Dallas snapped and bit, maybe the only reason Thurman was unharmed so far.

Jeff was back up and taking grabs for them and the other men, but also had re-focused on Gina and Katie.

Gina screamed.

George swung again at the boy coming after him, this time making contact with the head. "Go down," he yelled, swinging.

"Hey, you bitch." Neal 'Tink' Tinkersley slammed out of the house and strode over the porch, leveling and pulling the trigger to his Remington 700 at Mr. Perez. The back of the man's head flew off in a mess of blood and brain pulp.

As the teen boy shot up to his feet again, threatening George, Tink shot twice, taking out his throat, almost decapitating him, and taking off the side of his head in a crimson spray.

George went over and slammed his tree branch at Mrs. Perez's head.

"What're they doing trying to bite people?" Tink grumbled.

"And trying to bite Dallas," Benny added angrily.

As they wondered what to do next, Thurman, George, and Benny numbly stared at the woman on the ground as George popped her periodically in the head to keep her down.

Dallas barked at the man, Jeff, who was making his way closer to the porch, somewhat distracted by the dog.

Glancing behind to be sure the woman and girl were still in the house, Tink scowled.

Benny retrieved the dropped limb and whacked Jeff across the back; he didn't even moan but turned angrily, reaching for Benny. Benny kept solidly swatting at the man's arms; breaking bones and tearing skin, but the man didn't stop coming after Benny, just as Mrs. Perez, who was still on the ground, never stopped trying to get up. Her jaws, arms, and head were dented, broken, oozing, shredded, and her face was a messy, red pudding of flesh.

George, sickened by the violence, was also angry.

"Are y'all about done playing with the zombies?" Thurman questioned, brushing off his pants.

"Thurman...what are you callin' 'em zombies for? They're sick people."

"Yeah, they always said those hopped-up drug freaks were sick, too, and they sure tried to kill us same as Viet Cong. Nuts tried to bite Bennie's dog and me."

"And they stink."

Winded, Benny paused in hitting Jeff; the smelly man lunged at Benny like lightning, causing Benny to stumble and go down on his backside.

All four realized that they had luck, training, each other, and a gun on their side, plus Dallas, and if not for even one of these, they might not have survived. It was sobering. But they were old men who had no business fighting hand-to-hand like this unless they wanted to break their bones or have heart attacks.

Tink shot the man once in the head. "Okay, now we are way too old to be knocked on the ground...broken hips are no playing matter, and with the hospital not taking sick people..."

"Maybe they take broken hips." Thurman, cursing quietly, helped his friend to his feet again. "George?"

"They may not take broken hips."

"No...what do you think about these things?"

"They don't feel pain...it's like they said on the news in Europe, Zombies." Benny nodded to himself. He had just said minutes ago that he didn't believe the news, but seeing it now, made him a believer.

"They're callin' 'em zeds, though." George stepped back, motioning to Tink to finish up, which the man was happy to do. Benny was tired of smelling the stinky people and shooting. "They wouldn't stop coming," George said it for himself, for his friends, but mostly for Tink who had just shot four people.

Patting the big man on the shoulders, he looked at his normally well-manicured lawn in disgust. "Let's catch our breath, calm down, and meet our visitors, and then we can get this cleaned up." Thurman and Bennie went inside the house.

Tink surveyed the area. "No movement."

"I still bet some people were peeking out at the gunfire."

"If they are able to. I think most got sick, 'cept for those of us soaked in Agent Orange."

"And we're too old to do much, except we sure as hell fought a good battle here. Good job, Tink."

"You, too, Brother." They had been best friends and then partners on the police force for almost sixty years. Benny and Thurman had been partners, and all four were close buddies, each having served sometime in the Vietnam Conflict, their Agent Orange discussions and theories were deep.

Inside, the little girl, Katie, was hugged up on the sofa with Dallas, who shared a doggie laugh: he wasn't being shooed off the furniture and could nap happily with the child.

George gave him a mock dirty look.

Bennie brought in hot tea, one of the few men who could pour tea into a cup, and still be masculine. He added honey for Katie and urged her to sip, nodding at her mother. Both were in shock.

"Can you tell us what happened? If you feel like it?"

George had thought to send the girl and dog to the other room, but Katie screwed up her face miserably and sighed, "It was terrible. Which one are you?"

"I'm George, Honey."

"Daddy was all sick...it was stinky." She cried again, sucking her thumb and hiding her face against her mother's shoulder. "I want Daddy fixed."

Big Tink grinned at Gina. "Let me rock her." Tink was a massive man, six and a half feet tall, still with much of his muscle tone, big boned, and heavy, but children never feared him; he was a giant teddy bear to them. He took Katie and she allowed him to rock her as he sang softly.

"He has...had Red," Gina said softly. The virus had some technical mumbo-jumbo name, but no one ever said its name, just called it Red for all the bleeding it produced.

"They said on TV that almost everyone does," Thurman said. He was a dark-skinned black man with warm amber eyes and his hair and light beard were white. Everyone found him confusing since he didn't understand racial lines; for whatever reason, he simply didn't get the concept of prejudice and always just shrugged and claimed, "Folks don't know better" or "Weren't raised right." If someone showed judgment, Thurman would not allow it to be based on learned racial reasons, but on just having a bad soul.

George told Gina that they had a theory about Agent Orange, and, if they were right, it had left a bunch of old war vets that were once a strong generation, unable to reproduce. "And if you notice, lots of times, siblings or a parent and child are immune. A genetic thing, maybe."

"I heard that, too," Gina said. "Jeff got worse and went into a coma or a deep sleep maybe…"

"And you can't get to a hospital."

"No hospitals," Benny agreed. He came across as the scatterbrain of the foursome but was, in fact, the brightest of the group, the most widely read, and had a surprisingly high IQ. Also the smallest, he was the most inclined to aches and pains of advanced age. "I'm Bennie," he reminded Katie.

"I had the back door open, airing out the smell…and went in…Oh, my, God, Jeff attacked me, came after me. If he hadn't tripped over the bedding…" She glanced at Katie to get her meaning across.

"Daddy was playing monster," Katie said, "but it wasn't funny then, was it, Mommy, not a bit funny?"

"Not at all." Gina wiped her nose on her sleeve and sighed. "I grabbed Katie and the keys, but Mr. and Mrs. Perez were blocking the door. We circled the rooms and got out, but that boy was there. We just ran." She again thanked the four men for saving their lives. She looked exhausted.

"The boy and the man were attacked and…turned…whatever you call it, infected, I guess. They take a while with Red, but they turn fast…get infected, if bitten." Tink looked the bodies over. He didn't say more with Katie listening.

Gina winced.

"Where's daddy?"

"Katie, love," Gina was helpless to continue. She wept.

"Your Mama can explain it better to you later, but he's gone now; he went on to another place and is at peace," Thurman said.

"Heaven?"

"I 'spect so."

"Okay." Katie took a deep breath after hugging her mother and laid her head on Dallas.

Tink, George, and Thurman went out to pull the bodies over to the next yard where they covered them with a tarp. For them, digging graves was almost more than they could handle; the smell was vile.

Benny arranged things upstairs and down so Gina and her daughter would have a safer place to sleep.

After washing up, Gina and the men worked on securing the house. Storm shutters had been installed since George was a bit of a survivalist. Until that moment, seeing those things chasing the pair hadn't seemed real; it had been like some never-ending movie on the television.

"It's real," George said to Thurman.

"Seems so. I was hopin' it wasn't…no cure, people turning into those things…they've known a while we had no hope…that's why it was easy to close hospitals and shelters…or to shoot looters and all….'cause they knew we weren't gonna make it. Half the country is sick."

"Some of us will."

"It's looking bad, G."

"Yep. And ya know this was like the movies, but those weren't dead people coming at us. Kind of liked 'em though."

"You're right. I never watched those movies though. They were alive, kind of… but messed up. They didn't feel pain and were like…"

"Alive, but only sort of. Half alive," Thurman said.

"That's worse and better, I think. I can see why they said they were sick, but I also see why they called 'em zombies."

"Zeds."

George chuckled. "Too new-fangled for me. Monsters."

He and Thurman sat down on the porch, watching for movement, knowing the smell outside would soon go foul.

Benny came out, silently closing the door. "We have a problem."

"Besides the zombies attacking us today?"

"Besides that."

"Lay it on us; what's wrong now?"

"Gina showed me under her sleeve; she's been bitten."

George ran his fingers through what remained of his hair, sighing. That was a big problem.

2
HOSPITAL

In another time, news would have been slow with a lack of collective knowledge about the virus that swept the world; however, the Internet was a modern wealth of information. Like lightning, savvy teens and nerds alike have viral videos and Face Book pages up with not only theories, but also trendy terms and helpful nicknames for the ill. The Red Zed page was swamped by 'likes.'

An infected was called a zed, short for the z in zombie. Because of the nature of the illness, the one who went through the stages would almost always bleed out and be called a red zed. Later, the ones dispatched were dead zeds, and those decapitated were zed heads. A friend who succumbed was Fred Zed. One who attacked or was in the midst of an attack and cannibalized was a fed zed. A person in the medical field in uniform and sick, was a med zed.

It was very creative.

Beginning in Asia, the infection was reported to be a hemorrhagic virus, a type of Lyssa virus that mated with another Lyssa virus which may or may not have joined a prion, in other words, bleeding meets rabies meets mad cow. What they knew was that people contracted hemorrhagic symptoms and bled viciously, and then suffered a coma-sleep-like state while the viruses mutated.

In the third stage, the patient awakened with rabies-like symptoms, anger, and violence. The brain showed holes like mad cow disease, but was also functioning to support the anger and the attacks on others in order to transmit the virus, and to show the lack of pain and recognition of friends and family. It seemed to wipe away everything but the most basic of life's functions, and the need to reproduce the virus. Technically, the resurrected victims were alive, but were left as puppets to the mutated virus.

All anyone knew was from the Internet and news reporters, and mostly, the reporters had only rumors and reports from other places, but, yes, a vaccination was in the works. Maybe. Possibly. They doubted anything would be available soon if all those things had indeed joined to become one super virus.

No one knew where the virus had come from, but everyone whispered about a terror attack.

The virus began with swollen, painful joints that locked up, tiredness, fever, and headaches; then, the bad stuff started with stiffness in the face and jaw, drooling, diarrhea, vomiting blood and nose bleeds, anger and violence, frenzy, and finally a coma. The hospitals, with military help, had set up emergency stations for all of the ill, clearing the hospital buildings of all usual illnesses; all of the victims of the virus had the same symptoms, had to be cared for, and then had to be isolated.

But the medical staff was over-whelmed and was overcome with so many patients that the doors had to be closed to the infected, who had to be guarded by the few military that were healthy. Everyone had been told to stay home by the order of martial law. It was already brutal. The only thing that kept the remaining military from being over-run was that most were simply too sick to leave their beds, much less their homes.

It was devastating as more had succumbed, but the worst part was laying in wait in the brains of the victims. After lying in a coma, the patients woke, angry and violent, alive, but no longer in control of themselves, and they had attacked others, biting, clawing, and even eating parts of their victims with an insatiable hunger. Or so the reporters claimed that the victims did this across the ocean.

Those who had been immune to Red as an air-born virus, had not been immune to the deadly saliva that had dripped from the mouths of the attackers. The viruses, with their prion hitchhiker, had entered the bloodstream and turned the new host into a shambling, frenzied monster, quickly. Hence, the terms: "zed or zombie."

Eyes glued to the television or computer screen, people watched as North Americans had begun falling ill; in Atlanta, Tampa, New York, Los Angeles, Seattle, Houston, Dallas, and everywhere in between. It was in the air. Within forty-eight hours, most of the US population was in some stage of the illness.

Reports said the first victims of the plague were out of their comas and attacking people. The military was under orders to shoot.

Beth watched the television in the cafeteria, seeing people biting, taking down others, eating them, and armed soldiers killing them with shots to the brain and heart. The screen was filled with screams, panicking reporters, images from nightmares of raging, uncontrolled fires, massive car pile-ups, carnage on the streets, looting, and terror. She, like everyone else that was watching, stared at the screen in disbelief.

It was the way he had turned his head, pulled down his yellow-tinted Hank Williams, Junior, glasses to watch something behind her that had forced Beth to turn around against her will.

Behind her was a young, black man, clad in shapeless, white pants that billowed around his legs, his feet and chest were bare. In one hand, he held a big bottle of beer wrapped in a wrinkled, brown paper bag; he took a drink from the bottle, grinned at people in the cafeteria, and then vanished around a corner, giggling to himself.

The man in the yellow glasses was left to mumble to another man close by. On his head was a large black cowboy hat; his belly hung over a belt that had "Roy" stamped on it; his jeans were too tight, his boots too pointed, and his mouth underneath the droopy mustache, cruel looking. He kept looking everyone over, commenting to himself or to the other man. Maybe to both.

Beth was tired, she had never been more tired, and wanted to lie down and sleep. Instead of just curling up and hiding in her apartment, she went to the hospital to donate her blood, but then couldn't leave. She found herself with scores of others who were also donating their blood, answering questions about their immune system, being examined, being punctured by needles, and then being told they had to remain as no one was allowed on the streets. They didn't know what else to do.

After a while, there were fewer technicians and doctors to do research, fewer military, no one really keeping the order, but a lot of people had stayed at the hospital willingly, the one place where there had been plenty of living and awake people. No one had wanted to be alone.

Rumors had it that patients in the makeshift hospitals were either still in the first stage of the disease, bleeding from all of their orifices, or in comas.

The news from Great Britain was that the ill were awake, angry, in a frenzy, and attacking everyone they could find. The news from Europe was that the people were being attacked by their own residents, while Africa, the Asian countries, the South American countries, and the Middle East, were completely overrun by what the media had called zeds. The disease hit America after most of the other continents had been hit.

Beth wasn't positive whether that was true or not. She was scared that people she knew would get up to wander the streets, hungrily. It was a nightmare that she couldn't stand to think about.

The hospital had been cleared of most Red patients and was now being used by the few doctors and nurses who had been left to do research. Schools and other public buildings still, supposedly, were being used for the ill.

For the first time in history, there wasn't a positive message being given out, or hopeful promises, and no real instructions. There was only martial law. Everyone was told to stay at home, to isolate or avoid the infected, to barricade the house, and to prepare to defend their home, property, and self.

It was pretty hopeless.

Beth smiled weakly as Kimball came over to join her at her table. He was an intelligent, tall, long legged man with reddish-brown hair, and ocean blue eyes. In the absence of her brother, Kim was a real find, and it was to him she confided her concerns and the desperation she felt. He and everyone else there felt the same. They walked around, drank coffee, and stared at the television.

"Heard anything?"

"No, you?" she asked. "I'm watching the reports. There are a lot fewer people left to report now."

"I heard some rumors. Someone said that the US military was considering retaliation."

"Is there even enough military to fight?"

"I think they mean big weapons."

Beth shivered. "The people who were sick…do you think that they died? Or do you believe the rumor that they have become zombies?"

"Zombies. That sounds pretty stupid."

"Zeds."

"No, I know that they're calling them zeds, but I'm saying the whole idea sounds stupid. It's impossible."

"Technically, they are dead, so they aren't zombies, but the disease makes them go crazy." Beth leaned forward, "I heard it's like rabies, the mad cow disease, and something else, all mixed up together."

"Sounds right that some scientist cooked this up in a lab, and someone else used it for terrorism. That's why they're talking about using massive weapons."

"Against whom?"

"I'm sure we're blaming it on the Middle East or some other country across the water. I think what's left of our government is just pissed off and wants to do something," Kimball said.

The large cafeteria in the hospital, along with some offices, long hallways, the generator, the morgue, the pharmacy, supply vaults, exam rooms, the radiology department, and several lobbies, were located in the basement, and that's where most of the people spent their time. Even one of the lobbies had been set up with cots as a place for all of them to sleep.

"New face," Kim said.

Beth looked up and followed his gaze. "No, that's the guy I told you about… one of the military guys assigned here." She had spoken to the man, Bryan, before; he was smart, interesting, and deadly; it was like being caught in an electrical storm, exciting and edgy.

Brian saw Beth and began to walk over. He was dressed in a Marine Corps combat uniform with an M4 slung on his back, his M9 on his hip.

"He's coming over. You want me to get rid of him?" Kim offered.

"So he can kill you right here?"

Kim laughed.

Bryan walked over and lit a cigarette. When he saw the questioning look on their faces, he shrugged. "I think the rules have changed and we can smoke in a hospital now. No one cares. I saw a fellow in the elevator drinking beer from a quart bottle."

"Yeah, I saw him, too. Things are changing real fast."

They all watched as a female doctor, her clothing stained and rumpled, grabbed a cup of coffee and hurried out of the cafeteria, hardly glancing around as she left.

Sally, the youngest doctor on staff, was frequently told she looked too young to be a doctor. Normally, she had to turn down dates, but right now, she doubted if any man would look at her. Her hair was a rat's nest pulled up into a ponytail, left over mascara was smudged beneath her eyes, and her armpits were sweat- stained; she felt filthy. Drinking hot black coffee, she hurried down the hallway, back to a new patient.

Technically, the medical staff wasn't taking any more patients infected with Red, but this one was the last to come in. Here at the hospital, they were operating with a skeleton crew, and Sally was one of the few doctors available.

A patient, named Jana, had come in with the usual symptoms, swollen and painful joints, high fever, and a headache. Jana should have been sent home like the rest of the people demanding medical treatment, but because she also had a rash, she was admitted. It was something that a nurse had noted and referred to Sally.

Sally went into Jana's room, set her coffee down, and quickly read the chart. Although the diarrhea had almost stopped, Jana still complained of stomach pain and intestinal cramping, her nose had been packed with gauze that leaked blood down to her upper lip, and a kidney-shaped bowl full of bloody vomit sat nearby. Her fever was still high, her blood pressure was low, and the diaper-like garment that they had put on her was full of blood. She moaned; saliva was dripping from her tense jaws. Sally had been trained to handle anything without emotion, but she felt a wave of pity and disgust.

She made a note to get Jana another blanket and set up a new IV bag. The rash had vanished, and Sally decided that this was something else, not related to the disease. According to the CDC, Sally needed to send her home, but the woman wasn't in any condition to walk, and Sally didn't know how she would get her home anyway.

To be honest, when Sally had been assigned to stay at the hospital, she was curious to see how the disease had worked. All the people who had come in to donate blood, be tested to see why they had been immune, should have been sent home by now, but Sally said they could stay, had cots brought in, and had made sure they were fed for free. They could still take quite a few more for shelter.

And the CDC was no longer in contact with anyone.

Millions, with family or alone, were sick all over the world, bleeding and pouring bodily fluids. In a few hours, those same people would be violent, intent on biting those who were immune so the virus could replicate.

The CDC reported that the infection levels were over ninety-nine percent and that the reports from other countries showed that 100 percent of those infected, would go into a coma and then would awaken with the sort of brain damage that induced violent behavior, biting, and cannibalism.

Sally had read the reports and watched the news coverage, she had seen people in other countries attack and bite people, yet it had seemed medically impossible. People were sick, not dead, not the living dead, not zombies or zeds, but that's what they were being called, Zeds.

The smell of blood, vomit, and feces, suddenly overwhelmed Sally, so she stepped outside the room to get some fresh air. She was fighting a losing battle, and she knew it. This seemed like the end of the world.

Maybe this was how the world would end, with a gush of blood.

3
VICTIMS

Damn, Karen thought as she curled herself into a fetal position, clenching her face so tightly that her nails dug little semicircles; her lower stomach was knotted tightly. Walking on aching joints, she stumbled to the bathroom, barely reaching the toilet before vomit blew out of her mouth in a rush. Shivering violently, she sat and reached for the toilet paper to wipe her mouth and blow her nose.

Nelwynn was there to hand her a wet washcloth. "Mom, are you okay?"

"Better now." Karen wiped her fevered face, enjoying the coolness of the cloth, now spotted with blood from her nose. Karen stood, pulled down her underwear to pee, and changed the pad in her panties. She was bleeding from everywhere, just like the people on television. God, she was afraid.

"I'm scared," Nelwynn said.

Karen felt worse, knowing that her daughter was worrying about her. Although she felt guilty, Karen kind of blamed Ed, her late husband, for Nelwynn's extra misery. She missed Ed terribly. He had always promised her and the kids that he'd take care of them forever; he had enjoyed being the breadwinner, the man who could fix it all, and the one who could take care of all of his girls' problems. He'd wiped their leaky noses, given them a shoulder to cry on, understood female problems, had explained algebra, and he always had known the best gifts to buy. Ed had been the best Dad and husband in the world.

Karen had worried that they were too overprotective, babying the girls, spoiling them, and not even letting them scrape a knee to learn a lesson. Ed had been the kind of man who would follow Polly when she was learning to ride her bicycle, and grabbing her before the bike could wobble twice.

When Nelwynn turned fourteen a few months before he died and had complained that her peers had more privileges, Karen just laughed; Nelwynn had no privileges. Ed hadn't allowed her to wear makeup, to go out with friends, or to go to movies unless she was with the family.

Nelwynn had been a model student, and the best daughter that any parent could ever have asked for. And he'd been right in how he had wanted to raise their daughters; they had never had a bit of trouble with either, but the children had never been prepared for the real world, the cold, cruel, hard world that had been all too likely to spit right in one's face.

Ed had always said that he didn't want them to be exposed to what he had seen every day, a bad side of the world, and it had spit in his face a lot. He had worked vice division on the police force, wallowed in the filth, but had preferred to meet it head-on rather than have it happen behind his back. No matter how bad it had gotten, he had managed to stay apart, to somehow separate himself emotionally, until the porn movie case.

Ed had been undercover, and it had taken him two months to set up the sting: he had gone into the investigation, pretending to be a porn movie producer and managing to seem bored and businesslike about it. The operation he had infiltrated specialized in the worst of that industry; bestiality, sadomasochism, snuff films, and necrophilia. It had been the most difficult thing in his life to watch women and children being tortured, degraded, and abused while pretending not to care. Finally, he had been offered women for a snuff film, and he lured the thugs into the trap.

One of the runaways offered him a girl named, Deanna. She was only fourteen, the same age as his daughter, and wore too large blue jeans, a soft T-shirt, and sneakers; her hair was honey-colored and baby fine, and her eyes were a pale, sea green. Thin, she looked underdeveloped, without much figure, long, coltish legs, and no bosom to speak of. The pimp in the industry used Deanna, and had been looking to get rid of her because she was too difficult to handle, he said. She was unreliable and headstrong; refused to use the drugs he supplied, and was prone to fighting. Even the porn industry hadn't wanted the girl.

She seemed not to care about the movies, being in them, degrading herself, it just never had touched her. She did what she was told to do so that she wouldn't get beaten, but there was no emotion from her; she seemed dead in many ways. After so many experiences, she hardly noticed what was being done to her or even what she was doing, unless there was physical pain.

When Ed and his team made the arrest, Deanna had been lost. She did not know what to do, but she wouldn't go back home because her stepfather had beaten the hell out of her and he didn't want her back. Without the movie people to abuse her, she had nowhere to go and no one to be with. As soon as she had been placed her back in her home, she ran away, again.

Social workers tried to find her a foster family, but each time, there were problems within days; she was a smart girl, a good girl, but too willful and too accustomed to freedom. She hadn't known how to be a child, how to be taken care of, or how to be watched over. She was a too-often kicked puppy with fear in her eyes and no trust. She had run away again and again.

Ed lost track of her, but he thought of her often.

A few months later, during a routine bust of a prostitution ring, Ed found her with the pimps and hookers, her lips were been painted bright red, her skinny body was dressed in a slinky, neon purple miniskirt and halter top. Ed let the rest be taken, but asked an officer to keep Deanna there so he could talk to her.

He had been thinking of what they could do to help her, and his mind had not been on his duties. From an unsecured doorway, a man bolted. Ed took a deep breath and started to chase after him. The pimp topped mid-stride, and the split second before Ed fired his gun, the man fired his own, turning Ed's stomach into a fury of burning, and acidic pain.

Ed's partner had taken the pimp out.

Ed tried to move his legs but felt tired, exhausted so badly that he had fallen to the ground; he wanted to find a more comfortable position, but there was a strange sensation, a burning, pulling, sliding feeling. Heat. Reaching with his hand to his midsection, he found the mess of his stomach, the slimy intestines slipping out between his fingers as blood soaked the ground around him.

His partner, the other officer, and Deanna, stood close to him while a fourth officer caught and tried to stuff Ed's intestines back inside of him and to stop the blood flow. Ed let the man help while he had looked up at Deanna, "Well, look who it is."

"Yup, I guess you have found me again." She looked at him curiously. "You sure as hell have been hurt."

"No shit. So have you." He looked at her bruises and cuts.

She smiled.

The scene had been chaotic. While the officers yelled for paramedics to hurry and they had waited for the siren to draw closer, Deanna sat down beside him, and reaching out, she squeezed his hand. But in his mind, it seemed as if his daughter, Nelwynn, had been there with him.

This little hooker smiled at him, as if she cared.

Ed didn't want to let go of her hand, but the paramedics pushed her away as they tried to save his life. He died before they could strap him in.

Deanna looked at one of the officers, "You know what he said to me? He said he loved me; no one's ever said that before. I guess he thought I was someone else."

"You will be fine," the officer told her, wondering why this little prostitute had even been talking.

She squeezed her eyes shut and said, "I sure will be."

Karen met Deanna at Ed's funeral. Although Karen had mixed feelings about the girl and didn't want her own daughters exposed to her, she was gracious, listening to how the girl had known her husband. It made her proud of Ed, but she also thought his life had been wasted for people like this. To Karen's surprise, she found herself scared of what and who Deanna was, but also caring enough to accept the girl's persistence, and willing to keep in touch with Deanna at her next foster home.

Maybe it had been a connection to Ed that the girl was with him when he died. It had been something.

As Karen sat in her bathroom, sick, she thought of how she needed Ed and how worried she was for her girls, yet wondered about Deanna, too. She worried about Nelwynn and Polly since they didn't have the skills to survive as someone like Deanna would have. They had no street smarts, but who would have thought they would need them? She was terrified for her daughters.

Deanna called to check on Karen, and the girls whom she had never met. Finding out that Karen was ill, Deanna went to the house in a taxi to help Nelwynn take care of Polly. Karen didn't want her daughters around someone jaded like Deanna, but she passed out and had been helped to her bed right after Deanna arrived. When Karen came to, Deanna asked her to call for help next time.

As Karen lay back, she knew that she was dehydrated and had lost a lot of blood. She wasn't stupid. She knew she was dying, and that part didn't scare her because according to the news, millions were also dying. It was the end of times as foretold. She had her faith and her religion, and she never had been afraid of death, though this apocalypse of the plague scared her badly for her girls. Karen faked strength for Nelwynn, telling her to be strong and that she loved her, and asking her to please take care of Polly, but when her vision cleared a little, she saw it wasn't Nelwynn standing there; it was Deanna.

"Deanna, would you tell Nelwynn to come in here, please. I need her."

"I can't." Deanna looked around the room, straightened the bed covers and refused to make eye contact.

Stubborn girl, go home, Karen thought. "Bring her to me," Karen raised her voice, blood rising up in a clout from her mouth and almost strangling her.

Deanna looked at her sadly. "I can't, Karen," she cried, "Nelwynn is asleep…unconscious… she was bleeding out. She's not immune, either."

Karen felt herself spiraling away, falling into a vacuum; darkness descending.

"I'll take care of Polly," Deanna promised.

"What? No, this is wrong."

The girl's voice was far-away sounding to Karen. *No*, she thought, *no, not you; we sheltered the girls so much; I don't want you.* But Karen slipped away.

4
HOSPITAL AND NEIGHBORHOOD

Everyone had gathered for breakfast but was hardly able to eat, just watching the news coverage.

Len and Hagan sat with Beth and Kim, all offering theories. Bryan and his buddies patrolled the hospital. Groups of people sat talking, crying softly, commenting on the news, and finding chores to keep them busy.

Most could no longer reach loved ones by telephone or cell phone, and reports from those who did manage to reach people across town, told a totally unbelievable story that the sick were rising up to attack, bite, and sometimes eat the immune people.

The television had shown that very thing, but in a nation of avid movie fans, things were not-so-concrete-believable, just because they saw them. Most distrusted the media, mainly, because those actions were impossible, so the actions were dismissed. And even if they had happened in every other country, this was America, and America had provisions and plans for this kind of action, with FEMA and the military ready to help. Right?

Scientists speculated, and cameras showed sick people. Then, scientists warned and offered ideas, and cameras showed attacks. Finally, scientists said that it was all FUBAR and they had no idea of what to do, but were headed to bunkers. Cameras showed bloody cannibals, eating the guts and flesh of people, ripping muscles away, feasting on belly fat, and swallowing fingers; they showed camera-people and the newscasters running, the military being ripped apart, and that was that.

Someone decided they should organize, while some wanted to leave; they did leave but were warned that they might not be allowed back, so they didn't try to return.

Len, retired as a major in the Marine Corps, began to talk about security; Hagan, the hospital security guard; Mark, a young deputy in training; and Kimball, a former police officer-turned-PI, were interested. Without a military structure, civilization was doomed.

Roy, with the pointed cowboy boots, Hank Williams, Jr, yellow-tinted glasses, sat to the side, poking holes in everything they heard. "Last thing we need is more military."

"I disagree," Len said.

"We need security and more," Mark said. "Military or police force, they're all sick...so who, besides us, does that leave?"

It was decided that they would hole up there with the benefits the hospital offered, but some pointed out they wanted items from their homes, and if the state of the country was an indication, they had little time to get them before being besieged by deadly predators and looters. Some said they didn't need anything, but the debate got heated.

Bobby, a self-proclaimed redneck with an easy grin, a ball cap, checkered shirt, jeans and boots, told them he was the most valuable asset they had, that he and his brother owned the gun and survival shop in town.

After a lot more debate, one team decided to drive several streets over to the gun shop and the hardware store to fill SUVs and trucks with supplies. Another team would strip the grocery stores and fill more trucks. For that trip, the soldier, Bryan, offered to go so no one would be shot for looting and to help with guard duty. He gathered a huge group to do the job.

At Bobby and Billy's store, Bucks and Ducks, Bobby warned them to stay calm, keep weapons out of sight, and keep their hands in full view. "Hold the steering wheel, unroll the window, play drums on the car roof, stand by the vehicle, or have your hands on your hips, but don't let your hands look as if they're going for a hidden gun." He motioned Len to come with him so that his brother would see he wasn't kidnapped.

Once inside, Bobby and Billy discussed the present situation as Billy looked Len over carefully.

"I thought we'd fight from here," Billy said.

"Well, the hospital has supplies and a generator."

"So do we."

"And a doctor or two, one is female," Bobby said, "and while we're gathering supplies here, they are fixing things up there. We have a bunch...over a hundred. Some of them females, anyway."

"Ya' don't say...hmmm." Billy scratched his head.

"I guess I'd rather hole up with some females around, waiting for the end of the world if I had my druthers," Billy agreed.

"So, I'm thinking we pack it all in, go hang out there with the rest, and teach them some survival stuff."

"It'd make us real heroes." Billy directed some to load boxes and bags with every firearm he set on the counter, while others were to load the heavy ammo, and a few were to gather items such as crossbows, mace, cleaning kits, water bottles, and MRE's. "We don't need the more unusual guns or ammo that we can't get more of."

"Basic is always best," Len stated. "I'm thinking to outfit a group and train them military-style camouflage, guns, bug-out packs, you know, the basics."

"Sounds good," Bobby agreed, "training military teams is about the only way to survive this clusterfuck."

"We'll get you a room and stock all this there, and it will be yours...with a lock, so you can hand things out as you see fit," Kimball told Bobby and Billy.

Although the men were seeing their hard work destroyed and the money they had invested evaporate, there was pride in both of the men's eyes as they watched their supplies being appreciated. If the world were ending, it was far better to show off their great planning than to hole up and have no one know, or to be over run and robbed by raiders.

"What about clothing? We need pockets; can we use this?" Beth looked at the garments. "I like these pants."

"We'll take it all and them boots, too. And socks. There's a changing room; load yourself up."

Beth grabbed some clothing, darted into the room, and changed quickly. Clean clothing felt great. She laced the boots, thinking they were comfortable, light, and sturdy. She put on a long sleeved tee and a pair of pants, where she found tons of pockets.

Len appraised her. "I like the camo." Then he handed her a holster, a small backpack, a K-Bar knife to go into her boot, and nodded. Len thought his first recruit looked like a really bad ass. "Grab things for the pack; keep it light and smart. Find a bandana, too; we're taking those."

Beth picked a small first aid kit, added a tiny roll of duct tape, some wire, a bottle for water, dried food packets, another pair of socks, matches and a lighter, toilet paper, a rain poncho, rope, flashlight and extra batteries, and a compass. The pack was still lighter than she expected. Gloves went into a side pocket and boxes of ammo into her other pockets on her shirt and pants. She found a small knife with a thin sheath that she threaded into her braid, using elastic to secure it. It might never be needed, but she liked having a secret, a last resort weapon. In a way, she felt silly, like an actress in some bad apocalyptic movie, but she also felt tough and then guilty for feeling that. She felt strange with the AR-15 hanging on her back. She added a P226.

"Oh, *Chica*, help me get in an outfit like that," Julia demanded. "I wanna be in Len's Military, too." With her lean, muscled frame, she would look fantastic, strong, and dependable.

Beth showed her what to get, and while Julia dressed, Beth loaded several backpacks the same way she had loaded hers; each person could then add personal items or more that they needed to carry.

"How'd you know what to pick out?" Billy admired her work.

"I watch television, survivalist stuff." She laughed. "I may have missed a lot though."

"Add a whistle and those tiny bottles of insect repellent."

Beth nodded.

"We're gonna get all those plastic bottles and jars, too. When we get back to the hospital, I want you to soak cotton balls in Vaseline and seal them in a jar, adding one to each pack. Do you know why?"

"Waterproof…but…no…Why?"

"One ball can help you start a fire in bad conditions."

Julia walked out of the dressing room in her combat gear, all the clothing a size too small, hugging her curves. "*Gracias.*" She managed to look great. "You got scissors?"

Beth grabbed a pair and handed them over. Julia, without a word, cut her long, glossy, dark ponytail, and tossed it to the side. "Now, can you cut it short right fast? I don't want one of them grabbing my hair."

Beth cut the beautiful hair down to short spikes all over, in kind of a buzz-cut. Amazingly, the harsh and bare style highlighted Julia's angular face, sharp cheekbones, strong, square jaw, and strong nose, while juxtaposing it against her soft, big brown eyes and lush lips. Beth felt a quick wave of envy.

"We change with the world; if you don't adapt; you get left behind, yes?" Julia smiled grimly. "Dinosaurs didn't adapt; we'll do better."

Despite any jealousy of Julia's good looks and capable attitude, Beth liked her immensely.

The rest changed outfits, some immodestly, and then outfitted quickly; they finished loading everything from the store. More supplies from the back room storage filled the two SUVs.

"Hagan, you, Bobby, and Billy, can get them a room for all this and then supervise it being unloaded into the area. We'll leave these and get two more vehicles," Len said.

They quickly drove back to the hospital; Len gave orders, and they grabbed new SUVs. The group at the hardware store had filled their trucks. Two of the men, Chauncey and a guy they called, Big Bill, raced down a side street and got their own cars, and while they didn't hold as much, both were filled with nails, hammers, saws, machetes, buckets, pans, and much more.

"We're done," Roy said, drinking from a bottle of water.

"Us, too. Now, we're gonna do the five minutes in for personal shit and get out," Len said. "Any of you need to do that?"

Some did. Roy didn't say anything. Chauncey and Big Bill had gotten their things when they ran for the cars. That left the two trucks to be driven to the hospital. The two men would get rides and drive the trucks back.

"If this goes like the rest of the world, we can't be running around like this much longer...maybe a day...maybe less."

"I think it's all bullshit," Roy said. "Zombies. That's stupid."

"Call 'em something else, then," Kim said.

"Zeds."

Roy glared at Julia. "That's stupid, too, Taco Bella."

"*Chingada Madre.*"

"Spick chick."

She was lunging before anyone could move; luckily, Len's reactions were like a cat, and he yanked her off her feet to calm her.

"Knock it off, Roy. We don't need that on top of all the rest we've got going." Len didn't know yet if the man was crazy, mean, scared, acting a fool, or a dangerous combination, but for now, Len needed everyone working together. "Get off the racist remarks, and I mean now."

"Bitch called me a name."

"Pendejo," she said.

"Okay, now she called you a name. Before, she made a suggestion. You knock off the nasty remarks, and she'll stop calling you names," Len said, staring them both down. They finally nodded.

"You have a bad temper, Julia." Beth laughed.

"I do when I hear stuff like that; I have no patience with rude people who say racist things and pick on people...bullies."

"He is a bully."

The first neighborhood was close. They parked both SUVs and gathered courage; this was a first foray into the chaos the news said was going on, yet it was quiet on the street. "Keep calm; stay together; follow directions, five minutes in and out. I want it by the book."

"Ummm." Misty raised her hand like a schoolgirl, baffled by what he had said. "What book?" She was only sixteen with long brown hair and a pretty face with womanly curves. Roy had called her, in his nasty way, 'trailer trash', but luckily few had heard. She didn't like him at all.

Len realized again these were civilians, even if half were in combat gear. He told them that he, Kim, Roy, and Misty, would go into her trailer. That left Julia, Beth, Warren, and Mark to watch all four directions. "And I mean don't be jacking around. You keep watch."

Julia saluted, half in jest. The other four would sit in the SUV.

"No noise," Kim added. He took his place as rear guard, Len as point, Roy second, and Misty third. Kim admired Len's training as the man quietly said, 'Clear', to allow the rest to enter the trailer. An awful smell assaulted them.

Len and Roy moved ahead, clearing each room until they saw the master bedroom where Len walked in. He came back out, closed the door, and tapping his watch, held up five fingers.

Misty knew the smell, and Roy's behavior indicated that her parents, although not sick at first and encouraging her to donate blood and help out, had, in fact, gotten very ill later.

Red had progressed in the ones who had caught it late, like a whirlwind, doing in hours what it had done in days to others. When one was infected with Red and went into the coma stage, it was all over. Misty had planned to get them and take them back to the hospital with her. She wanted to see them, but then again, she didn't.

Len held up four fingers. Kim stood in her room while she threw pictures, a few items from her dresser and bathroom, and papers into a pillowcase. Len showed three fingers. She could hardly think. Her parents were dying in the next room, and she had to decide what to take; she smashed underwear into the bag then went back to pile make-up into a bag and into the pillowcase. Len held up one finger. Tears streamed down her face. With time ticking away, she snatched frame photos and shoved them in. Len refused to let her into the room, whispering her parents were about to go through the horrible change.

She was thinking about demanding to stay and care for them, but Kim whispered that they were already gone.

"Move," Kim said, business-like. She could barely carry the load; it was so heavy, but he had the gun, and she had been warned. She grabbed sneakers as she walked out, hanging the laces around her neck.

In the kitchen, Roy finished loading cans and dried goods into sacks as Len stayed on guard. As a unit, they left the house.

"Everything okay?"

"Quiet."

"A bunch of sick people and we're playing military ops? Come on, I could have used help carrying that," Roy complained.

"Did you see the streets of London on TV? They were chasing people and biting them, eating them," Beth snapped.

"Not here."

"You missed the camera people being knocked down and one having an arm torn off in Los Angeles?"

Roy shrugged, "Gangs do that shit."

"Gangs tear off arms and eat people? Since when?"

"Media lies." Roy threw the food in the back.

Misty thought again about arguing, but she knew that when they had sent her away, that was good-bye, and she had mourned then. She sniffed back tears. She got into that vehicle, and both moved on to the next stop.

In Beth's car, Julia was bashing Roy's stupidity with colorful words that no one could translate. Kim asked them both to calm down.

Misty kept her eyes on Mark who had given her a hug and a kind smile. He was handsome and classy, wasn't the type she might have dated before. She planned to write in her diary a little about how cute he was.

The next stop was for Roy, and Mark joined the operation, seeing it as further training for his hopes to be a deputy sheriff.

Len made note of Mark's calm stealth and gave him a pat; he was an eager kid, pretty well countrified, and would have made a fine deputy. So far, this made three he could count on, including Hagan and Kimball. Rita and then Warren got their things. As they filed out, there was a scream in the distance.

"Anything on visual?"

"Nothing, Major," Julia quipped.

"I am retired, smart-ass."

"Sir, yes, Sir."

Len thought she was a pretty quick study, and despite her smart mouth, she would be a real asset; she was a good girl, had recently moved to the city, and could handle a gun like a pro.

Len's nerves were jumping.

Kim grabbed his things from an out-of-the-way, seedy motel on the edge of town as Len led them in a big circle. Kim shrugged and reminded them he was a PI now and in town for a case. They heard bumps and distant moans and screams, but saw nothing.

"Did you solve the case?" Beth asked.

"I guess. Both the husband and mistress had caught Red, but he had panicked, and it became a murder-suicide. That's why I ended up at the hospital, waiting to see if the forensics showed anything unusual."

"Besides a zed virus?" Julia smirked.

Jeri, an older woman, had left her roommate and the roommate's two kids feeling fine. Her face drained of color when she saw the door covered with drying blood and a trail to the rooms both in blood and feces, ground into the carpet. Jeri gagged. Pausing, Len followed the blood splatter with his eyes, rifle ready to go. It trailed off into the grass.

"Keep a close watch," he mouthed to Beth and then saw her whisper to her other three guards. He motioned Beth to come to him and for Warren to stand guard in her place. She wasn't trained, but she was smart and rational and wouldn't panic. He whispered for her to remain at the doorway and to watch the street and the open door of the house; to her credit, she didn't ask how to manage both.

In the bedrooms and bath, the roommate and kids had left brown stains and puddles, vomit all over the floor, and blood trails. It reeked. "Where are they?" Jeri whispered.

Roy looked more concerned. "Maybe they went for help."

Kim rolled his eyes. "Five minutes. Go."

Jeri gathered her things with a minute to spare, saying she wanted out of there. As she slid into her seat, the roommate, two kids, and two more bloody people rounded the side of the house next door, saw them, and moaned loudly.

Beth saw them first, moving her body to aim her gun. Mark and Kim were seconds behind her. Len calculated. Several houses away, five torn bodies moved in their direction. "Hold fire. Warren, you and Julia watch behind us."

"I don't know how to shoot," Warren said.

"Hells bells." Misty ran from the car and took the Sig from him, pushed him towards the car, and told them, "My Daddy took me to the range a few times."

Thank, God, we're in Texas, Len thought.

"Beth and Mark, hold fire. Kim, me, Roy…one, two, three, pick a target and put them down if they don't stop. You need to stop right there," Len called. He fired a warning shot into the air.

One child was missing an arm and most of his face, while the other had slimy, grey, intestines leaking from his partially eaten stomach. The mother had gotten sick, turned, and attacked her own children. Beth leaned over to vomit. No one blamed her; they all had wanted to heave.

"Hold." Len placed a shot into the mother. She didn't react to the wound. He took out her leg, and she struggled to get back to her feet, stumbling on the mangled limb.

"Acquire target. Go." Kim hit the child mid-section, Len hit the mother in the head, and Roy used two shots to drop a man. The other man kept coming, as did the man Roy had shot twice, and the child shambled along, again.

"My God," Mark muttered.

"Are they zombies…dead people?"

"Dunno. Acquire and go again," Len ordered, "head shots." The walkers were close now, and Kim, Len, and Roy, all got headshots easily.

"Len," Beth warned, her finger ready to pull the trigger. She watched the five approaching. Many would have turned and run after seeing their cloudy eyes and knowing they wanted nothing more than to eat.

"Julia? Sitrep?"

"Nothing moving here."

Len leaned closer to Beth, saying, "Exhale, and gently pull the trigger. Keep it on your target. Go."

Beth almost closed her eyes and fired, hitting the man three out of four times. Body shots. She mentally kicked herself.

Len finished him with a shot to the head, motioning Roy and Kim to hit one each. Two kept coming, bodies torn to shreds with bite marks, clothing tattered, just like in one of the movies Len had seen. But these bled. Not a lot, but some, and he thought it might be true that they were just barely alive, a few functions still working in order to keep them going so the virus could spread.

Mark calmly sighted in, quickly dropped an obese woman with a headshot, and then turned and took out a black man who still gripped a hammer in one fist.

"Load up. Let's move," Len ordered. He spoke calmly, but he was as shaken as the rest.

Roy scowled, mumbling beneath his breath. Beth felt sick. She tried to say something, but Len again gave the same order.

She did as he asked, with a "Sir, yes, Major," flipping from her mouth as she got in the SUV. She had a case of Julia's smart mouth. Nausea abating, she knew she would think about this and talk of it later, analyzing her feelings and maybe getting sick again, but right now, she felt strangely like part of a team, no, a machine that should be run a specific way. This calmed her.

"Damned fine job," Len said in his vehicle. Kim and Mark said the same in theirs.

"Can you teach me to shoot like that, Mark?" Beth asked.

"Me too, *Chica*."

"Sure." Mark was flattered; they didn't know how sick he felt after killing two people.

Len knew they wanted to run back to the safety of the hospital, but the god-damned virus had changed things, and whether he wanted it or not, he was leading a rag-tag group of civvies whom he needed trained for this, yesterday. It felt hopeless until he had seen them in action, responding calmly.

Later, they would feel shock and despair probably; he'd have to counsel the ones who did the shooting. So far, half were acting like good soldiers in-training. Maybe more could rise up. Roy would have to be watched.

Tom and Ben, after seeing all of this, didn't want anything from their homes, but Len drove there, the other SUV following, so his team could gather things for both of the men. Part of him wanted to make the men go in, but these were just regular, scared people. He did it himself to encourage the team. Underwear, pictures, personal items, all went quickly into pillowcases, and they were out fast, both times.

Beth got her things, the operation was going smoothly although she was jumpy as more screams echoed down the street. She came out with her pillowcase full. "It's as if they all left." She motioned to the trails of bloody footprints.

"Maybe third stage," Len said.

"But where are they all going? Where are they? And why?" Julia fumed.

"No idea, but let's get this finished." They drove, not seeing but a few shambling around. They were Reds, heading for someplace only they knew. No one could tell if they had turned yet or not.

"Last stop," Len said. "Let's get this finished; then, we can go." They were in the final neighborhood.

Each took a place, the routine sinking in, as Len, Kim, and Roy, walked with Julia Perez.

5
HOSPITAL

Hagan helped Billy and Bobby and a few more volunteers as they unloaded the firearms, ammunition, and anything else related from the vehicles. The clothing and survival gear went into another room.

Another group loaded the already-full pantries with food from the grocery store; they had enough canned and dried food to feed all of them for weeks, but the fresh vegetables, fresh fruit, and fresh meat would be missed. From the cafeteria and grocery store, they had picked up huge cans of all kinds of vegetables, soups, rice and pasta, sauces, canned meat, fruit, nuts, and boxes of instant breakfast foods and potatoes, along with junk food such as, chips, sodas and juice, and sports drinks.

Hagan had spent the last few hours with his time neatly divided; every week there were forty hours working, five hours commuting, five hours getting ready, fifty-six hours sleeping, two hours attending church, and twenty hours working out. Anything left might be for something fun. A year ago, he was spending almost all of his time, except for the forty-five hours needed for work, with his sick mother.

Red was a bad disease, but the cancer and treatments Hagan's mother endured were every bit as bad. She became a thin, shrieking, raging woman who cried piteously with the pain, vomiting helplessly from chemotherapy, and unable to eat because her mouth and throat were filled with blisters. She had been a nanny to three rich, white children, grown now, who were like brothers and a sister to Hagan; they had cried bitterly and as hard as he had at her funeral.

Now, he was security in the hospital where his mother had died, and for the first time, he understood why she had passed years before; so he would have time to learn to be a guard and to sculpt his body, making it strong and healthy, and then being here to get work. Hagan believed in God, and he figured that it was true that God had purposes and big plans; each person was a small dot on the wheel of that grand plan. Each had to do what was planned for him.

Hagan gathered a group and asked them to bring bed mattresses and linens. For some reason, he felt they should store the resources and sleep close to the generator in the basement where the cafeteria and many other rooms were located. Maybe from others such as Len, they wouldn't understand that Hagan thought his feeling was a whisper from God; they might not even believe in God, but Hagan was sure it was the right thing to do.

Hagan asked Sally if her nurses could help move more supplies which might be needed. Few doctors and patients were left, and Hagan thought the rest of the medical staff was at the relief station, sick.

Sally sighed, "I heard from them a while ago…maybe it was hours…"

"Are they sick?"

Sally nodded. "Yeah. They couldn't even get back here; no one is left tending the sick but a few nurses and doctors who are immune."

She didn't mention the few, such as her patient, Jana, who had come back to the hospital and who were now comatose. Taking a break from watching them, she made a list for Hagan and told him where everything could be found; he could get another group to gather those supplies for the basement.

It was amazing that no one had complained, yet, about his organization, and he figured it was the chores that kept their minds off what was happening outside. They were glad to have anyone in charge.

A woman, Hagan forgot her name, had made a list of everyone there so the staff could note ages and medical needs. She assigned rooms, as mattresses were put down like in a dormitory, but there was enough room in some of the tiny rooms for people to sleep alone.

When several people trickled in and asked for sanctuary, Hagan okayed it and had the woman put them in rooms on the first floor. He was in charge of not just the army guys, and he wasn't going to turn healthy people away. But he did tell the woman, whose name slipped his memory, to check each one for bites. No one with bites could come in.

6
IN THE NEIGHBORHOOD

Julia's strong personality lagged when she was finally inside her house; she wiped tears from her cheeks. All over the kitchen, it looked as if a battle had taken place; blood covered the floor, along with flour splattered on the walls, and all kinds of food and trash were thrown on the floor. Of her parents, there was no further sign, but the backdoor was opened, and the blood trail went that way.

Julia gathered her things, stoically saying that they would have to go without her, she intended to see if she could find her family. "I can't leave my parents like that…wandering around."

"You can't just stay," Beth protested.

Julia shrugged, "I have no choice."

Len, unhappy with this turn of events, tried to decide what was best. He saw her point, but seeing her parents put down was going to be bad as well. Before he could think, two men across the street waved for their attention; one, a huge bear of a man, an older gentleman carrying a big Remington pointed towards the ground; and his friend carrying a .30.06. Len motioned his team to stay watchful as he and Kim walked over.

"Good-looking gun," he said.

George turned it and allowed Len a closer look at the smooth walnut finish, glossy with wear, and the blue steel finish, fancy with its scrollwork.

"Man, that's a beauty." Len shook his head. "I've never seen one so nice."

Tink winked, "Mine ain't pretty, but she's a monster. You military? They aren't." He used his chin to point to the people next to the vehicles.

"They're in training; I'm retired. I was retired, back in business now." Len introduced himself and Kim; they all nodded to one another. Len explained why they were there and for whom they were looking.

"Oh." George had a wary look. "Mr. and Mrs. Perez? They just moved in, and I didn't recognize them. I think she turned him, nasty, sad thing that. In a normal life, I doubt she would have raised a hand to him, but it made her do what she did. I'm sorry."

"It looked as if she was sick, and he was tending her when she changed," Tink added.

"Did you…?" Kim asked.

"Yeah, those two and a teen boy from somewhere, and a man who attacked the man's wife and little girl, and then us."

"You held them off?" Len was a little shocked and impressed at the ability of these old guys. "All four of them?"

"We had the help of two more of our friends." George laughed a little. "Until a few seconds ago, one of my friends was above you upstairs with a rifle on your friends. No offense."

"None taken…sounds smart," Len said. "I'm sorry you were attacked by my friend's family and sorrier you had to take them out. Bad business all around. I'm hating this." Len waved Julia over.

Len introduced her and nodded to George.

"Honey," George said, "I'm awfully sorry to have to tell you, but your momma and daddy got really sick and were out in the neighborhood with some more people, chasing a little girl and her mama. Scared them and us pretty badly. We tried to get them to stop, but they were mighty sick and unable to quit trying to bite; they were gone, Honey, those weren't your parents anymore."

Julia wiped away fresh tears as Kim patted her shoulder and said, "Mom and Dad?"

"Yes. But those weren't my parents."

"I'm sure when they were healthy, they were fine people, but they were with a teen boy and a man and very sick."

"My cousin, Michael, was checking on them. I guess it was him?"

"Maybe so. I'm very sorry."

"Did you?" she asked now.

"Yes, Honey, those were their bodies. They were gone...the parts of them who were your parents. We released them is all...they wouldn't wanna be chasing little girls and hurting people."

Len waited for her anger, but she smiled.

"Thank you. Thank you for setting them free and giving us the closure." She took a deep breath, "Where are they? The bodies?" She wept.

"Waiting to be buried," George told her, "but you are not going to see what's not them anymore. I mean it. No viewing today or any day."

Len and Kim heard an amazing strength in George's words.

After a lot of discussion, they decided Benny would stay with Gina, Katie, and Julia on the porch while Kim, Thurman, George, and Tink stood guard.

The rest helped to dig a deep hole on the front lawn, wrap the bodies in sheets, and watch the vehicles. Some were unable to help much and sat with Julia on the porch.

Beth re-bandaged Gina's bite, noting the reddish-purple color around the mark; the green, smelly pus leaking; and the severity of the pain. Gina was feverish and pale. Smudges beneath her eyes were now deep bruises, and she moved with a pained gait, her joints screaming. "I got sick so fast."

"Sorry, if I'm hurting you." Beth had used a full bottle of hydrogen peroxide on the bite, letting the bloody, stinking foam flow down into the sink's drain, then swabbed the area with cream, and added tons of gauze for padding and soaking up the fluids.

"It hurts around it bad, but the bite is numb now. I guess as it infects more skin, it causes the pain. It was a tiny bite." Her entire arm was now red, more purple and green above and below her elbow. The bite had spread open, gone mushy, and was now raw and open, the size of a palm.

"Keep it immobile," Beth made a sling, "not sure what else to do."

They had both seen the discoloration spreading past Gina's shoulder and along her back. "Thanks, anyway. I feel rough."

"We'll get you fixed up; don't worry."

"Thanks, but I doubt there's anything you can do for me."

When the grave was finished, all four bodies were side-by-side, buried, the rich earth smell finally covering the smell of the bodies. The rest stood around uncomfortably, with Kim, Len, and Tink on nervous guard.

No one knew what to say; everyone looked at one another. People passed away, and there were family gatherings, a time for a comforting process and for closure with support. These people had been sick, then had been shot, and now had been buried, but it had been only a few hours. Grief was blocked by shock. Dealing with death should be a process, and being thrown into situations, where loved ones had to be put down like rabid animals, was beyond comprehension.

Finally, clearing his throat, Warren said a few words, asking for peace for the dead and strength for the survivors. He hadn't thought to ask about religion, so sudden were the events, so he just muttered through, figuring it didn't matter what was said, only that something had been said. Julia, weeping, prayed aloud, grasping the hands of Gina and Katie.

Tink, off to the side of the huge, rough old man who looked as if he could eat nails and spit them out his ass, began to sing "Amazing Grace" in a rich baritone. Voices joined him after a bit, saying goodbye to their own family and friends. When it was finished, Julia kissed Tink's cheek to his embarrassment.

"*Vaya con Dios*," Julia said to the graves. Len came to help her as she glanced around, unsure of what to do or say next.

All four men said they wanted to go to the hospital with the other survivors when they were invited.

With help, Gina got things for Katie while the rest helped the four other men gather everything from the basement; the large amount of stockpiled food and ammo was staggering. George said he was somewhat of a "city survivalist." They filled two SUVs that George and Tink owned and then a third that belonged to Thurman.

Len shot one of the shamblers while he worked, a man they called a 'Red Zed' that had been ill.

"You get your stuff?" George asked Gina.

"No, and we need to talk about it."

"I'd rather we didn't."

She shook her head, reaching for his hand. He and Kimball sat next to her. "I'm sick, and I don't wanna be one of those *things*." She cried quietly. "I don't wanna hurt Katie or anyone or wander around."

"Aw, Gina," George said sadly.

Gina called for Beth. "You can tell them I'm getting sicker and fast."

Beth nodded. "I'm no medical expert, but the infection is moving really fast. She said it was a tiny puncture; it seems to have spread like lightning."

Kim asked, "What can we do, Gina?"

"Katie will need a godmother and godfather to look to. Will you and George take care of my baby girl?" She choked out the last words, begging Beth with her eyes.

"I will, Gina. I'll do my very best," Beth promised. George nodded.

"We'll all protect her," Kimball spoke.

"And you can trust a Blue," George said.

Kim looked at him quizzically, "I'm a barely-making-it private investigator, boring and simple."

"Then how'd you know what I meant?" George asked, "I'll eat my boxers if I'm wrong on your being a former cop."

"Well, I guess you don't have to eat underwear," Kim said, getting slight smiles from Gina and Beth. "Former. How'd you know?"

"You can smell it. Didn't you smell it on me?"

"Yeah, but you told us that you guys had all been cops. I didn't know it showed on me."

"It shows even if you're quiet about it, and Gina, that means you have five cops looking out for Katie."

"And Mark is…was training to be a deputy, plus Len, and Hagan, he's with us at the hospital as a security guard, and we have a few military guys there, too. The ones who made it," Beth explained.

"It sounds safe. And some nice women?"

"Some very nice ones. Julia and Misty are super; no one can replace a mama, but we'll watch out for her, and she'll find whom she wants to fill in for you, and we'll talk about you, and we won't let her forget you." Beth was crying.

"Keep her safe. She deserves a chance, and please don't let her get hurt, God, she needs me, and I had to get bitten."

Kim glanced around. "Len's getting antsy to move. Maybe you can go with us and decide this later."

"I doubt Len is gonna let someone sick go along. I'm sorry, Gina, but that's a fact," George said. "One of us can stay back with you; I will, then go alone, later."

"I'll stay," Kim offered. "We both could."

"And what if a bunch comes along like before, only more?" Gina asked.

"Then we put them down," Kim said. "These four fellows did a fine job, so I figure we can keep safe."

"I hurt; my whole arm throbs. And inside, I feel weak and cold; it really hurts," Gina said. "I can't stand the pain much longer, but I think it's all going numb anyway…which is even worse. My head feels fuzzy, like I can't think about things long. They drift away like wisps."

"You're feverish."

"It's more than fever. My head feels angry, hard to explain, but it feels as if sometimes I just want to run screaming, tearing my hair out…and…well, it feels really angry in my head."

She jumped as they heard Len and Tink shoot several times.

Len asked Mark to ride with Thurman and provide protection for Warren's SUV with Jeri, Rita, Ben, and Tom.

Benny was to follow with Misty. George, Tink, and Len, would follow with Kim, Beth, and Katie. Len was ready to be the bad guy, but an infected person was not going to threaten the entire group.

Benny asked for a few moments.

They got Dallas ready to go as they ran nervously from room to room.

Benny showed Gina what he had left for her on the polished oak table in the dining room: a bottle of pain killers and a tall glass of clear liquid filled with ice, sparkling, as it danced about a fat, fragrant wedge of lime. "Gin and tonic."

"Wait a minute." Kim scowled.

"She's in pain," Beth said simply, but she shook her head, "but not alcohol…Oh, my God, Benny…"

George rubbed Beth's back, "Shhh."

"Adapt or fail."

Gina gave Beth a hug and told her to stop worrying.

"You're sick, and I'm the one you are all comforting now." Beth sniffled. "I understand, I think. I guess. But this just sucks. It sucks bad."

Benny called to Katie, and the little girl and her mother sat down to talk.

George turned gentle eyes to both. "This thing we call Red doesn't care about religion or race or age. It makes people sick without caring who we are, who loves us, or whom we love. Whatever this new virus is, it only cares for replicating itself…multiplying 'cause that's what it does; it lives to re-produce itself and win so it can be at the top."

"We've been killing viruses for years."

"Yes, and this virus doesn't intend to die. We can't beat it; the men who could have beaten it died. And it's so set on reproducing that it makes us get up from a semi-death and attack people we care for so it can spread. I know and you know it's just a virus…but doesn't that sound cruel and intelligent? Evil?"

"It isn't smart; it's a virus."

"Seems it is smarter than we are. It's taken out most of the human race, all but for a few of us. And we're complaining now, but what about when the rest rise up and start coming after us? It'll come until we're all gone, if we let it."

George watched Katie, crying in her mother's arms. "What kind of evil makes a momma fear biting her baby girl? And she will, once she turns."

"But it isn't a thinking virus."

"How do you know, Kim? What do we know? In my mind, it's an evil, selfish son of a bitch. I wish it were a man I could fight and tear to pieces. I tell you this: I will be damned if that evil thing makes me turn on friends and help it reproduce…I won't be a part of that."

"Jesus, help us," Beth whispered, "me neither."

"When I know how things are going, I'm gonna go out on my own terms. I refuse to let the cock-knocker win. I'll go out on 'George's terms.'" He used a finger to point at his own chest.

"But she's alive." Kim complained. He sounded less sure.

"But we know she's going to turn; no, don't shake your head at me; we *know*. It's her choice, and she has made it. 'George's terms' are that she gets to decide. I'd support you the same. It's what is right. It's what makes us human."

Kim looked miserable, "But I hate it."

"So do I, son, but it is what it is; isn't that what kids say these days? Beth is right. It sucks. I hate the virus, and if anyone made it in a lab, I hope he or she burns in hell. I hate him, too. I hate having to have my own terms or standing by that poor woman in this. I hate a lot. But that hate will ruin us if we let it. I suggest we do like in a war…we don't hate…we do our job, stand by what is right, execute the enemy with extreme prejudice, and move on as best we can. We are Americans, son, and we are gonna damn sure act like it."

"Amen." Len had walked in. "I may steal that speech."

"Well, you can, but it stays 'George's terms.'" He looked sad. "I wanna take credit for making a pact to take out that evil, whatever it is."

"Agreed."

"Too much, too fast." Beth sighed. "I can't get my head around one thing before there is another."

"Please come get Katie. I'm feeling worse," Gina called.

Beth and Kim had to take Katie from Gina amid screams and kicking, but Gina grimaced in pain now, already swallowing pills and washing them down with gin and tonic. With a squeeze of their hands, she whispered incoherently, walked out to the backyard, and lay on a chaise. She smiled at the sky as she swallowed pills and drank. She looked peaceful. Kim came back to watch her, ready when it was time, but George said he would do it.

"Len…we have a problem." Misty ran in, her face contorted with fear. "There are zeds headed this way."

"How many?"

"A bunch."

"What…a half dozen? A dozen?"

Misty looked at him, baffled. "No… a bunch."

Len sighed. She was not good at Intel. "More than a dozen?"

"About fifty, Len."

"Stay with her, George." Len spun, running to the front yard, "Beth, take care of the little girl. Kim, inside…if any get past us…"

Kim barked an okay, although if they got past all them, he wasn't sure what he, Beth, and George would do. Len locked Dallas back in the downstairs bedroom, warning him to stay quiet. He got a doggie "*woof*" in return.

"Major!" Julia was calling from the front.

At the end of the street and heading right towards them, was a crowd of moaning, angry people. Some had surrounded a home, and a few had entered, with a few stumbling back out, fresh blood covering them; two more joined them in a minute, chewed almost to pieces, following, adding to the ranks.

In seconds, a man ran from his house too late, tripping and falling as zeds grabbed at him. He had run too close to the group without a weapon, carrying only bags with clothing and food, rolling out. Several immediately bit into his neck, ripped at his stomach, and in a frenzy, tore off an arm, amid biting at his elbow. He wailed, rolling around the slick, blood-gored ground, unable to get to his feet.

Thurman and Tink took shots, but the distance was causing most shots to stray. "I can't hit much from here, Major," Tink reported as he *did* land an expert head shot, putting the man down so that the screams finally stopped.

Len made a circle motion at Warren, "Go. Back way. Get yourself and the others back to the hospital, and don't stop for anyone or anything."

Warren launched into the vehicle with some of the others, speeding the opposite way of the crowd, his people inside the car, fearfully staring out the windows.

"Get everyone loaded and moving," he told Mark.

"Go," he told Tink and Thurman. "Let's move, people." He thought that many could easily overturn an SUV, trapping them. It was harder to run people over than the movies portrayed. Plus, it was a nasty business that none were trained for; if they hesitated and the crowd broke a window, it would be a violent, painful death.

Someone yelled, drawing Len's attention back as they heard the SUV that Warren was driving, screech to a stop, do a three-point turn, and roar back to them, slamming to a stop. All five jumped out. Len knew at once why they were back, feeling a knot form in his gut.

"There's a crowd of them at the next intersection; we saw a bunch, but it looked as if twice as many were joining them."

Len could have screamed. How much was a bunch?

"That many." Warren shouted, pointing to the crowd still shuffling towards them. The smell, from both directions, was already there, thick and revolting.

Len barked for them to grab their guns and get into the house.

"I don't like this," Tink said, "retreats are not always good ideas."

Len didn't know. He didn't want to be pinned in a car under a mob of them, but retreat did sound just as bad. No one had trained him for this, and he had never asked to be the leader. Alone, he would make a run for it out the back; he was in good condition, and a few of them could make it on foot, but now they had a dog, a child, and four old men.

He wasn't such a good man that he didn't think about that for a few seconds. He and whoever could keep up would run, maybe even draw the horde away, and then double back. Or keep going. He wasn't active duty, didn't have a trained bunch who could barely shoot a gun, and wasn't under any obligation. Who said he had to be a hero? He had already been brave and honorable for these people and gotten them into a good way. Well, it had been a good way until the crowds of zeds came that way.

But it wasn't his job. Or Beth's, Kim's, Mark's, or Julia's...they could bolt for safety.

A gun sounded from the back. Once. Twice. Now, four shots.

Was the old guy that bad of a shot? Len wondered. It was one woman. Why didn't George just put her down?

"Zeds in the backyard," Kim stated, joining Len.

They could get past them.

"We aren't gonna be going on foot either. George got three, and Gina...but...Major, we need a plan."

George had once said something... *'I suggest we do like in a war...we don't hate...we do our job, stand by what is right, execute the enemy with extreme prejudice, and move on as best we can. We are Americans, son, and we are gonna damned sure act like it,'* and Len agreed.

Len knew they had less than five minutes.

He ordered Julia, Beth, and Rita upstairs to shoot from the second floor when the herd got closer and told them every shot better be in the head; they weren't trained, but sometimes when you ordered people, believed they could do what was asked, and accepted no less, they did it.

The rest began removing interior doors and cabinet doors from their hinges, to be placed across the wooden shutters already on the windows. It was best to nail from the outside since it was harder to push the wood *through* the window than to push it *off* as if it had been nailed on the inside. Luckily, the men already had nailed some up outside. This was a secondary provision. Len ordered weight to be added at each window to reinforce them, lifting a door into place as he gave orders.

Beth saw a zed approaching, took aim, and used three rounds before she hit her target.

"Beth, unacceptable. One shot, one kill," Len yelled.

She blinked. How had he known it was she? Across the room, Julia shrugged and tried her skill.

"Julia, I said one shot, not four."

"One went down on two...the other two shots were body shots," she whispered to Beth, "you're right, *Chica*; he has a scary talent."

"Body shots don't help," Len thundered back. He sent Benny, Thurman, and Tink to help the women. "And you wish you had my talent."

Beth flew down the stairs. "Where's Katie?"

Jeri screamed from the kitchen, calling for help.

Kim, Ben, and George, the closest, got there first.

In conclusion, Katie had opened the back door, looking for her mother. "I saw her, hurt. Her head 'bleeded'," she cried. She had looked into the backyard from an upstairs window and saw her mother lying on the chaise, amid the dead zeds, her head bleeding from the single shot placed there; her arm had soaked the bandage with pus and blood.

Seeing and hearing Katie, Jeri was a half second behind the child, grabbing her and pushing her back, as a stinking, bloody woman was reaching for Katie.

Ben scooped Katie to him and then tossed her backwards to George who caught the girl in one arm and held her close to him.

A man, infection dripping from a bite wound to the head, clawed at Jeri, moaning, snapping his teeth at her arm, and hissing with fury in her face. Jeri froze for a second as the smell of decomposition, pus, blood, feces, and vomit, surrounded her and bluish intestines slinked from his belly in slimy coils. It was straight out of the worst nightmare one could imagine; only it was real.

The woman grabbed Jeri's arm and yanked her out the door, clamping bloody teeth down into Jeri's throat.

Kim shot the woman through the head, awkwardly dodging the man; Ben and he were blocking the way of anyone else's helping as Ben tried to fire.

Ben, losing his grip on Jeri's shirt, stumbled, falling on all fours in front of the man; two more red zeds tore into Ben's arms and scalp. They pulled at him, and he slid belly-down, swatting at them. A woman bit into his face, ripping away his nose with a bloody sweep; a teen snarled as he tore away Ben's lips and chin. It was all that fast.

Mark slid like a runner coming into home plate, firing upwards, while George got behind to help in case he could get a shot.

Kim and Mark put all of them down and added a round each for Jeri and Ben so they didn't get back up. While it made sense to fire at once, it was difficult to fire at a healthy, live person, fighting with zeds. Training was hard to override.

Once the door was slammed and locked, the rest, faces full of shock and horror, had two doors to hammer into place. Kim slid down the wall next to Beth who was holding Katie. Mark crawled to the side.

"Damn fine work," George told Mark and Kim. "Very good move there, Son." He patted Mark's shoulder.

"My God, we lost two people." Mark was pale.

"And you protected every one of the people in here," Len said.

"Major? George?" Tink yelled.

"We're good, Tink," George called back.

Len frowned as he understood he was being called 'Major' by most of them now. Damn that Julia. "Could have been any one of us. They were brave folks." That was his simple salute to the two who had died. He had to get his team moving forward again. It was hell seeing friends die, worse to see them viciously chewed to pieces.

Misty and Rita sat in the dining room crying, and Len asked Rita to take Katie upstairs and not let the little girl out of her sight. He wanted Rita to explain, in a milder tone than he would have used, to Katie how serious the situation was and to extract a promise that she would not do that fucking shit, again. With his jaw tight and eyes staring, Len dared Rita to say she couldn't handle that one chore. He had Rita take Dallas with her for Katie. Maybe the damned dog could watch the kid better than they could.

"Beth, upstairs with George...one shot, one kill, Beth. Don't waste the ammo." He glared at her. "Cover the backyard. Misty, you and Tom stand duty on the stairs. Anything happens, you cover until the rest can back you up." Upstairs, sporadic shots were fired as they acquired targets.

"Major, Len." Beth tried, eyes sad.

He had to snap her out of it, or she'd take the blame, and it would eat her alive. Like the zeds would. "Beth, you have a job to do, carry on. Good job on noticing the kid was out of your sight, way to be alert. I need you watching the backyard."

"Incoming, Major. Almost all of them," Julia called down.

"I'm going up to shoot. Kim, Tom, and Warren, I want you patrolling the house down here. All rooms. If you hear or see anything hinky...do not...I repeat, do not engage, but call us immediately. Mark and I will come down to help. Kim, you're point man down here; stay alert."

Len ran up the stairs with Mark, yelling for a sitrep as he went.

Julia and Beth called back, making him feel a wash of pride in them. He didn't ask for this, but here he was with a rag-tag bunch of civvies: some were poor shots, cried too much, and couldn't keep an eye on one child; others were old men, but all were surrounded by crazies who wanted nothing more than to disembowel and eat them. Yet, he was just as proud of them as he had been of any other of his subordinates. They didn't ask to be in his company but followed loyally, learning quickly what he demanded, and showing dependability.

He blamed himself for the loss of Jeri and Ben, reacting with self-anger and growls at others. So be it. He would shoulder the blame. He might have fared better with well-trained soldiers, but this group had heart.

"Julia, stop jerking the trigger," he called out to the other room, earning a weak grin from Mark and Tink. "Drives her crazy," he whispered to Mark.

"How does he do that?" Julia complained.

"Quit yer bitchin' and hit the target," Len sighed. If they survived this siege, he had a helluva team.

If.

7
THE PRESIDENT

He had not been where most thought he would be; he was still alive, was immune, it seemed. His small staff had looked at him in silent expectation. What did they expect? He had a tiny military to command, few advisors, a concern for his own family, and little hope.

Fact: The scientists who were left, few that they were, had no cure, only a vaccination that worked some of the time, no idea why the red zeds had been biting, had been crazed cannibals now, or *zombies*. The scientists had not known why it had spread so fast to those bitten, had claimed that they were not *all* undead, but had not been positive about that or anything else, anymore. Few were not even in touch anymore.

Fact: All who had been bitten by Red turned.

Fact: All countries had been over-taken, including the US.

Fact: Reds were still turning and might be for another week.

Fact: The power grids, all water, and every resource: everything had been finished. Nuclear reactors had been shut down. Nothing was expected to be working in the near future, if ever.

Fact: He had a headache.

Not one piece of positive information had been shared with him. If he didn't do as the rest demanded, he would be relieved of duty, maybe via a bullet. It made no sense to him that they had wanted to destroy the rest of the world and their own soil in waves of mass destruction, taking out every zombie, every sick person, and even those survivors who had been trying their best to recover.

With anger, retaliation, and fury at an enemy they wouldn't otherwise harm, they had sought to hit back.

Fact: He had had no real hope, despite being the president and had been expected to tell everyone to pull together and rebuild, to have hope and be strong, and to wait for rescue. Rescue wouldn't be coming.

He looked at the map again. Maybe there was hope.

The youngest president ever elected, he was strong, determined, and scared to die like this. There had been no fair chance at fixing this national crisis. There hadn't been a budget problem or a war, a health crisis or an education situation. This had been a plague of *zombies*. Really unfair.

They had wanted the infected wiped off of the earth.

"Mr. President…" He had been urged. Or maybe it had been a veiled threat.

Fact: This was a situation he could not win.

"I have chosen a time," he had said aloud. Then he had looked at them with sad eyes that had held a spark of raw fury, "May God damn you all to hell."

He had issued the order.

8
BACK IN THE NEIGHBORHOOD

Benny, Misty, and Julia served food to those who were ready to eat; some were upstairs on duty. While he worked, Benny outlined his theory, "It's gotta be the smell. Some of those didn't have eyes left, and they still headed this way."

"Sound," Beth said, grabbing the beans to serve.

"Possible…that moaning calls them…they call each other when they find us, I mean. They flock like birds."

"Like the movies," Mark agreed.

"But then, they started going away…so that makes no sense."

Mark thought, "'Cause they couldn't get to us."

"Really? Is that in the movies, *Chica*?"

"No."

"So if we assume they can call one another, then assume they can smell us…as if we were…food…"

"That's sick, Benny," Tink argued.

"Sick, yes, but maybe true. So what I'm thinking is…maybe they can't really smell us anymore."

"Why not?"

"Look at the ones we killed out there…there has gotta be…a hundred? That's what they smell now. They can't see us or hear us…we stay hidden, and now they can't smell us."

Mark nodded, "That makes sense."

"I thought of it while watching Dallas. He uses his nose," Benny told them.

"They don't do it out of hunger," Julia said, "George says they attack and bite to get the virus spread. Bigger bite area, more saliva, faster change."

"The fuckers swallow." Mark grimaced. "They bite and eat...it's not as if they spit the flesh back out."

"Well, not as if they can fix meals and eat like normal, now. They're more like animals the way they hunt," Benny suggested.

Len was scribbling on paper, looking up to think occasionally and listening to the theories. They needed their minds and bodies busy. He had a plan for four guards upstairs, two downstairs, and one with Katie, in shifts of four hours each. They would leave the house, hopefully, a little after dawn.

They used the fresh beef, vegetables, the rice and beans that Julia seasoned to fill themselves, aware that fresh food was about to become a thing of the past until they could make their own gardens. The smell of the sick and events had left them sick to their stomachs, but Len encouraged them to eat.

Beth watched the front beside Kim. "I keep thinking that later, I'll have a good cry when this hits me."

"That might make you feel better."

"Or worse. Len is keeping us busy, which is pretty smart."

"We have several smart ones here," Kim said.

Beth stretched. "The shower felt so good; do you think he's right that we have a good team?"

"Sure. And we have the others from the hospital. Roy's an ass, but he's helpful...Hagan...several."

"Julia is a star pupil."

Kim laughed. "She is trying. The old guys have it going on."

"I like them. You and Mark are good shots. I dropped the ball in not watching Katie. I caused two people to get killed."

"If you had, Len would have yelled at you; it was an accident that Katie opened the door; we all dropped the ball if anything. We didn't tell her not to. It could've been any one person, and we can look at how many things have gone wrong or at what we didn't do right to cause this."

"I feel as if I caused it."

"Really, whoever caused the virus caused the deaths. The *virus* caused the deaths. Beth, sorry, but people are gonna make mistakes, and people are going to die. We just have to always be a step ahead of what could go wrong."

"I'm a bad shot."

"You just need practice and confidence. Misty is a possibility, too."

Kim moved to watch shadows across the street. He pointed to his eyes and then to the window; Beth nodded and shifted to see better, as Kim darted from the room.

Downstairs, George, Len, and Warren, laboriously opened the front door and took positions with Julia and Kim behind them.

Beth shivered, realizing Kim had left her to cover the front alone. The shadows darted across and to the end of the lawn, hesitating when they saw three guns pointed at them. Three teens. In a second, they moved forward again, closer to the men. She could faintly hear them talking.

A zed moved into the light, into range, missing an arm and hand, along with parts of its stomach and face. Only the long hair told Beth it might be a female, dressed in tattered clothing, and barefoot. She looked into the scope, breathed out, squeezed, and saw the zed drop with a hole neatly through the forehead.

The front door closed and was sealed again; the shadows had been three young people who crept away down the street in the opposite direction on the other side of the street.

"Good shot," Kimball said, returning.

"I got lucky. It just stood there. What about those people?"

"Len is watching them in the other room; we couldn't let them in; one was bitten, one might have been bitten but was hiding it, hiding something anyway, and the other wouldn't leave the two."

"I feel bad for them."

"Len told them about Gina and what she did and how she turned." The guys didn't look real happy about that outcome, but they didn't want to be here with us so much after they found out that we weren't allowing sick people to go with us."

"No kidding. They don't wanna have to take their own lives or get shot by us. I don't blame them."

"But they'll turn, and that girl with them will get bitten and torn up. But then, didn't George explain it? We all have our own terms. Maybe she prefers that."

"That's bad. How does Len feel about having to do that?"

"Probably terrible, but he can't dwell on it. They were about to argue when you took your shot; that convinced them we were not playing."

"Oh."

"You did good."

"Never thought I'd be shooting people." Beth was an interior designer before, a cushy job, and now she was a zed killer. It was laughable. She silently thanked her dad again for teaching her how to use a gun. She tucked in her undershirt again and thought about the way she was dressed.

People often told her she resembled Demi Moore, with her long, almost-black hair, big green eyes, and pale skin; and yes, she was in combat camouflage like in the movie *GI Jane*, which Moore starred in, but Beth's hair wasn't going to be shaved off although Julia looked amazing with her short spikes of hair. Beth was a bit heavier than Moore had been in the movie, but she knew the activity and days ahead would slim her down fast. The issue was that Beth didn't feel as bad assed as Moore had been.

"What are you thinking about?" Kim asked, noting her wry smile.

She told him, making him chuckle.

"I'd be Nicolas Cage in one of his movies when he was pretty tough, but still a bit unsure of himself."

"I can imagine that easily," Beth told him. They made up whom each person with them would be, laughing hard when they argued about Roy. When they switched duty, Mark and Julia commented that they didn't know guard duty was so funny, making Beth blush as she tried to explain.

"Hey, why didn't I get Salma? I want a redo," Julia complained.

Beth washed her face and brushed her teeth. All at once, she felt a wave of dizziness, weakness in her legs, and chills. In horror, she whispered for Kim, asking him to come into the bathroom and then closed the door as she sank to the floor on her butt.

"I'm scared...maybe I got infected when I was helping Gina with her wound." She frantically searched her hands for cuts, seeing a few scratches. Had she gotten the poison in her skin? "I don't feel so good."

Kim watched Beth's teeth chatter and her face pale, felt of her forehead, and looked over her hands carefully. "Do you hurt anywhere?"

She shook her head.

He felt her pulse and wiped damp hair from her brow, "Beth, what kind of car did you get when you were sixteen? Did you get one?"

Instead of confusion over a strange question, she looked at him blankly, not interested. He stood, and she clutched his hand in a near death-grip. Opening the door a crack, he called Len.

"What's wrong?"

"Take a look, and tell me what you think. She's scared she's infected."

Len, in fear and concern, knelt by her, but she didn't respond to his questions, just shivered. He looked her over, talking very softly. "Hang on."

He vanished and then returned with a quilt, which he wrapped around Beth. He stepped back and motioned to Kim. "We've got you, Beth."

Kim scooped her up in his arms and followed Len to a bedroom.

"What's going on?" Julia demanded as she followed.

"Delayed shock. Suspect she's freaking out over Jeri and Ben earlier; she was talking about it," Kim said. She still didn't let go of his hand.

"Poor thing. I should stay with her?"

"You're not letting go of Kim, are you, Beth? He feels safe to you?" Len rubbed her arms. "Kim?"

"I'll stay here with her."

Julia and Len helped remove her boots, and then Julia made the men look away as she removed Beth's pants and wrapped her in the bed covers, pulling pillows along Beth's back to make a cocoon. "You be a gentleman, or I'll kill you, even though I like you," she warned Kim.

"Beth trusts me." He frowned.

"Keep her warm and comfortable. Julia, can you get her something to drink? She needs to be re-hydrated, too. Don't leave her alone."

Kim gave him a wry smile, looking at his hand still in her vise-grip. "I won't leave her." Beth pulled at his arm as she rolled to her side away from him, so he stretched out beside her, looking uncomfortable. Len got his boots for him and shrugged.

As the door closed, Beth jumped a little, shaking, and Kim turned towards her, spooning her body with his, wrapping his arms around her to keep her warm.

In minutes, she was quiet, relaxing against him, and he felt her warming. In less than fifteen minutes, she was asleep.

Kim slept, too, waking only when Len checked on them and then when Beth turned over, staying close to him, her head on his chest as she slept. She mumbled, "Thanks."

Strange, that she thought to thank him; her presence, the fact she had needed him and trusted him made Kim relax enough to sleep when otherwise he would have paced the rooms.

Usually a loner by nature and kind of shy, Kim felt as if he were changing and as if the world had gone to hell, but he was more socially comfortable now than he had ever been.

On a personal level, his only worry was that he hadn't minded a bit taking care of and sleeping next to her; he felt a quickening in his stomach when he looked at her, when he inhaled how good she smelled, and when she moved closer. If ever there were a bad time to be interested in a woman, this was the worst of times.

For the next seven hours, they were roused only by occasional shots fired.

Len gave up his schedule as some couldn't sleep or had slept all they could and stood duty while others were exhausted.

Kim woke at daybreak to slip away and save them both the discomfort of waking up together in bed.

"I took your pants off for you." Julia breezed in to wake Beth.

"Thanks."

"Just know that maybe it will be me next time, and if so, don't get my pants for me. You let whoever the man is help and then don't stick around." Julia winked.

Beth chuckled, "Noted. Unless it's Roy?"

"*Cabeza de meirda.* No, please, save me from him, racist *pendejo*. He makes me angrier than anyone I've ever met. I don't usually get this mean toward people."

Katie bounded in, and Beth hugged her close. "I like your hair." Beth cocked her head, "Did you do this, Julia?"

"Yep."

Beth held back a grimace as she surveyed Katie's hair, neatly braided into five strands down her back, the sides in elaborate French-style braiding. "It's very unique."

"I want hair like Jules. Choppy, choppy."

"I told Katie how you chopped mine and that maybe you'd chop hers."

Beth frowned and groaned this time, making Katie giggle, "No chop chop, and 'Jules' is no hair stylist."

"She wouldn't let me come get you. Were you sick?"

"Yes. But I'm better now."

"Is Mommy? Her head 'bleeded.'"

Julia hugged the little girl. "I explained that this morning, again...how Mommy is in Heaven now with Daddy. You have to help me watch out for Beth, remember?"

"Yes, Jules said you are naughty and I have to help keep you out of the time out chair." Katie giggled again.

Beth, tying her bootlaces, had to laugh. "Jules is in the time out chair far more than I am." They ushered Katie downstairs where the food smelled good. Misty and Mark were chatting quietly.

Len went over the plan again.

After they ate, they opened the front door with guards upstairs and covered the area so that Warren, Rita, Tom, and Mark could pile into the SUV parked at the street.

The four almost froze when they saw all the bodies littering the lawn, but Mark told them to hurry. Bodies lay everywhere. The smell made them think again of Benny's theory that it drove away the zeds with the scent of death.

Tink drove for Beth, Katie, Julia, and Kim. Beth kept Katie's eyes covered as they walked out to the SUV.

Benny drove for Dallas, and Len came around the rest to take the lead.

George rode with Misty and Thurman as the last in line. In a caravan, they headed across town, resisting the urge to stop when they saw a house surrounded, but there were hordes, and to stop might mean being over taken.

Len said they might come back and do rescues, but they needed to get the supplies and people to a place where it was safe.

Kim thought, had he been trapped in a house surrounded, he would want one of them to stop a car and save him; the sight of their zooming away had to be beyond depressing, but he couldn't imagine stopping, either. While he and Tink were good shots, the two couldn't hold off as many as they had seen in the hordes even long enough to get anyone out of the house. He might be cold enough to leave the rest and grab Beth to run to safety, but the thought of that made him feel sick. That's why Len had said no stops.

In another car, George worried for the people in the car that Warren drove; Mark was the only one who could shoot for that group.

That thought about Mark had not escaped Misty; George suspected she had a little crush on the man, ten years her senior. She was jumpy as a cat and unreliable because of the separation. George made a note to mention that to Len; when civvies were separated from their significant others or crushes, they got nervous and became undependable.

George watched people.

Len chucked a few times in admiration of Benny's driving. "You a race car driver?"

"No, but I always drove on patrol. Thurman always kept his eyes shut." Benny laughed. "Not bad for an old man, huh?"

Dallas barked in a laugh.

Despite not having any mishaps, they hardly dared to breathe until they were within sight of the hospital.

9
HOSPITAL

Everyone was welcomed back, and people stopped to hear news from the outside although all of it was basically bad news. People seemed stunned when they heard the stories of what the group had been through; from Julia's parents, to the herd that attacked, to losing members, to what the conditions were outside the hospital. For those in the shelters, it was a hard reality.

Hagan said he had been worried when they hadn't returned but had not known where to look for them. At once, Hagan said they should have reinforced the hospital, easier than it could have been, as they were staying in the huge basement floor area as much as possible with families of the hospitalized, moving from there and back to rooms above.

The news was off, but they had a radio they listened to for the sparse information they could get.

"I didn't think you were coming back," Bryan said, appraising Len and the rest in their camo.

"Me, either," Beth said, "it was really rough out there." Sometimes she thought he flirted with her, and so appreciated that this time, she was now dressed like one of the men.

"Hey, they're saying on the radio that something happened to New York City and a few other big cities."

"What happened?"

"No one knows. It sounds serious though. Something about explosions."

A man, who looked like Billy, of Bucks and Ducks fame, was looking towards Bryan and Beth, his mouth hanging open; he was standing in the hallway that led to the pharmacy.

"I'll be back," Bryan said. For some reason, the hairs on the back of his neck were standing on end, and he got that little feeling that he usually got when he was in danger.

"Do you like him?" Beth asked Kim, watching Bryan walk away.

"He's okay. You always seem to be frowning at him."

"He rubs me wrong. I think he's a sexist pig."

Kim chuckled.

Beth motioned for Kim to follow her as she felt something was off, just sitting wrong for her, a feeling about the way Billy had looked, as if his face seemed to reflect the shock she had gone through the night before.

As she walked toward the pharmacy, others began following, curious, as they heard voices from the pharmacy that was being guarded by one of the military. Some liked to stand and look out as they watched for zeds.

They walked up the stairs and into the pharmacy. There was a crowd, staring out the front doors and windows, some crying, and some muttering and mumbling.

Beth scooted forward to look, whispering, "Oh, dear God." On the horizon, she saw it, a small mushroom-shaped cloud; it looked like pictures she had seen of atomic tests and of Hiroshima. She backed away.

"Where is that?" a man asked.

Someone answered, "I'm not sure how far we can see, but it could be Barksdale if we can see that far."

"We can see that far. Maybe. No."

"Those things are big, and they would get Barksdale since it's an Air Force Base, you know."

"It could be Doddridge; doesn't it have that tank manufacturer? We could see that far."

"Why would anybody bomb there?"

"Maybe big cities such as Dallas or Little Rock…unless someone is hitting the military bases, refineries, and manufacturers."

"We couldn't see a bomb hitting Dallas."

"What, it's not enough for everybody to die of fucking Red? They have to bomb us, too?"

Someone muttered, "Hell, why not hit us when we're down?"

"Knock off the language. We have women here."

Bryan said, "Those mushroom clouds are about six miles high…maybe twenty million degrees."

"Damn."

"If we were closer, the wind would be hundreds of miles per hour, and if you looked at one closely, it would burn your retinas."

"We're okay, right? Nobody would want a hospital."

Kim suddenly felt his stomach drop. "Lone Star Army Ordinance Plant or Red River Army Depot."

Ammunition plants.

The man from the military pressed the pharmacist to get out, yelling at everyone to move faster.

Kim grabbed Beth's arm and swung her around. "Go."

Bryan yelled for everyone to get back into the hospital, away from the windows and out of the pharmacy. As Bryan jogged behind the people he was ushering out and up the stairs, he saw his shadow clearly against the wall in front of him. The light around him was brighter than anything he had ever seen, and his back was hot, like the August sun beating down on him.

They ran for the hall. In the incandescent light, people, who were staring out of the window and refusing to move, continued to stare, screaming in agony and fear.

Beth almost froze when she heard the screams, but several people were pushing her forward.

As the ground began shaking, Bryan and the military guy grabbed the metal doors, swinging them closed, bolting them shut. Even the closest people to the doors were too far away to make it. It was too late for them.

In the pharmacy, hot air singed hair, and screams wailed louder as people reached for the metal doors, blisters popping up on their fingers.

A roaring fireball, driven by wind, hit the hospital like the hand of a giant. Window glass flew like daggers, as metal bent like paper clips; the concrete cracked, and ceilings tumbled. Rooms spilled into one another, tossing everything into the first floor and some below into the basement. It sounded like hundreds of trains crashing; then, like the climax, concrete slabs came sliding, breaking through like huge behemoths. Some of the ceilings poured downward in showers of rubble. Like an earthquake, it was as if it went on forever, rolling, sliding, and falling.

When everything else finally stopped shaking and falling, the hospital wasn't finished, as debris continued to settle, and it seemed possible that the plaster and dust would fill the rest of the basement. Luckily, most of the rubble canted backwards to fill the parking lot and crush the biggest lobby instead of dropping straight downward.

As noise continued randomly, no one dared to make a sound, frozen in place, waiting; then, when it was totally quiet, they called out. Cries broke out all over.

Outside, the wind was screeching and forming small tornadoes, trying to drown out the inside noises. When the tortured metal screamed, there were echoes.

While everything was shaking and falling, both Bryan and Kim tried to pull Beth underneath each of them, not that their bodies would have offered much protection from falling concrete.

Kim won as Beth yanked away from Bryan and allowed herself to be cradled protectively. When it was finally quiet, Kim pulled Beth against him so she could rest against his shoulder. "Shhh. Are you hurt?"

"I'm okay," Bryan chirped.

"I was talking to her."

"I'm alright, thanks," she whispered, "Only Bryan could be cheerful at a time like this."

"We still have lights," Bryan said, amused.

"I'm guessing it's the backup generator that kicked on; we're lucky it wasn't crushed," Kim said. "This would be worse in the dark."

"Listen," Beth said.

"People are crying."

"No," Beth protested, "not that. Listen. It sounds as if somebody were calling for help from outside the metal doors."

They all looked at the doors. Others sat up to listen.

"It's the howling of the wind and this building moaning. That's all you hear," Bryan told them.

"No, I hear someone out there."

Something hit the door. Kim looked confused. "Maybe."

"It's just the wind," Bryan said. "There would be radiation falling back to earth out there, depending on what bombs were used. Now if someone were really out there or still in the pharmacy, he would be really hurt, cut up, and burned horribly. He wouldn't even look human. And if you opened the doors and let something like that in, it would bring in radiation that could kill every one of us. Maybe there are several of those monsters out there, but if we open the doors to see, we might all die."

Kim looked at Bryan straight in the eyes, squaring his shoulders. "I think you're right; it's just the wind."

No one else argued; they just sat and rested for a few moments and then got up to help people around them.

They tried not to look at the other military guy whose head had been crushed by a chunk of concrete and whose blood was seeping out onto the floor. Kim checked his pulse, shaking his head negatively. Bryan didn't look cheerful then.

Following Bryan past piles of debris, they moved into the cafeteria where they saw large slabs of cement. Crying, people were beginning to crawl out of corners and from underneath rubble; some walked around in a daze.

Roy was gathering some of the people at one of the tables, brushing trash to the side, righting the tables and chairs, and asking them to sit down; he stopped and nodded to Kim as he walked by.

Sally, who had been getting more coffee, had been fortunate in that she was down there and alive. "If they have bruises, cuts, scrapes, things such as that, get them seated at a table out of the way. If it's worse, call me. We're going to have some dead, some dying, and some with bad injuries; I'll need help with those." She nodded approval to Roy and motioned for help from Beth, Kim, and Bryan. Sally brushed her hand over her forehead, pushing back stray hair, "What the hell just happened?"

"What do you need us to do?" Bryan asked.

"Bomb?" Kim said softly.

Beth noted that most were asking what had happened; she told the others that she would explain to those seated at the table. She told them there had been a bomb explosion nearby.

Len gathered people to help with the injured.

A hard-looking woman in black leather pants, black boots, and a Harley Davidson tank top walked over. Her face was heavily lined and bare of makeup, and her hair was hacked short, bleached white-blonde with dark roots. "I'm Johnny, and I'll help if I can."

She looked unsure, glancing at Beth and feeling out of place. She was a fool for even thinking they would need her help.

"Thank, God, yes, we need more help." Beth pulled her over to help the young woman who had gone white and was staring into nothing. "She's ice cold."

Johnny spoke softly to the girl, rubbing her arms briskly, while Beth brushed her off, cleaning away debris.

On the other side of the room, Len found a man dead in big pieces of rubble.

Out of nowhere, Mark came over with Misty to help Kim move chunks of concrete where they found a man's legs crushed, shattered beyond help. Kim called for Beth to talk to the man even though his face was gray and his eyes were opened and going glassy; there was nothing that could be done for him, but she could sit with him as he died.

The hallway, leading to the rest of the basement with all of its many rooms, was clear.

Sally and her volunteers came from that direction with beds on wheels and medical supplies. She reported that the rest of the area, ten or twenty times as large as the cafeteria, storage rooms, and more, didn't take much damage and no one had been hurt. She said that the pharmacy and a lobby on the other side of the hospital had been hit the worst, and from what they could tell, the upper floors were destroyed, as well.

With Len's help, Sally applied pressure to a woman's wounds, grumbling about what they didn't have. She gave the woman shots and said they didn't have nearly enough painkillers, antibiotics, or other medication. "I'd kill for more valium."

"For yourself?"

Sally grimaced, "That, too."

"If you give me a needle and thread, I can do stitches," Len told her confidently. To his surprise, she got the supplies, handing him what he needed and pointing to a long gash on the woman's arm. "Sterilize, inject lidocaine, stitch her. Bandage."

Soon, Sally called him to handle another stitching job, and Beth joined him as a nurse.

Julia approached them and sat down to wait her turn, saying Sally had told her to super-glue her forehead, while watching for a concussion since she had been knocked unconscious. "Luckily, I have a hard head."

Chauncey and Big Bill had gotten body bags, as directed by Sally, and were carrying the bodies down to the morgue. Johnny, the woman in leather, and Billy, of Bucks and Ducks, joined them to help; Bobby, Billy's brother, had been killed in the pharmacy. Bryan said all who had been in the pharmacy were dead, and no one disagreed.

In a corner, Thurman and Tink applied antibiotic cream and bandages to those sent over by Sally, while Benny and Kim found that Dallas was a great dog to sniff out the dead and injured. Katie, uninjured, was scared and was being watched by several friends in a separate room. She had found several children to play with.

It took hours to sort the scared from the wounded and the severely injured from the dead. It was difficult to keep going with all the death and dying, but they did, at some point collapsing into chairs to rest. Some of the volunteers had cleared a path to the kitchen; water, coffee, and soda were there. Some went to cook food for the rest.

Roy blinked his eyes behind his yellow glasses and said, "I've never been in an earthquake before."

"I told you what it was," Beth said, "and it wasn't an earthquake."

"Of course, it was," Roy chuckled, spreading his arms wide.

Bryan brought his face up from his folded arms. "It was a bomb. That's what the radio was saying about New York before this happened to us."

Roy got everyone quiet again as the alarm spread, "Buddy, you're scaring people with that talk."

"It's not my intention to scare anyone, but I'm trying to be honest with all of you."

"You're full of shit."

Bryan snapped, "We saw it out the windows of the pharmacy, we saw the mushroom cloud, and then Lone Star and Red River got hit; we just caught the side blast."

"So this was nothing?"

"It could have left nothing of us but stone and ash," Bryan said.

"Well, bad as it is, we have no proof yet," Roy snarled.

"Man, you are in serious denial." Bryan marveled. "Hell, it was a bomb."

"Well, it might've been a bomb, or it might've been an earthquake," Roy still protested.

Bryan thought about dragging the loud cowboy through the metal doors so he could see the burned people and destruction from the explosion.

"Damn, you're stubborn." Len stepped forward. "You all saw the mushroom cloud?"

"Yes, I told you that just minutes ago… a few hours ago, I mean…or whenever it was; we saw the cloud towards Doddridge or Shreveport." Beth was furious now. "I told him, I mean." She pointed to Roy.

Len shook his head, "I never thought it would happen."

"You believe this?" Roy was surprised.

Thinking, Len rubbed his chin and frowned. "Well, I don't see why we wouldn't believe it; I can't give ya any reason why not to believe it. Beth doesn't make up shit."

Roy glared at her. "I'm not totally convinced that that's true, but if it were, we should get the hell out of here. We need to go where they can find us easier."

"They?" Bryan leaned back in his chair and lit a cigarette. "Who the hell is 'they'?"

Roy was unable to answer.

"There's someone out there coming to help us," someone said.

"Maybe we should get out of here and go to the mountains. We don't need to stay here. You said there were sick, crazy nuts out there, biting people, and now we have a bomb on top of us."

"It wasn't on top of us, or we wouldn't be having this conversation. Okay, look, there's radiation falling from the sky in dust, and it's dangerous, and if more of the United States has been hit, such as New York, it's gonna be snowing, and the radiation will be falling with it. And it'll be cold."

"Snow?"

"Yes, all that dust and crap will get thrown up into the sky and cover up the sun, and then the weather will turn cold. That causes what is called 'nuclear winter'." I don't understand it all, but it was on TV."

"For how long?"

Bryan shrugged, "Possibly years. Maybe months. It's been all speculation until now, and then we have a virus out there that we don't understand, though we know it causes people to want to hurt and eat us." He lit a second cigarette right behind the first one. "Leaving here is not only unwise, but also is dangerous for anyone out there; he would die of radiation while being chased down by the crazy cannibals. It's worse than what you're imagining."

"How long do we have to stay in here?"

"At least a month, but we have to stay in here anyway because we're trying to stay away from the sick people." Bryan wanted to bang his head against the table; they just didn't get it; even before the bomb, they had a big problem. The word 'nuclear' was panicking them. He backed up, "It was a bomb…maybe not like an atom bomb, maybe some other kind of bomb, but we have to assume we need to stay inside a few weeks."

"Maybe somebody will come for us before then."

Roy agreed. "Maybe."

"Unreal." Bryan almost screamed. "You saw what the outside was like before those who caught Red. Now, people with it are gonna be chasing the survivors who didn't get smashed by the damned bombs."

Roy glared again.

"Look, we have the generator for heat and light and to keep the food from going over," Len said calmly. "We were stockpiling and using this sanctuary against whatever was out there already. That said, I've been out there; I know how important it is to stay somewhere safe where we can set up security... where we can meet our basic needs...where we have medical help. Here we have people. It's worse out there now, but it's nothing we can change, only adapt to and make better. In here." Len stood.

He had their attention in a way Bryan could not get.

"Okay, we had a list of everybody who came in. We need to make a new list of everyone still here and those we lost, cross checking so that we know who is missing and whom to look for. I need some people working on that.

Sally needs some people with her, helping tend to those who got hurt. We need a group to finish clearing out this cafeteria so that we all still have our meeting place, and we need a team to continue searching for the dead and injured."

"Mark, get a few for security, will you? There is already a team busting their asses, hauling out those who didn't make it, a selfless, honorable way for them to show those people respect."

Everyone went about his chores with new energy, Len's speech having made everyone see what was right. Humans have a need to earn praise; most wanted to hear Len say that they, too, were doing honorable work.

He wasn't unaware of that, having led troops, so he knew his old work was done and his new job was to go around, lending a hand when needed. Mostly, his job was to praise those working tirelessly, reminding them that their dirty, sad jobs, while horrifying, were important. They needed a pat on the back.

Right now, he missed trained troops, not that Bryan did not know how to encourage and lead.

George waved for Len's attention, moving close to him, he said, "There was a lady who sat over by Roy; she was crying a lot, I mean really crying a lot."

"I think I know who you're talking about," Len said.

"She went to the ladies' room a while ago, still crying. After a while, she didn't come out, so I went over and called out. No answer."

"Have you checked on her, yet?"

"I came to get you."

Len knew the old man didn't want to be alone when he saw whatever had happened.

George and Len went to the ladies' room while the groups worked.

Inside, was the woman, lying where she had fallen, her wrists cut deeply, and awash in scarlet. There was also broken glass, with the sharp edges bloody. She had no pulse.

"This is a real shame."

George stared down at her. "You couldn't take it, could you? You couldn't stand what the world had become, could you? You took the easy way out, leaving us to hammer it out and to struggle through it. I can't blame you. But I can't join you, either."

"Maybe she lost someone just now in the blast, or maybe it was all of it together," Len suggested. He walked out.

George looked at himself in the mirror. "I can handle this. I can do this." The man in the mirror agreed.

Working with the others, Beth held off for a long time, but her bladder was about to burst, or so it felt. For some odd reason, she felt as if the bathroom might slam the door and lock it behind her, holding her captive. There she would sit in silence until she died. It was crazy, she realized, but she still thought about it.

Finally, her discomfort won her over. She headed for the door, marked 'ladies.' George and Len came out, startling her.

She did a double take, checking the sign on the door again. "The sign says ladies; you two are men." She smiled.

They smiled back, but Len seemed to be grimacing.

"You don't wanna go in there."

"Yes, I do want to go in since I'm about to pop."

"Use the men's, instead."

"Len, George, what's the problem? You need to go on and just tell me; what's going on?"

"There's a body in there."

For a second, she stared at both men as if they had spoken a foreign language. "And? Len, you know how many bodies I've seen lately since I've been around you? How many did I shoot?" She was flummoxed.

"This one is different. Suicide."

"Who was it?"

George told her, and she used the men's restroom without another word. She said she would stand guard outside the ladies' restroom until they could return with a body bag and mops. As she came out, Bryan approached, and they told him what had happened.

"Did you check the men's restroom first?" he asked George and Len.

They admitted they hadn't.

"They were nice to have saved me from having to see that, but I didn't need them to check the room first. If there had been anything in there, I would've handled it."

"It's still best to let a man check."

"A man? Do you have any idea what I was doing all those hours when I was with Len? What in the hell do I need a man for now?"

For the first time in hours, Len was enjoying himself again. George snickered.

"Women need men. Until you drop your pants and show me you're a man, then you're a woman whom we have to watch out for," Bryan said as Len began shaking his head with dread and George stared at the floor.

Beth went red with anger. "You would love for me to drop my pants, you douche," she yelled at Bryan while shooting George and Len dirty looks.

"I didn't say it," Len protested.

"Well," Beth pushed past him roughly, hearing him chuckle as she went back down the hallway, "You're bad, too, George."

"Next time you mouth off and she whips your ass, I'm gonna be watching and laughing," Len promised Bryan.

10

HAGAN

Things were bad enough, and now, there was a damned earthquake. Hagan lost his balance and rode the hallway like a bucking bronco until the movement stopped, seemingly a lifetime of shaking and hearing noise. A shower of rubble knocked him to his stomach, pounding his head into the floor. He passed out.

When he awoke, the noise was gone. Nausea gripped him as he tried to stand in the confined space that canted to the side. One half of the hall was completely covered in a pile of trash. Prying the remaining bit of the door open, he found that the hall ended at a ragged slab of concrete. He was buried alive. Pressing his back against one side of the hall, he looked around, trying his damnedest to stay calm.

That's when he noticed a foot, bloody and grey, peeking from the rubble, crushed under the slab of concrete. Hagan crawled back to where he had been, noticing a closet that had its door snapped in half, seemingly as if it had been compressed to half its size.

He rested for while and then went back to where the slab and foot were. Inching forward, he saw the floor disappear into a wide crack. "Hello," he called into the maw of the black hole. He regretted having come up here instead of staying in the basement.

For a long time, he lay on his stomach, staring into the ink; he had lost track of time, but when he came back to his senses, his neck ached, he was thirsty, and his bladder felt full to bursting. His watch was shattered, so he had no idea how much time had passed.

Hagan relieved himself in the closet. He looked over the inventory again. Sheets. Scrubs. Nothing useful. He went back to the hall, dragging things to make a pallet, his entire body aching. His head throbbed with each heartbeat; Hagan figured he had a concussion.

For a while, he begged the big crack in the floor to leave him alone, telling it that he would not feed it. As soon as he said that, he came to, wondering why he had said it.

Next, he listened to the sounds of rescuers, thinking that it might take them a while with the hospital like this, but he decided it was his imagination. Slowly, he remembered there were zombies and that many were infected with Red, but, then, he figured he had imagined all that as well. Nothing sounded plausible at that point, whether it was the big black crack in the floor demanding to be fed, or rescuers, or zombies, or the damned tooth fairy, dancing the Charleston.

"They're coming to get you, Barbara," he quoted.

He wondered if he might run out of air. He gasped a while.

Hagan went over the little area in minute detail. He drifted. When he awakened again, he felt a little better and that he might know what was real and what was claustrophobia and concussion. The fairies and rescuers were false; zombies and big cracks were real. The jury was still out on the flying monkeys.

Hagan crawled back to the mouth-like crevice. "You gonna eat me all up?" He shined his flashlight into the maw, the beam lit nothing but rubble and ink, and he could see nothing, but when he turned the beam off, he was positive that he could see a pinpoint of light far below.

He blinked. He was afraid that this might be his imagination or in his aching head, but he *knew* it was real.

After a while, Hagan had made a rope of braided strips of bed sheets from the closet. "Just like the movies...getting out of Alcatraz," he told the mouth. But there was no other way out. At least this was a chance. If he waited too long, he would be too weak to try anything. His claustrophobia was making him feel stark-raving-Lord-hand-me-a-bucket crazy.

Tying the end of his makeshift rope to a piece of iron bulging from the wall, he pulled, testing it. The other end, he tied around his waist and retested. "I'm comin' down, so don't bite."

Taking in a deep breath, he got ready to climb down. He thought of something and told the crack in the hallway, "Reminds me of that movie, *The Poseidon Adventure*, where all those fools were running around inside the upside-down ship, up one side and down the other... and into the worst messes, trying to escape; maybe this was a good sign since none of them were black folks." He laughed at himself.

He had to get out.

He found footholds and handholds, which made it a little easier; then, he felt swallowed whole in the belly of the beast. At times, the wall narrowed so much that he needed to force himself to squirm through, shredding his shirt and one of his shoulders. Next, there was a wide space.

Next, there was a slide to his side, where a sharp piece of protruding metal had dug into his muscular arm. He raved, talking to people he imagined, played word games, and listed trivia. He pictured a single black thread in a white room, and he grasped it. He was almost stuck again.

At this time and stuck tightly, he inched down, fighting not to lose control, because if he did, he would stay in that tunnel, screaming until he died, like some Poe character. He listed stories and characters by Poe. He went on deeper.

At one point, the space was too tiny, so he felt to the left, finding nothing, then to the right where a block shifted, allowing him to crawl downwards again.

The makeshift rope was given up, but he knew that either he would find a way out or would have to give up anyway; he had come down a long way. His hold on his imaginary thread grew tenuous.

The tunnel he used cut hard to the left; panels flew away; then, Hagan's feet were hanging in mid-air. Although he stretched his legs in all directions, he couldn't feel anything; the ground had simply disappeared, and he wondered if this were a deep, dark crack in the earth. He'd come so far and dreaded climbing back up, wasn't sure he could even make it. The thought of going back to that small tomb was too depressing. The big black crack was gonna eat him all up, yes, sir and slap-my-ass-and-call-me-Bob.

He took a deep breath.

Like going off the high dive, Hagan didn't think about it, he just let go, praying and visualizing the big white teeth the shark had in that movie when it ate that fellow on a boat.

"Ya' damned big fish," he yelled.

With bent knees to absorb the impact, he landed solidly in the hall. A few steps after that to the side, he could see ceiling tiles which he dug through like a rat. It was a miracle that he had landed safely and a miracle that he hadn't fallen on rubble or sharp iron that could've possibly killed him. The biggest miracle was that he hadn't died to begin with in the initial cave-in.

Hagan just sat for a second, feeling literally as if tons had been lifted off his back. He could move. He knew how close he had been to sheer insanity; it wasn't a bad place at all; insanity is a prison of freedom. He shuddered and took time to settle down.

As he looked around, he grinned big time. He knew this place. Somehow he had landed in the basement, close to a hallway that branched into another hallway, which led right to the cafeteria.

He walked that way until he saw someone.

"Where did you come from?"

"I climbed down from the upper floor." Hagan shrugged as if it were the most natural thing on earth. "Tight in some places."

From across the room, he heard Len hail him. "Where the hell have you been? Thought we lost you." Len shook his hand.

"I was up there." Hagan pointed upward.

"You gotta be kidding me," Len said.

"Since when does Texas have earthquakes?" Hagan asked.

"It wasn't a quake."

"Huh? Sure it was; what else could have done it?"

"Hi, Hagan, good to see you didn't get burned or crushed." Beth smiled.

"Burned? Is there a fire?" Hagan was getting more confused. Were these people crazy, or was he?

Kim walked over, looking at Hagan closely.

"I'm not burned," Hagan blurted as if that were some secret password that he didn't understand.

"No, you sure aren't. Where did you come from?" Kim asked.

"Up there," Hagan said. This conversation was making less sense as it went on. Maybe he was dead, imagining this whole thing. "The earthquake knocked everything over up there and almost squashed me like a bug, but I got out and climbed down here." Hagan showed him his tattered shirt and the cuts and scrapes he had. Why did they think he had been burned?

"I can't believe anyone on the upper floors could have survived. You're lucky," Beth said. "He doesn't know what happened; he thinks it was an earthquake." She really hated to be the one to tell him the truth.

This made no sense to Hagan. "What was it?"

"A bomb."

Hagan waited a second. "Excuse me? A bomb?"

"Like a missile. None of us know exactly, probably hit Red River or somewhere," Len explained. "You know that guy with a yellow-tinted Hank Williams, Junior, glasses on? That asshole? He wouldn't believe for the longest that it was a bomb even though he saw the mushroom cloud."

"You saw it?" Hagan felt that someone had knocked the breath out of him.

"Yes, Kim and I, and the military douche, Bryan, saw it," Beth said.

"Glad you crawled down here and saved us the trouble, Hagan," Kim laughed, "No, seriously, we have so much going on down here, who knows when we would've been able to find you."

Hagan flinched as Len touched the wound on his head. "You have a knot the size of a goose egg. Go get Sally to check it and bandage up those cuts for you. With your head and that lump, I'm surprised you were thinking clearly enough to get here."

"Glad you made it, Hagan. We lost Billy to the bomb and some black lady to suicide, maybe two dozen in all."

"Hate to hear it, my Brother." Hagan patted Len, shook hands with Kim and an older man, introduced as Benny. He hugged Beth. "Lost someone up there? I just saw a foot."

"That's bad."

"Len, who do you think did this?"

"Dunno, Hagan, North Korea or Iraq, maybe we did it to ourselves to clear out the infected. I don't think we'll ever really know if it's like this all over, and I don't guess it matters."

Beth snarled, "Matters to me, I'd kill to kick someone in the balls for this."

11
STATE OF THE STATES

The destruction in the United States was immense. New York City and the DC area had disappeared in firestorms, so huge, and so hot that even those underground and prepared, were incinerated.

Two missiles that had hit the ocean bottom, right off the coast of Florida, exploded on impact, carving out huge craters. Water had vaporized. A ball of fire with a temperature approaching 25,000,000°F had blown across the ocean, slamming over the land within seconds after the detonation, burning everything in its path with winds rising to three hundred miles an hour and squashing buildings as if they were children's blocks. Glass had shattered, melted, and had flowed.

The mushroom cloud of dust and dirt that had been sucked up rose above the ocean, eight miles high. All the fish, for twenty miles around the blast instantly died, sharks sinking into the muck with crustaceans, others bellying up on the surface.

Houston, Texas, had been hit by two hundred mega tons of TNT, and it was as if Johnson Space Center had never existed; five million, mostly Reds or zeds by now, that had been gathering towards the middle of the city, had vanished, leaving two million more behind to be burned, killed by debris, or face the concussion.

Cities such as Albuquerque, Phoenix, El Paso, Atlanta, Detroit, and Seattle, along with the main cities of Dallas, Little Rock,

Arkansas, and Colorado Springs, an important part of United States military system, had disappeared.

California, unable to take the damage done to San Diego, San Francisco, Los Angeles, Sacramento, and the Valley had shuddered; the area west of the San Andreas' fault had slipped right off from the rest of the continent, submerging burning cities.

Although the cost was astronomical in terms of the lack of survivors, the resulting elimination of so many infected who might have traveled east, spreading the virus, was the one action that may have saved parts of the remaining United States.

Missile silos released spears of destruction, going in another direction.

There had been many places, safely between one and point zero, that were directly hit by the missiles. People had seen the mushroom-shaped clouds in the distance and had been glad that they were safe.

But the deadly clouds from the detonation, tornadoes, and raging fires had sent millions of tons of radioactive dust and debris into the sky, and once there, had done two things; first, much of it would remain in the sky for months, if not years, blocking out the sun's rays so that nothing would grow in the cold, brown snow and gray rain that would fall. Just as dangerous, the dust that was deadly with radiation, had sifted back to the earth to poison humans, animals, and plant life; everything that it touched, had been covered by an oily, dusty film.

In Nebraska, Kansas, Oklahoma, and Missouri, tornadoes had crisscrossed over the land, cutting paths like no one could imagine. Floods from the ocean and rivers had drowned seaport cities.

Oddly enough, those infected with Red had been the largest population to be taken out by the bombs, and while there had been mass destruction with radiation that had killed many survivors, the Red in the cities, had been greatly thinned out. It could be said that the cure had been as bad as the original illness, but some would argue that even the bombs and the radiation had been preferable to being eaten alive by the Red Zeds.

Shockingly, with all this destruction, the United States had suffered the least, as other countries had seen the remaining survivors infected and eaten alive and then were lost over the next few months.

12
A SURVIVOR

When it had happened, Tina had been in a hospital room with her sister, two brothers, father, and her mother. Her mother had appendicitis. Amazingly, they all were immune to the Red. They had been in and out of the room but had been standing around her bed, willing her to get well.

All of this was unsettling to Tina. She had been a librarian who excelled in her job mainly because of her OCD, having a specific place for each book and allowing no dust or dirt in the library. It had been perfect for her, as her environment stayed in absolute order: cross-indexed, clean, pristinely neat, the way it should have been.

The hospital hadn't been orderly or very clean, and she suspected that there had been a spider web in one corner. In the little bathroom off of the hospital room, baseboards had been scuffed, counters had been chipped, and a stray hair had been on the floor close to the toilet.

She had taken Xanax to keep from screaming about everything that she had seen in the hospital days earlier; blood, mucus, urine, and worse. Those fluids had been everywhere. It had nauseated her. Television reports she had seen from the cafeteria horrified her with the images of disorder, filth, and humans, running all around, doing unclean things.

Her mother's fever and sweating almost had driven Tin insane. One of her brothers stared out the window into the parking lot, not really seeing it.

Tina glanced out the window at the lines of perfectly parked cars, columns, and rows neatly formed. She had seen imperfections. Now, she saw a voluminous dark cloud, rolling and billowing with smoke and debris, rise up on the horizon; it was huge, larger than anything she had ever seen.

Tina turned to tell her father that he should look out, just as the room roared with incandescent light. The floor swayed outwards and then inwards. Concrete fell as metal twisted, screaming, and equipment rained down from the upper floors. An enormous crack yawned open in the floor, and Tina watched with horror as her mother's bed began sliding into it, too large to fit. The ceiling bulged, and along the wall, cracks formed.

Tina felt something incredibly hard snap the back of her head, neck, and shoulders, dropping her to her hands and knees and then to her stomach, like a giant flicking at her with a big fingernail. Right before she passed out, the dark rushed at her with the sound of the ocean's voice. Tina heard the most heart-wrenching wail and a sob that echoed emptiness.

Even when she awoke, she kept her eyes closed, thinking. She knew that for some reason, the hospital building collapsed, and abstractly, she connected the mushroom cloud to the hospital's falling.

She opened her eyes slowly, lying on her stomach in the rubble, paper, and a dribble of water. It was coffin-like where she was laying, a tiny, oblong space where she could barely wiggle her feet. She could only move her head a few inches. Pointing her toes on only one foot, as the other was numb; she found the end of her coffin. Light showed from there. To either side, she could move her arms and hands.

Under her face was dirty water and grime that made her feel horrible; she painfully rolled over on her back, her skirt scrunching up beneath her, making her more uncomfortable. Her virginal white blouse had come loose and had pulled out from the waistband, so she could feel her back, scraped and dirty. Her Peter Pan collar was pulled to the side.

It felt as if the numbness was leaving her other foot; it was aching now.

Light filtered in from the hole close to her feet, so she was able to see in terms of gray. She froze in absolute horror. Her bladder almost let go. Right above her was the back of a head, an arm that was shredded, and a bluish-grey hand with fingers, pointed down at her accusingly, telling her she had no right to still be alive. No right at all. She thought it was her brother.

She saw a fat black spider on one of the blue-tinged fingernails, crawling closer, and inches above her face.

Not a spider.

A big drop of blood.

It fell, hitting her neck and sliding slowly across her skin to her back. She could almost feel legs scuttling, causing goose pimples.

Without a doubt, Tina knew that the water she had fallen into was probably blood. Her bladder let go, burning, but also feeling good. Hot, searing urine gushed between her legs, stinging her scratches and her scraped back. The blood and urine terrified her.

It was *on* her.

She screamed hysterically, thrashing and kicking, so disgusted by the nastiness that she felt herself going mad. With dust and pebbles falling across her chest, she stopped moving; screaming now as her foot and ankle throbbed, sending sharp spikes of pain to her brain that threatened to steal her breath.

She made herself calm down, felt in her pocket, and with a lot of maneuvering that caused pain all over, she managed to get a few pills to her lips and dry swallow her Xanax. She waited until she could think again. How many did she have left?

Carefully inching her hands across her thighs and her hurting stomach, then across her breasts, chest, and face, she brushed away the dirt. Tina began to explore her surroundings again, steeling herself against the panic. Toward her feet where plaster had fallen and the ceiling had opened up, she saw her sister's face; one ear, an eye, and a cheek, torn to the bone. With the hole in her head, it looked as if her brains were oozing through it.

Disgusting.

She scooted plaster over to the side with one foot, and running her bare foot along the floor beneath her, she felt a pillow or wadded sheet but possibly something worse. With the other foot still hurting, she wiggled it a little, experiencing an odd sliding-scraping-thumping-groaning pain in her heel. She didn't think she could take much more.

Another big drop of blood left the fingernail to plop right into Tina's open mouth. Her eyes promptly rolled up in their sockets as her world went black.

As she lay unconscious, the building shifted again, making changes. The little hole, which had let in the light, elongated to three feet tall and six inches wide, a big window but too small to use as a door. Her sister's head disappeared as her body fell down below. Her brother's body moved upwards, giving Tina more room. Dirty water fell into the hole where the light was dribbling through the cracks, and a thin stream trickled close to her head.

She awoke, imagining the trickle of dirty water was a pure, little spring which she greedily sucked down. Then, she slept, again.

The next time she was awake, she looked around, but all she could think about was getting a scalding hot shower that would make her skin lobster-red; she would use disinfectant straight on her flesh. Her fantasy was a shower with lots of clean, hot water and nice-smelling bath gel. Tina was hit by pain that took her breath away. Blinding pain.

She ate another two Xanax, emptying the bottle.

She could sit up a little even with her head heavy as lead. She decided that her ankle was probably shattered, and it felt as if the bones were grinding nauseatingly.

Even with the changes that had occurred while she was unconscious, she found that she was able to rise up a little to look down; her neck muscles ached with the strain of holding her head up. When she wiggled her big toe, it hurt terribly, worse in her ankle. Something was very wrong; she blinked. *Big toe?* She laid her head back quickly before she could pass out, again. Her bloody, smashed foot was missing its big toe; in its place was just a spongy spot, covered with dirt.

The pain was terrible, she was buried alive with the dead, but somehow, the worst of all was that she was just so dirty. Her bowels cramped painfully, sending fear through her stomach that they would release, leaving her trapped in her own waste. That thought was the worst she had ever had.

Sometimes she wasn't conscious, but when she was awake, her ankle and foot brought the worst pain she could have imagined. Smells were beginning to overwhelm Tina, as the dead had released their bowels and were beginning to smell of decomposition.

While unconscious, again, Tina had fouled herself, and unable to escape the stench and the sticky-mud feeling in her panties, she sobbed and prayed that the next time she was unconscious, she would just die.

No one could live with such filth in her nose and all over her body. The pain was unbearable, and she was so scared here, alone. Oh, and her family was dead.

No one could ever be okay after something like this. Why didn't she just die? She begged her body to let go.

The next time Tina awakened, there was something new. There were little blisters lining her mouth and throat, and she was blazing hot with fever. Half out of her mind in pain, she thought about the water that trickled in; she knew it had been a terrible mistake to drink it. Cramping, nasty diarrhea was more humiliation than she could bear; she wailed through each wave.

The smell of rotting meat made her salivate; with her stomach growling, she screamed with disgust and desperation. She thought there was an odor coming from her foot, and when she reached up to feel her face, to check the fever, she felt little blisters popping, as if she had a bad sunburn. Nausea rose, and she turned her head to the side to vomit.

What did I do to deserve this? What was my terrible sin? She would die in this disgusting, terrible, stinking place. She began looking around for something with which to hurry her death along.

Voices.

"Hello?" she called, knowing it was a hallucination.

She thought she heard some type of muffled reply. Then there were hands reaching, pulling plaster, concrete, and debris. The hole widened. "There."

"It stinks."

I do, thought Tina.

"Shhhh."

"It's gonna hurt like a bitch." Somebody was doing something down close to her foot and ankle.

Tina vomited again.

"We're going to ease you out; keep your eyes closed."

"Look at her."

"Shut up."

Tina squinted at the people standing around her.

"It's going to be okay," someone lied to her.

Tina tried to smile, dreaming of the hot shower again. "I need a bath," she said, her voice raspy and rough.

A man shook his head in disbelief.

"A bath."

Tina sank into unconsciousness.

13
ANOTHER SURVIVOR

When the hospital began shaking, shuddering into itself, Bridget was in a restroom close to the lobby. She held on to the sink as she rode it out, bumping her head soundly, knocking herself out for some time.

When she awoke, she winced as she scrubbed blood from a cut in her hairline. Opening her bag, she meticulously patted expensive powder onto her face, clucking at the shiny places she was erasing. Her Crimson Delight, cherry red, lipstick ran smoothly over her lips, making them full and smooth. She used a sweep of brown-black Super Plump Mascara on the upper and lower lashes with a quick line of blue-grey eye pencil applied to her inner eyelid at the bottom to make the whites appear whiter.

Perfect.

In the department store where she worked, her perfume named Guinevere, smelled lovely, sensuous, and yet innocent. She immersed herself in a cloud of the fragrance.

Bridget swirled her brushed, bright blonde curls about her finger, giving them quick spritzes of hairspray, then rubbed lotion into her hands and down her taut claves, and finally straightened her designer skirt, blouse, and jacket. After she was finished, she neatly refilled her bag.

She moved to sit doll-like in the hard backed chair, a slight smile on her face; when they came to rescue her, she would be waiting as pretty as a picture.

14
AND ANOTHER SURVIVOR

Her first trial had been surviving the car accident, and that had left her blind, her second trial. Now, she knew she faced her third. In the lobby, she had listened to her brother-in-law say that he had seen a mushroom cloud on the horizon, rising angrily to the sky. She had a feeling something even worse than Red was coming, and now it had.

"Why would there be a bomb?" she asked uselessly.

"Maybe we did it, or they did it, but it's a bomb. People were buzzing around her, fear rising like a cloud, making her stomach knot in waves of uncertainty.

Someone shouted when incandescence filled the lobby; Maryanne didn't see the light, but she felt the air change. Voices went shrill. The floor shifted, and the wall tilted at an angle, giving her protection from the searing, hot wind, burning light, and death.

Cooler air was vacuumed from around her, and she broke into a sweat, her eyes pulsing blindly, throbbing. Instinctively, she flopped to her stomach to gasp, fish-like at the little oxygen there. Around her, the roar of winds eclipsed the screams; moaning and screeching of the rubble that pelted Maryanne.

Cocooned in her eternal darkness, she lay there, riding waves of upheaval until she lost consciousness.

When she awoke, it took a few seconds before she had her bearings; she sadly thought of her brother-in-law, sister, and the new baby and wondered if they had survived. There were sounds, but she was alone. She knew they hadn't survived this; it was a feeling she had.

Carefully, she began to explore her surroundings. Glass and sharp concrete, twisted metal, all tore at her hands.

Finding a cooling body close to her that had no pulse and a hand that ended at the elbow, she shivered, moaning as she threw it away from her. Sure that the man was beyond caring, Maryanne stripped the man of his shirt to wrap her hands.

After much trial and error, she crawled and stumbled into less debris. She squirmed through tight spaces, climbed up, down, over, and under trash that scratched and scraped her skin.

A half-opened, crushed door allowed her to creep into a small bathroom that she recalled being not far from the lobby. She was able to quench her thirst, relieve herself, wash, and re-bandage her hands. Those few actions did amazing things for her mood.

She hummed to herself while she searched for a way out. Squeezing through blocks and slabs, she thought or told herself she was following faint voices.

She rested.

Yes, those were voices. Maryanne crawled through more of the collapsed building until she could stand. "Hello? Is someone there?"

"Stay where you are," returned a strong voice.

"Thank you. I'm blind. Can you help me?"

"She was blinded by the blast?" someone asked.

Maryanne remembered to breathe, scared of being left by these people. "I was already blind. It was a head injury long ago. I need help. Please."

"Are you hurt?" Closer now.

"My hands, I cut them a little. I got scraped up pretty bad."

"Are you burned?"

"No," she said.

She felt a woman's hands on her arms, looking at her hands. "I'm Beth. Kim is here; you heard him first. And George is here; Mark, Chauncey, and Big Bill are behind me."

"Thank you. Are you from the cafeteria?" She felt safe.

"Yes. Some of us are from the group that went out for supplies. The hospital collapsed around us."

"There was a bomb. Dale said that."

"Is he with you?"

"No. He was way back there with some others, but none of them got out unless you've seen one of them. We were in the lobby."

"No, only you."

The one named Kim whistled. "You're lucky to get out of that. Sorry about Dale." He had strong hands that she felt as he patted her arm lightly. In spite of herself, she felt herself falling into his arms as her legs gave out.

She tried to form a mental image for each person who spoke to her; she felt positive energy radiating from each one of them, but she couldn't speak anymore. Finally, she felt safe and began to cry for her losses.

Kim carried her to the cafeteria.

Maryanne just cried.

15
WALKING DEAD

"I wonder if we'll find more survivors?"

"I'm surprised we found this many," Sally told them. "This has caused a lot of trauma; the ones we have found are fortunate." She set up make-shift clinics in some of the rooms.

"No one has given up looking for survivors."

"They won't last much longer unless we find them," Sally noted.

"We all need to stay on work details."

A man snorted.

"That seems smart," Roy agreed, surprising everyone. "If we are staying here a while where it's safer, then we need to be comfortable."

Paul and his wife, Donna, looked unsure. "Maybe we should try to find where the military is massing to help us."

"There is no military, but me. Maybe some had scattered around the country, but there is no place to go; after all, we're in a hospital," Bryan pointed out.

"He's scaring me," Donna said, clutching her husband's arm.

"We are not the only ones left," Paul growled.

"No. We have plenty of Reds out there. And yanno, you're right. There are millions of survivors, just like us, but the radiation will take some, and the disease and injuries will take others…and the Reds are going to be hunting the survivors."

"That's crazy talk. They don't turn into monsters."

"Really? Did you see them coming at you, moaning, and trying to grab you and take a chomp? Tell Jeri and Ben there aren't monsters."

"That's crazy talk."

"Why did they bomb us?"

"Maybe it wasn't a 'they'; maybe we did it to ourselves. Maybe that was how 'they' thought to get rid of the masses of Reds in the big cities," Bryan said.

"We only saw a small herd of them...hundreds, imagine thousands out hunting," Len agreed. "Even one can be deadly if it gets you." He thought of Gina. "Johnny, hand me a smoke; I need a fresh pack."

The woman shot him a dirty look. "You have your own." But she offered him one from her pack. Bryan and Kim held hands out. "You want me to fix a fancy pitcher of girly drinks for you, too? Add the fancy umbrellas?"

"I'd like that if you put enough vodka in it," Len chuckled.

"How can you people laugh and make jokes?" Donna dramatically waved smoke away from her face. Since the bomb, she and her husband had stayed close to Roy.

"'Cause we aren't dead, yet," George said quietly.

One of the other men, along with Donna, and Paul, drifted away with Roy, heads together, talking quietly.

"Division?" Bryan asked.

"Human nature," Len reminded him.

"Roy is building his own camp, I think," Beth said, "small so far, but it'll grow. On this side, we have those following Major Len."

"I'm in this camp," Johnny said, her voice rough.

Bryan held an arm up, and they did a fast high-five.

"You have me and the boys," George added.

"And us, Misty and Julia, Mark and Bobby, and Hagan. I think Chauncey and Big Bill, too," Kim added.

Len raked a hand through his short hair, "You people are amazing, but about stupid, electing me a leader."

They laughed.

"How's the generator?"

Kim shrugged at Len. "With this place going down, I figure we can make it a month with lights if we conserve. I'm no expert. Mark knows more than I."

"Ah, but you're smart, farm boy."

Kim laughed. He was still ropey, muscled the same as when he had grown up working his dad's farm. His reddish hair and slow grin, along with his tendency to remain quiet until he warmed up to people, let his secret weapon, intelligence, remain hidden. In his Wranglers and tee shirt, roper boots and hat, he personified the term 'goat-roper' look. He hadn't adopted the camouflage style that most had.

He tipped his hat to Johnny, making her cackle.

In one hall, the half-wall hid most of the view, but they could see where a dark tunnel snaked upwards. Len held his hands out for them to halt.

"Another survivor," Bryan said quietly.

Beth cocked her head. "It sounds…"

Len pushed them back. "Get back." Only he and Bryan still carried weapons. The moaning might have been someone injured, but Len had heard that infernal noise outside. It sounded like a Red Zed.

Fists pounded from behind a fallen door.

"Get them out." A man named Arnie had heard and brought Sally running. Several others filled the hall behind them, trying to call to survivors.

"We need to be sure."

"What the hell is wrong with you?" Arnie and another man rushed forward to move the door, side-stepping Len, as he listened.

"Wait."

"It sounds wrong," Kim said as the moaning intensified. He pulled his pistol from his back, surprising Len.

"Help us, why do ya wanna shoot a survivor?" The man snapped and then went back to clearing rubble. "Asshole. We need help."

"Stop digging," Len ordered.

"Hey, Len says to wait," Johnny yelled.

The two men heaved the door to the side, and everyone waited a heartbeat to see what was in the dark.

The smell assaulted them first. Beth's eyes went wide as she took in the smell and the moaning. She grabbed Sally before the doctor could move closer; everything went to slow motion. A torn body shoved forward, shambling out of the dark, hands reaching; it wore jeans and a shirt that were once blue, both garments shredded now.

"My God, are you okay?" Arnie was slack-jawed at the staggering form that managed to keep on its feet despite missing flesh from its thigh and chunks from both arms; the stomach was torn open, showing the white ribs bones protruding boldly.

"Get back," Len yelled.

But Arnie wanted to be a hero and save this one. He moved closer to help, accidentally allowing the zed to snatch his arm and sink his teeth in, lightning fast. Arnie screamed as his flesh disappeared into the mouth, down the gullet, and out again, back to the floor.

The second man tripped, trying to get away.

Kim motioned for everyone to retreat, but people blocked the hallway, screaming and staring blankly at the carnage.

Another partially eaten body, a woman in a dress with her arms chewed to yellowish bones, shambled out from the dark, and a male Red Zed came out, his mouth solidly covered in dried blood. Both had oozing sores that dripped. All three moaned.

Len fired, taking out the one who had come out last, but the other two in his line of fire were tangled with the two men now, biting. A fourth and fifth appeared, sending some of the survivors bolting down the hall as others ran forward to see why there was a shot being fired. Chaos ruled.

A family with a victim of Red, Beth thought. Why was a family here? Why was a Red here?

Blood spurted as the zed bit into his stomach, pooling fast beneath him, and making it impossible for him and the other man to get to their feet in the slick liquid. Both men howled.

Unnerved, Kim fired, finally putting a second one down.

Kim handed his handgun to Beth and swung down low, scooting forward and grasping the man's feet to pull him to safety. She could have screamed with fear and frustration at Kim for this suicidal move.

"Man up, Beth. Acquire," Len yelled as he hit a third. With an unexpected wash of anger at Len for making her do this, Beth took a breath, firing at her target, and taking it out in two quick shots to his head. Her ears rang.

Amid blood and other liquids washing out from all his wounds into a slimy mess, the man was yanked by Kim to safety.

Bryan took the final shot.

The fight had lasted mere seconds.

Johnny held Sally back this time as Len nodded to Bryan, and Arnie fell back with a single shot to the forehead.

"Why?"

"Sally, look how torn up Arnie is, and he was infected with the first bite," Johnny reminded her.

They all looked at the other man whose name they didn't know, wounds gushing blood as he convulsed with pain.

"You don't wanna see this." Len motioned everyone back. "Go on back. It's over."

"But he's alive," someone muttered.

"No he's not; he just doesn't know it yet." George and Johnny walked over to herd the on-looking crowd back down the hallway.

Kim sat back, frustrated. Bryan and Len let Mark and Tink, both armed, back them up as they carefully searched the dark space, watching for more movement and listening for moaning.

Tink fired once.

Beth's ears were still ringing. She handed Kim his pistol. Sally walked over to check Kim for bites, yanking his shirt and sleeves up, then checking his legs and going over his hands carefully.

"Clear," Len called back

"He's clear, too," Sally announced, allowing Kim to redress.

"Looks as if the Red and the others were on a floor above and slid down. The Red then infected the others. But that doesn't make sense." Tink scratched his head.

All heads turned to Sally.

She shrugged, "We had a few infected." She went to the dead ones and felt for their pulses, felt around, poked.

"If they aren't dead…" Len checked each again, with one eye on Sally.

"They're dead," she said, rocking back on her heels as she crouched there. "But, this is impossible. They have *been* dead."

"What?"

"I mean, they were dead before they attacked."

"That isn't possible, Sally," Len told her. "I mean none sounds possible, but I gotta draw the line when you say we had dead people, biting and attacking."

"Draw a line then, but they were dead. I'm sure."

"No way. 'Cause that would mean…"

"That the bombs were for nothing and there's still just as many." Beth sank to the floor next to Kim.

"That's what I thought. I mean, I figured it out when they were attacking; they looked dead," Kim said. He took a cigarette as Johnny, hands shaking, passed out more cigarettes.

Bryan squatted, looking at Sally, "And we have Red in the hospital?"

"Yeah. His temperature and the *rigor*; he's been dead half a day. You can smell decomp over the rest of the smells."

"And they really are zombies."

"Zombies, zeds. We're seriously screwed," George said.

16
KNOCK AT THE DOOR

"Len?" Big Bill called, "Chauncey and I can get this taken care of; they need you at that other exit…not the pharmacy."

"What's up?"

"We hear people. People are outside beating on the door."

Kim got to his feet and pulled Sally and Beth to theirs. Len pointed at George and Beth. "Get your weapon, and tell any of the rest with us to get theirs. Hurry." He motioned for Sally, Bryan, Tink, Kim, and Mark, to come with him.

"When it rains…" Roy stepped aside, to give Len authority. He had gained a follower who stood close to him now.

"What is it?"

"Listen. Voices."

Len stepped closer to the closed metal doors. "Hello?"

"We need in. Please. We need help. "

"How many do you have?"

"Five." Pause. "Seven. Please."

Len, Kim, and Bryan traded glances. Tink muttered they couldn't count.

"Were you exposed?"

They heard a discussion. "Some of us. We don't have Red. We're immune. None of us were bitten. We need food and water, and we have injuries."

"Are you bitten?"

"None of us are bitten…it was the bomb that got us."

"We could vote," Tink offered.

"Those people will go for rationing food 'cause it is necessary. They will live around guns and our shooting the infected 'cause it's necessary. They won't like many of the things we will have to do, but those actions will be necessary. I don't think many in here will vote to leave them out there when we have food, water, and a doctor," Len grumbled.

"I might," Bryan stated.

"If they are bitten, they can't come in," Kim said.

"We helped Gina."

"Len, we knew her. We don't know them."

Len nodded. He wanted everyone to say what was on his mind. Johnny, George, and Beth had come back with Hagan and a few more. "It isn't a democracy anymore," George said, "we need a leader."

"Not a dictator either," Len protested.

"Are you there?" the voice called.

"We're here. Give us a second." Len looked at Sally, "Tell us how to do this."

Len called back to the seven that they would have to follow every instruction given to them. They agreed.

Sally said that they had to remove every stitch of clothing and all jewelry, even wedding rings. "I can't think," Sally complained.

"You're all we have."

She grimaced. "All wallets…absolutely nothing personal can come inside."

The voice outside argued that they didn't want to leave jewelry and wallets behind; Len responded that they couldn't come in until they discarded all of those items; all they had was poisoned, now.

"We have some hurt bad."

"Then stop your bitchin', and drop your pants so our doctor can help you," Johnny yelled back.

"If you're bitten, we won't let you in," Len added.

The people agreed.

Sally told Len the next part, and he relayed the message: "I am tossing scissors out a crack in the door. The doc said to cut your hair down to the scalp. If anyone rushes the door, he will be shot, and the doors will stay sealed. "

The people outside howled in frustration and anger.

Sally directed people to bring in wheelchairs, along with lead aprons that would be used to protect themselves when the people came in.

Reddy came in first, his hair and eyebrows already burned off, and blisters covered his face, hands, and arms. Sally ordered a hot shower for him before she could apply soothing creams. He told her who the rest were, thanking them for allowing them inside. "They need help fast."

The next man almost looked like a victim of Red, but he had been sliced up by flying glass; he was a black teen, who needed a shower and a few stitches. George said he would begin helping the teen with Mark's help. The teen kept smiling and thanking them, saying a shower sounded like Heaven. His name was Calvin.

The next one was like a pincushion, filled with slivers of glass. Sally shook her head, not expecting the woman to survive. "Shower her gently, and pick the glass out. If the glass is too big or is next to an artery or if she begins bleeding badly, we may not be able to do anything. Apply pressure if it happens, and call me. I'll stitch her in a bit."

The woman was missing fingers. Sally could hardly touch her because of the glass shards that were sticking out of her skin; she almost glittered with crimson. Sally handed her off to Johnny and Beth. "Give her some pain shots in those hands, then re-clean them, and apply antibiotic cream and the lidocaine gel in a heavy paste, covering with thick bandages of gauze where her fingers are missing. Use a flashlight to see all the tiny shards."

A Latino girl named Maria was handed to Misty and Julia, her body red from what looked like deep sunburn, blisters showing on parts of her. Her feet were mashed and torn, and she was cut deeply all over, blood covering her.

"Cool shower, 'lots of soap, and mind her poor feet." Sally winced in pity. "Cream and lotion for her body and for her feet…clean well but carefully, use antibiotic cream and lidocaine, and maybe some stitches. Bandage heavily. You've seen me stitch…" she sighed, "about time you did it. If you can't; it'll be a while before I can. Try the super glue, it will hurt like a bastard, but it works. Make sure the wounds are very, very clean and the bandages nice and loose but thick."

Someone heaved as the next one was brought in. This may have been one Reddy didn't count. No one moved. Sally sighed; she needed to pull 'Super Bitch' out now, "I need help. She needs help.... get your thumb outta your ass, and help this woman." Someone had said her name was Rachel.

Hagan and Kim reached for the gurney, both going pale.

The blistered skin was the best she had; half her body was charred; blackened skin slid off of muscle. Her legs were like burned twigs, fingers gone. She crackled as she was laid onto the gurney.

"They had her in a wheel barrel," Kim whispered. She moaned like a hurt puppy, sending chills up his spine.

"She can hear you," Sally shot him a dirty look. "Isn't that right, Rachel? And we're gonna get you all fixed up." She set her jaw. "Then we'll fix your hair." Sally shook her head. "I'll need an IV...not sure where to begin. Get her settled, see if she can take in some water, put some lidocaine cream on the blisters, clean the skin, don't rub too much, and don't touch anything burned badly... after ...leave the rest alone. I'll take her first and give her some pain relief."

Sally scraped and removed the charred skin, revealing the oozing, burned skin beneath; the pain was horrific. There was no way this one could possibly survive. Even in the old world in the best circumstances and with a hyperbaric chamber and experts with skin grafts, it would be almost impossible to save her life. She felt over-whelming despair.

"Rachel, I'm Kim, and this is Hagan. We're gonna be helping you, so you can relax. We aren't doctors, but we're gonna try very hard to help you until Sally can help."

Johnnie motioned them to follow her. "You, boys, go pick glass out of that gal. Hi, Rachel, I'm Johnnie, and I sure wish I had a pretty name like yours. I used to have a daughter named Candi, sweet as candy, and she was a fighter...would whoop ass just like me if she needed to...'til she fell in with a bad man."

Hagan had gone to help Beth, but Kim listened as he did what Sally had said.

"Do you have a man, Rachel? Is he a good man? Kim here is a good man and smart as he can be. He's a good lookin' man, too…a farm-boy-looking boy, but handsome like a movie star," Johnny crooned, and listening, Rachel stopped whimpering. "My girl, Candi run off when she was just fourteen with a no-account loser. I looked…Oh, Lord, how I searched…but he was twenty, and they were gone. She would've run again if I had found her…she was stubborn when she set her mind on something…so since I ain't got my baby girl, would you let me take care of you? Yes?"

As she came in to begin her work, Sally squeezed Johnny's shoulder in thanks, asking Johnny to please stay and help.

Kim, his nose full of cooked flesh that smelled like roasted pork, fled gratefully.

Roy and Paul tended to John, a man, who had been flash-burned. The fire had not done the damage; it was the intense light that had given him what looked like a severe sunburn and had blinded him, his retinas burned up. He needed a shower, creams, and bandages over scrapes and cuts, cool pads and gauze over his ruined eyes. They thought that somehow, his brain was cooked since he could hardly respond.

Len was with a man who mumbled to himself in between telling them he was Bart, a lawyer. His hands were lacerated and crushed in many places; one was broken; he had a big knot and cut on his head. Len got him clean and then bandaged the wounds, wrapping the hand loosely; it might have to be amputated.

It was a long time before most were able to gather again in the gloomy, windowless cafeteria. Sally took a quick break to report that while the seven still lived, two wouldn't make it. The other five had been given water and food, had been bandaged, stitched, cleaned, and had been made as comfortable as possible.

Theresa still bled from her many deep cuts, but the glass had been removed. Sally planned to stitch more to try to stop the blood, but the situation felt hopeless.

Rachel lay quietly, listening to Johnny talk, telling stories, describing the people who were around, and encouraging her to hang on to life, despite Rachel's agony.

"I haven't the heart to tell Johnny that Rachel most likely doesn't want to live and won't live. I keep hoping she goes soon; she's in misery," Sally said, laying her own head on her folded arms on the table to rest.

"I told you about Gina," George reminded her with an arched eyebrow. Benny looked sad, "Would we deny her because she can't get up and get whatever she needs?"

"I can't..." Sally said.

"My terms."

"'George's terms.'" Benny echoed.

Sally stood up to go back to her patients. "I won't get in your way, but it's her choice. Not ours. And wait until Johnny leaves her side; then speak to her. But you have to tell Johnny."

George nodded.

17
HOSPITAL HABITS

Work details provided food, moved rubble, helped arrange rooms, while Chauncey and Big Bill continued removing bodies and cleaning up the areas afterwards. They had distasteful jobs, but those were the jobs they had chosen so they could work together, pretending to toil mindlessly, but knowing what they did was vital in giving the dead respect and honor. Len made sure the guard duty continued, and with Billy's help and a long hallway, Len worked to train the others to shoot more accurately.

Kim watched as Bryan tried to flirt with Beth. He tried to dislike the man, but Bryan was likable, dependable, and determined. Bryan always seemed to be busy with one chore or another. He worked long into the night.

Mark approached Kim, "Have you seen that guy, Joe? He's the one always cracking jokes, with longish brown hair, about twenty, glasses; Len calls him 'Front-Row-Joe.'"

"I haven't seen him since last night maybe...if even then."

"That's what everyone says, and his cot is empty, wasn't slept in."

"Hmm."

"We've looked all over. Even in the morgue. I did find this." Mark set an empty bottle of codeine on the table. "It was on his cot."

Kim studied it.

He and Mark found that the doors to the pharmacy had been opened and closed back. This wasn't good.

With Len and Bryan with them, Kim and Mark got ready to go in, following instructions from Sally. Behind them, guns ready, stood Tink, Beth, Julia, Hagan, Thurman, Benny, George, and Billy. Holding a gun, ready to fire, was becoming a familiar feeling.

Joe had refused to let the destruction of the world get to him. Through it all, he had joked, smiled, and tried to make everyone he met feel a measure of happiness, if only for a few seconds.

From the beginning, he had been the unofficial cafeteria greeter, memorizing names, lending a hand when he could, and trying to keep spirits up. Never thinking himself attractive or particularly interesting, Joe had learned the joy in making others happy. He watched comedians, mimicked them, and now brought the humor into this unhappy place.

But, like many who seemed joyful, Joe was exquisitely lonely.

Joe's balm of choice was pills…codeine, Xanax, anything that relaxed him, and the monkey on his back was a gorilla. Now, in a hospital, he was without pills, having taken the last one the day before. The weight was too much; he shook, his stomach churned, and he felt panicked. He had tried to sleep, but there was so much to do, and he needed to relax so he could be social; he was actually making friends for once.

Almost jumping out of his skin and crawling with anxiety, Joe took a flashlight and sneaked to the metal doors. In and out of the pharmacy and who would know? He could bring back tons of pills, share them with those injured, and be a hero.

Len ran order now, but Joe had heard Roy and several more saying Len wasn't a good leader. He might have to choose sides soon, and it made him more nervous. He needed something to dull the edges. He needed to be able to think about all of this.

Inside, Joe closed the doors, kicking at something burned that was in the way, but almost retching as he saw it had once been a human who had crawled up to the doors from somewhere. Panic made his blood run cold. He was sick. If he didn't get a pill fast, he was going to start ripping his own hair out. He could ask Sally. But no, he couldn't. He was here now.

The pharmacy was a wreck, all the glass shattered and everything blistered, melted, and in ruins. Maybe the pills were melted. Clenching his jaw, Joe inched out, avoiding twisted metal. Dirty brown rain fell outside, bringing a chill with it.

Other things littered the floor, blackened things crackled.

Joe ducked into the area where all the drugs were kept in a kind of large, metal containers, much like in a candy store. He would be a hero for taking all of this back for Sally. First, he would rest and relax a bit. With a bottle of water from a pocket, he tried codeine with Xanax chasers. Valium followed. *Joy*. Okay. Now, they would help, and then he would load up and take the medicines back.

Things tittered, sounding closer.

Stealthy things whispered coyly.

Joe didn't move. He hardly breathed. Those things were there now, stalking him, waiting for him to make a sound so they could find him and pounce.

In fear, he swallowed more of the 'jewels.'

He began to feel better. If a few had helped this much…with a shrug, he added more of each. Sitting in a chair, he shivered with happiness. The noises were closer, but he didn't care. Someone moaned.

Another three pills went down like candy, then several more, this time Oxycontin. He wanted to rest a bit with his eyes closed as things moaned. Closer. Joe swallowed and refused to make a sound as he slipped away.

But by now, the others were looking for Joe.

Len and Kim took the lead, almost tripping over the burned and blackened, stinking thing lying close to the doors. "Damn," Kim muttered. They shivered. It was down right cold.

Other bodies were blistered and burned badly, but the blackened thing had crawled in from outside, from farther away; they wondered how it had made it this far. They took in the devastation. They used gloves to move the bodies away from the doors and then tossed the used gloves for fresh ones from their pockets.

"Here he is," Mark pointed.

Joe was dead, having choked on his own vomit.

"Suicide?" asked Kim.

"Or over zealous in his habit." Bryan shrugged. He and Mark moved Joe, covering him with sheets. They grabbed bags from their pockets, filling them with what Sally had said to get since most items had been protected from the blast.

When they heard the moaning, Len and Bryan set their bags down to watch. "Moaners," said Bryan.

Len grinned, "I like that...Moaners." Walking out to where the windows had once been, he raised his rifle; he took two shots; Bryan took one. The three who were moaning stopped.

In and out.

Grabbing the bags, Len and Bryan went back inside, grabbing clothing first, ducking in to grab towels. Len told them about the moaners and explained again that no one could ever go out the metal doors. "If you want to go out, then stay out," he told them, "but don't go playing self-medicator and putting all of us at risk for your selfishness."

With the rest working so hard, suicide and foolish behavior that led to death, was a slap in the face to the others; everyone should be grateful that he had survived.

The others took their guns and the medications as all four went for hot showers.

They had only been out for minutes and hoped for the best.

Sharing the information, they told the others what they had seen outside, down-playing the total annihilation of the world they had known. Roy asked a few questions, and the others noticed he had more standing and sitting close to him now.

One of the women, a schoolteacher, criticized Len for telling them what it was like outside. "Do you think we like hearing what it's like out there?"

"Do you think I like having to go out there and see it? Do you want to go looking for the next person who goes missing?"

"You're being depressing."

"I'm being honest. Do you want lies?"

"No, I want hope, or we'll all end up like Joe."

"You got truth."

A few left Roy's side, undecided again. Len, Kim, Mark, and Bryan were respected for going out to find Joe and for bringing back medication. They had put down zeds; their bravery did not go unnoticed.

18
RESOURCES

"What are you doing?" Bryan watched Beth as she counted and recorded in another section for ammo.

"You said it needed to be inventoried." She had columns and lists of every weapon, all ammunition, and every other item in the room.

Billy had helped her earlier when he and Len had taken everyone interested into one of the halls where they patiently had taught gun safety and marksmanship. With the clothing which had been brought back from the store and scrub uniforms from the hospital, they had something to sleep in. Some of the other women and men had an inventory going for the supplies of food, linens, and medical supplies.

"If I said I needed to be kissed, would you oblige me?"

"You really are a pig."

Kim and Len came in laughing. Bryan pulled a face, "Since when is it swinish to ask for a kiss? Isn't that extreme?"

"I think she's been taking lessons on a smart mouth from Julia."

"I already had my smart mouth, but I have learned new names to call people. Give it up, Bryan. Epic failure."

"I can't believe I'm failing."

"Bryan, I'm sure you've been shot down before...many...many...did I mention *many* times." Beth sat back.

"True, but you gals are more valuable now."

Len chuckled, "You have done stepped into it, now."

"Valuable?"

Bryan shrugged, "Well, I'm blunt if anything…and females are going to be a valued resource."

Beth cocked her head. "You have gotta be kidding me…"

"Boy, you have got more mouth than sense to be getting her wound up," Len warned.

"What? What'd I do?"

"You ran your mouth, but he's got a point, Beth. Women tend to care for the ill, care for children…do cooking and stuff, but if you think about it, not that I have any idea why I am even helping Bryan get out of this shit topic he waded into, he does have a point. Men are pigs. Men like women. Not all men are good pigs."

"True. But…you think…?"

"That some men will raid for supplies and women? Yes."

"See?"

Beth shot Bryan a dirty look. "Rape. Cave men."

"It's instinct, too, to rebuild population. The prime male will want to share his sperm and impregnate all the women he can."

Kim slid to the floor beside Beth, laughing at Len. "Share his sperm? Oh my, God, is that a nature channel commentary or what?"

"Well, that's what I meant, too." Bryan protested. "Survivors pairing off and repopulating…the fittest males and females. Len's right about males. You haven't seen Roy with his feathers fluffed out, pounding on his chest?"

"Okay, you just mixed two animals. Bad enough to be facing zombies, bombs falling out of the sky, and a virus killing, but adding a bunch of horny men, looking to pair off with the women left behind, and I am saying I'm not sure there is a damned thing to live for. Someone end it for me now," Beth complained.

"You'll get plenty of attention," Bryan said.

"Unreal if you think that is a compliment. We get to be the prizes?"

Len laughed harder. "I figured it as in *we* are the prizes…good, strong men…handsome, protective…I figure there must be a lottery among the gals, seeing who gets me."

"Johnny gets you 'cause she can whip your ass," Kim said.

"Wait 'til I tell Misty and Julia about all this…you may have more looking to whip your ass," Beth said. "And when Julia does it, she'll call you names in Mexican."

"She bi?"

"Bye?"

"Bisexual. Her hair is lopped off," Bryan said.

"Not to hear her talk…she likes men a whole lot. She just had me cut her hair off so the zeds couldn't grab her hair." Beth threw a shotgun shell at Kim's feet. "But I bet Bryan could love a woman straight."

"You're a cold one, Beth," he smiled.

Beth left the inventory list on a desk, going to look for her friends so she could share her humorous, newfound information with the other women. Misty went bright red, saying she thought Mark was attractive.

"You go for him, *Chica*. I'll see who wins, Bethy, and then I'll take the leftovers…all of them." Julia whooped; she laughed harder when Beth told her that the boys had asked if she were gay." Maybe I best grab one of them and show them how straight I am."

"I think they'd like that," Beth laughed. They teased Misty about her crush on Mark and then joined the rest.

Sally sobered up the group by letting them know that Rachel, the woman who had been so terribly burned, had passed on. A few glanced at George, but his eyes didn't betray a thing.

Three more came in uneventfully, following the routine that Sally had set in place.

Alex was unhurt but for a few cuts, and he and the third man helped another from a wheelchair that they had uneasily pushed from across town, even carrying it over the rubble. They transferred him to a new wheelchair as Alex explained that the injury was from long before. As a preacher, he created a big stir, for many had wanted some spiritual guidance and reassurance.

Sally was all but dancing in place over the other man.

Once he was cleaned up and seated, she hugged him repeatedly, introducing him as a fellow doctor who had been at one of the rescue stations. "Didn't anyone else make it?"

"I don't know. People kept trying to get in, and we were just over loaded; everyone had gone into that deep sleep or coma, and just a few were cleaning up and watching. We had a full house with family members helping and kind of camping out. A few military kept order, but it felt as if every thing were at a stand-still with a not-so-nice outcome." Doc shook his head.

"I've never smelled anything that bad...even working in medicine all my life...the people, we couldn't keep them clean from waste and blood...I was sure cholera and even worse was about to break out. I think it was like being in a war long ago with the smells of blood, sweat, and all..."

"It sounds horrible." Sally shuddered. "We just had a few here, and the smell was bad."

Doc told his story. All his patients were sinking into comas, and family members were increasingly worried and upset. Sanitation was failing, food was running out, and no one was bringing in supplies.

"My God, it was bad; they were just lying there, and the filth...nothing we could do with so little help. The floors that we washed down were a half-inch deep in water and gore. We just kind of hosed them off and hoped for the best; nothing was left that we could do."

"That many?"

Doc looked surprised. "Sally, we had maybe five hundred at the school."

"Five hundred people?"

"Patients! They came from the small towns, and the military brought them for a while...until they quit coming. Others showed up: gym full, classrooms full. We had some in an open courtyard. It was horrible. For every patient, we had two or three family members trying to help. "

He rubbed his eyes. "Then they...changed...like the reports said. Mothers attacking children, husbands attacking wives, children attacking...madness. Screams. Flesh ripped, sounded like duct tape being torn off or Velcro. Then everything went bright, and the building started to fall in. We ran like rats. Eight of us were huddled in a bathroom for hours."

It was hellish as they climbed out of the rubble of a downstairs bathroom, amid the debris.   Many had been crushed by the concrete and bricks.

"We dug out one, moaning and wiggling.   His arm was crushed, chest a mess; he had Red and was awake." Doc said.

"We had one that Sally said should have been dead: he was so torn up and so crushed and all; but he didn't react to pain and shock; he was trying to attack and bite us. If he hadn't had crushed legs, he would have gotten us," Alex said.   Doc said they were scared to dig people up but did so a few times, only to find moaning zeds. A few were uninfected, only injured, and their number had swollen to fifteen.

Then a horde came at them. They had been his patients, but now the doctor and the others had to fight them off with pieces of wood and pipes, smashing at their heads. They threw themselves at the survivors, bringing down those injured and bleeding.

More mangled and tattered zeds dug themselves out of the rubble and gathered to lurch at the doctor and others.

"Alex grabbed a wheelchair, and this big guy with us, Ed or Fred… something…picked up the Reverend and carried him. We ran."

"Amazing you made it, considering how they gang up or flock together like damned birds," Len told him.

"Ed saved my life," Bob said, "I owe him and Alex."

Alex joined in. "So we ran, and they kept coming. I never could have imagined hitting anyone with a piece of pipe, but I swatted those bastards right down. Some were burned; they smelled horrid. They smelled even worse when we popped their heads open."

They hid and ran, trying to stay ahead, with the hospital as their goal. "Most two stories fell in; one stories took damage; windows were blown out; pushing the wheel chair was a bitch," Doc said, "sorry, Reverend."

"I felt helpless in this damned chair; they were pushing me or carrying me. I asked them to leave me, but they wouldn't."

"Of course, we wouldn't leave you here alone."

The Red Zeds took down all the injured, causing bloody, violent battles that the survivors kept losing. "They are hardly human; these filthy things are covered in shit and blood, nasty smelly things. The Reds.

Then, after we had rested and eaten, we saw worse…bloody ones who had torn up bodies…missing parts and all…the ones they call dead zeds, but they were alive, just crazed." Alex shivered. "And they hunted us. We ran into a big herd of them, and we split up, just scrambling. Doc and Bob and I hid. The others ran, and we heard the most horrible screaming."

Sally told them about the ones who were not alive but yet attacked.

"That's bullshit," Roy added.

"Really? Did you check them and find them cold with decomp in place? Did you find rigor mortis?" Sally snapped at him. "I may not know everything, but those people were dead when they came out attacking us. I don't care what you believe. Facts are facts."

"Sally, that's impossible." Doc held a hand up. "Not saying you're wrong, just that it's insane and scary as hell. We know some things. The CDC was in touch. The hemorrhagic virus hit first, a Lyssa virus. It weakened the body, but Lyssa viruses are not really airborne, except for rabies found in caves where bats live; the rabies virus becomes concentrated in the air."

"So it was a combination?"

"Pretend you're a mad scientist cooking up a bad-ass disease. You see rabies has gone airborne in extreme circumstances, so that means it is *possible*. So if I am that scientist, I start with the rabies virus. It does double duty: it can go airborne, and it can cause increased saliva to more readily spread itself, causing aggression. I add a bit of hemorrhagic fever to my mix; now, I have a disease that is passed by air or bites. I knock down half of the population straight off with the hemorrhagic fever; then, what can stop me? No society can handle that many patients."

"But they become…zombies?"

"They go into a coma; both viruses affect the nervous system, and they are weakened. They are replicating at an unstoppable rate and affect ever tissue in the body."

"They said the problem was mad cow."

Doc chuckled. "Not really. That causes holes in the brain. We have people who can only shuffle, who can't speak, only moan; they piss themselves and have open ulcers that leak pus."

Sally gasped, "But that sounds like a prion…kuru."

Doc winked.

"What's kuru?" someone asked.

"It's a disease passed on by cannibalism. Prions are sneaky things and can actually communicate between cells in the brain. So it's simple; as a mad scientist, I piggy-back this prion, which I have tweaked for symptoms that I want on a virus, and send it on with an airborne virus I tweaked from rabies."

"That makes perfect sense except I know those were dead."

"Ninety-nine point ninety-nine percent dead. For all purposes, we can say dead, but the prion and virus become a puppeteer and keep the body moving to its last known point. It has one objective: to reproduce in more hosts."

"That's what George said." Len pointed out. "He says it is evil."

"George?"

"That's me."

"Are you a doctor?"

"No, I was a cop." He laughed.

Roy rolled his eyes dramatically, earning a few frowns.

"Well, in a way, you are right. It is evil. Not saying it thinks like we think, but it would like to be the top species, which means eliminating us."

George pondered that. "Well, then what? Once it's top dog, what does it do? It's stuck in people's bodies, and it's just a disease."

"I don't suppose it has a plan beyond that. It just wants to live, to reproduce, and to be the top life form. That isn't so different than we are. What do we really do besides that?"

Bob pointed at Doc, "Now that would be my cue to jump in with religion."

"You haven't told us anything to help." Roy sneered.

"I can tell you this: I appreciate the caution you took in taking us in, and we should keep that up a few days, but I don't think the bombs were meant for radiation, only to kill zeds. And it didn't, but that's beside the point. There isn't radiation like they had at Hiroshima; it wasn't a regular atomic bomb. That's good news."

"How do you know?"

"Before we dumped it, we had something from the military, a Geiger counter." Doc smiled like a Cheshire cat.

People went back to work on details so they could think that through. Doc asked if he could help Sally, and she sighed in relief. Several asked Bob to have prayer services and a gathering for them. For a while, Bob was the busiest person there.

19
MONSTERS

"What do you think?"

Len rubbed his jaw, thinking. In searching with Dallas for survivors, Len found a pocket in the destruction, an opening to a hallway full of closets and rooms, an oasis in the debris that offered hidden supplies and survivors as well as possible deadly adversaries.

It was a rough climb upwards and through a maze of fallen trash and concrete, metal spiking in places, but then seemingly easy-going into the mysteries of this newly found area.

"Sally and Doc need so much more than what they have now, and we can use more linens, scrubs, and blankets. The area looks enormous; I can't believe an area this big is still intact."

"We could find survivors."

"Or we could find zeds."

Len told them, "We are going in, but in very strictly organized teams who can follow the letter of orders. We take no chances but do this methodically. I'll tell everyone where I want each to be, and if you think you can't be on the team, tell me. Don't play hero."

He had them load up rifles, handguns, and extra ammo, and make a stash of some heavy pipes that they could use as melee weapons. They went over the plan.

Len, Kim, and Bryan would take point, exploring the area, slowly and quietly. Behind them, for backup, would be Hagen, Beth, Julia, Tink, George, and Mark.

Once an area was clear, a larger team made up of Johnny, Thurman, Benny, and Roy, would stand guard, while many more relayed any usable supplies to the rest of the survivors. He had more rifles if needed. Len checked and re-checked with them to see if they understood the team plan. He made it clear the plan could alter on a dime's turn.

"Stop second guessing. It's a good team plan. You have everyone where he or she is the strongest, with people you trust on the third section so nothing gets screwed up," George said.

"Okay. Remember…we stay stealthy if we can."

The first door was to a supply closet full of sheets and blankets that were needed. It was easy to secure a spot so close to the start and to insure they would at least have those supplies.

In the next room, the smell of decomposition from a corpse in the bed, turning into a messy black and green puddle, almost knocked them over: dead of some natural cause or lack of care over the last days. Fluids dripped from the bed to the floor, causing the group to retch.

Len closed the door and motioned to his back up. George quickly used a marker to make an x on the door, indicating clear, but to keep the door closed.

Beth snapped her fingers. When Len turned to her, she pointed to her ear, tapping twice and then to a room beside her. She had heard something. He motioned her to put her ear to the door. Yes, she heard noise but could not determine what caused it.

When the door swung open, again, the smell was bad, but it was a different bad, one that they later would come to understand as meaning a Red was inside; the smell of feces and vomit was always stronger with the Red victims.

A heavy woman stood by the window beside a skinny person, gender undetermined. Both moaned.

Len and Bryan fired. But there was still a moaning coming from a pile of lumpy, bloody clothing on the floor.

Len stepped over to look, gagging. He squeezed his eyes closed for a second, shivering in distaste and fear. It wasn't a pile of clothing, but the remains of what had once been a person, before the other two had eaten the poor sod down to the bone. Stringy tatters of flesh and blood coated the bones; some limbs had been torn off, and while parts of the head remained, the scalp was gone. Thus, this didn't fit the theory of their not being hungry for flesh but only for spreading the virus. He couldn't imagine being left with any kind of consciousness in a pile of gnawed bones and nerves.

It moaned.

Len almost jumped out of his skin before he put a bullet into the head. It was, by far, the worst thing he had ever seen. To the side, Bryan vomited, and Kim had turned greenish pale.

The door was marked by another x.

Several more rooms were empty, but the group, with tensed muscles, didn't relax.

Kim lunged backwards. "Zeds. A bunch in a lobby, glass doors."

"I'd rather they just not see us, but how do we get past the glass doors?"

George grinned.

From the last room the group had been in, he grabbed a screen and brought it out. Quickly, they got two more. Moving quietly and slowly, they managed to put the screens outside the doors of the lobby, blocking the view.

Len asked for the doors to be guarded and that if anyone heard a noise, he should indicate the zeds were coming out. Then, Len would gather the group and fight. It wasn't a great plan, but for now, the idea was to avoid the danger.

Mark slid next to Len, holding a heavy pipe. "I want to try some stealthiness if there is just one or two of them. I played baseball."

"It'll be nasty work."

"Don't we have to be quiet and get used to this sort of thing?"

Clubs and fists would put them much closer to snapping jaws, but ammunition wouldn't last forever; this might be the way of the future.

Inside, two small children were with their mother; one child was a Red. Mark went for the mother while Kim grabbed the child to restrain it.

Swinging back, Mark hit the woman in her head, causing skull shards, brains, and blood to fly. She went down in a gory mess, but still moved, trying to get to her feet; he swung twice more, making her head look like jelly, brains oozing out in a grey puddle.

Len asked for the pipe. "I'll get the kid; you did your job." He swallowed before he could puke. He wanted to use the gun, but it was his turn to use a melee weapon.

Shuddering, Kim pushed the child forward, its hissing, moaning, and odor of torn flesh made it a bit less than human.

Len swung hard. The group looked on the bed at the last child, trying to crawl down to bite them. Luckily, he was caught up, tangled in tubes and tape that once had helped him when he was alive.

"Fuckers." Kim took the pipe and finished the job, groaning each time he bashed the child in the head.

All four men had gone wide-eyed with disgust and horror at what they had seen or done; Bryan vomited, again. This united them in a terrible way, but they all had managed to take out zeds, using blunt objects, and sometimes, it might be necessary to do so again, without hesitating over the violence. Kim paused to vomit before they moved on.

Another x.

In the next room, Mark was a split second from using the pipe when he stopped in mid-step. A little girl sat in a chair, weeping. She looked up with her tear-stained face, filled with a look of horror and dread as she cringed away from the four, gore-soaked, tall men who stood over her, carrying big guns and looking very angry.

Her name was Toni, and while waiting to be rescued, she had survived on water from the sink and snacks in the room. She had been admitted to the hospital for bee stings, which were now healed. With only faint pinpoints covering her face and arms, he tried to show them where the bees had stung her.

"Mama went to get me a soda. Then everything fell in, and I waited." She was angry, crying pitifully. "Don't hurt me."

Len felt guilty about the bloody pipe and guns they carried, "We are looking for any bad guys. We can get you a soda and something to eat. I know you're hungry."

"Is Mama with you?"

"Let's get you out of here, and we can figure out about your mama, okay?"

"You're strangers." She shook in fear.

Len felt a temper tantrum coming on from Toni as she looked at them in stark fear.

They whispered for Tink, and after a few minutes, he collected Toni and her stuffed bear in his arms, promising her food, a visit with Dallas, and safety.

The gentle giant of a man had an instantly calming effect on Toni, as they knew he would. She allowed him to pick her up from the chair and carry her out.

In a few minutes, Julia reported that the others in the cafeteria and on the teams had almost cheered to see a survivor who raised spirits as they faced the rest of the search.

"A bright spot in all this mess," Kim mumbled.

"Wish there were brighter and less nasty," Bryan said.

Using Sally's keys, they found supplies that she and Doc needed; these were quietly relayed to where they were needed.

"Lobby is ahead with a hall branching off; then rooms are beyond the lobby. It's dark in there with a lot of downed rubble…a really big mess with hiding spots for bad guys, so we need to be careful of anything hiding in there. It isn't small either…so keep alert."

They angled to one side, seeing movement in the rubble.

It was amazing to see so many rooms that had fallen, mostly into an intact section of the huge hospital. This part had an uneven, buckled floor and was filled with trash from above, some of the trash six feet tall or more, chairs and tables, desks, and plaster tossed in all directions.

"Oh shit." Mark jumped to the side. They saw a hand, moving from beneath the trash, the hand that had grabbed at his boot. It searched and crawled like a spider. "Where's the head?"

Positioning around and searching, they found the rest of the person, his head hardly showing. Bryan took a turn, jabbed the pipe in hard through the eye, cracking the skull, popping the eyeball, and causing a wet plop sound. He dry heaved.

The back-up team moved in quietly, Roy leading after taking Tink's place. Without warning, a zed man lunged at them from behind concrete, making them scatter in response. Julia, Beth, and Hagan scrambled back and were now closer to the unexplored hallway.

Mark jabbed and swung at the man, but he didn't go down; Mark fell amid the trash.

Len and Bryan scrambled farther into the lobby, looking for a shot to help Mark as Kim swung in closer. No one could get a clear, unobstructed shot in the confusion.

Across the lobby, zeds began moaning, filing out from a room, and pulling themselves from rubble.

Bodies dug themselves up from bricks and metal and pushed chairs aside to stand, even though they had crushed, smashed, and torn arms and legs, bleeding holes in chests, and ripped open stomachs and breasts.

Fingers and hands had been mashed away, noses and the flesh of their faces hung in bits and pieces, joints were ripped to unnatural angles. Seeing the zeds dig themselves out was like watching corpses rise from graves.

Hagan and the women were pushed further the opposite way as they stepped away from the zeds.

"Hold your fire," Len yelled, "use the rifle stock. Check fire."

In their positions now, there were fewer shots that would hit one of their own. As jumpy and untrained as they were, Len waited, unhappily, for a shot to hit one of the team. He slammed his rifle down on a head, bursting it like a ripe melon.

Mark held back the man attacking him as Kim swung at his head, but the man luckily kept dodging as he tried to bite Mark. Everything was happening as fast as lightning, but also, at the speed of molasses. It was surreal.

When the third team asked what was happening, someone yelled that Mark was down, and after a wail, Misty ran into the lobby, screaming for Mark.

Len saw everything going straight to hell; it was a bag of dicks, but it could get worse.

And it did.

"I told you I heard rescuers."

A dozen people came pouring from the rooms across the lobby where the team had been headed. They called enthusiastically to their rescuers.

Now, the teams had no shots, almost two dozen excited people were in the middle, and zeds came out of the rubble, lurching at them from all over. There had to be thirty who had come from the rooms across the lobby, moaning as they shambled.

The newcomers didn't skirt the lobby but ran down the center where it was clear of trash; as Roy and George went to them, the retreat was effectively cut off but for Misty, who stood looking and wailing at Mark on the ground and Kim who couldn't get a sure swing.

"Do not fire. People, get back," Len yelled at everyone at the same time as he took a breath and fired, hoping his aim was good enough.

The man attacking Mark went down with a bullet to the head just as Kim cracked the man's skull. Unfortunately, it was seconds too late. Len should have let Kim fire.

Mark was up in a flash, grabbing Misty as he and Kim tried to get closer to George and Roy. Len and Bryan dodged rubble to get to the middle where several were fighting with zeds.

A woman went down with her throat ripped out, spraying blood everywhere while a teen screeched as his fingers were being torn off by the teeth of some gory man who shared the 'prize' with another man who was ripping at the teen's shoulder.

George and Roy were able to step in to swing at heads, hoping to crush them, but a woman, running manically, slammed into George, knocking him into the twisted metal and bricks.

Bryan and Len roughly grabbed the running people to push them back closer to the lobby walls, yelling for them to stop running and to be still.

Mark got George up, and they, with Kim and Roy, finished taking out each zed, searching the trash for any hidden zeds, and getting the new survivors to the relative safety of the wall. It felt as if the battle had lasted for hours, yet it had all happened in less than five minutes.

Their path of retreat was now open, guarded and defended by the third team who had rushed in and turned the tide. Chauncey,

Big Bill, and Johnny had fired so skillfully that they alone had provided George with the chance to get to his feet and for the second team to rally.

In the center, Kim had slammed skulls, beaten hands back that reached for them, and had known that he, Mark, Misty, and Roy were in a bad spot.

George had gone down, and they hadn't known immediately if the woman who crashed into him was a zed or a survivor. Chaos ruled. Kim had seen the woman snagged by a zed; George was finally able to shoot with his Sig.

The woman's face was partially torn open, and Misty, her pretty face in a grimace of anger and fear, shot the woman point blank with a small handgun. Misty hated these things, but it didn't dawn on her that the woman had not yet turned and was still human; she only saw blood and felt fury.

When Kim first heard the shots, he expected one to hit him, but the third team had been concentrating on the edges, thereby allowing Len and Bryan to get there to help.

When the last skull crumbled in a pie of yellow-white shards and mushy brains and the last shot went in, Kim called out, "I love you, Johnny, Big Bill, and Chauncey."

Bryan gathered the seven new survivors.

"Len, Guys," Johnny called.

"Just a sec." Len had wanted to get all of the people gathered, calm and safe, back to the cafeteria as soon as possible. He was still thinking of the lobby behind those screens and the danger, waiting there. There still might be zeds there, hiding in the junk that lay everywhere.

Nothing was going fast enough, and yet, it was flying by before he could even get his head around most of it. He had too much going on in his head. What did they need to do first?

"No, Len. I mean now," Johnny persisted.

"What?" he knew his tone was too short tempered. He was trying to think.

"Bobby and Warren went that way to help Hagan and the girls." Johnny pointed to the hall that branched away.

"Beth?" Kim called.

Nothing moved, and the hall was in shadows.

Something moaned.

20
BRINGING IT BACK HOME

"Slow down," Len ordered Kim. "I want the survivors briefed and taken back to Doc and Sally to be checked for bites. George goes with them to be checked, also. Mark, too. Get a team, Roy, and watch that lobby. Bryan, you handle all the rest but the lobby; after you get everyone to the cafeteria, join Roy. Don't start anything, but fight if necessary."

"Len."

"You do what I said, Mark, help Roy and Bryan." Len knew they all felt as if they should help him. "Kim goes with me, and I want Johnny, Big Bill, and Chauncey."

"You got it, Major," Johnny said. Big Bill, who never said much, glanced at Chauncey with pride at having been chosen.

Len felt shitty that any one would feel pride for having been picked to risk his life. "We're going to get Hagan and the ladies. And if you get into a fight, give Misty some practice since she's determined to jump into battles."

Kim was already moving towards the hallway. The rest followed, scanning the floor carefully, amazed at what they saw and didn't see. There were several zeds with skulls crushed and blood splattered, showing that the five had come this way, unable to get clear shots but dispatching threats. Yet none of the five were in the hall.

Johnny turned around in a circle. "Where are they?"

There were no doors, and the short hall ended in a wall of jagged cement, metal, and bricks, with no way through. It was as if the five had simply vanished. "Here." Kim stared into a dark maw next to the wall where the floor had fallen in.

It was apparent the floor had given way beneath the five as they retreated.

Len sent Chauncey for rope, hoping he could hurry, despite the other activities going on, the lobby full of zeds and the unruly survivors, trying to get to the cafeteria.

Kim was about to bolt through the hole and go on his own; Len knew because he felt the same way. To keep them both busy, Kim and he looked over the hallway again and found nothing but the zeds that had been taken down; there was nothing to indicate anyone had been injured. Len, Johnny, and Kim, smoked.

"We have to find them."

"And we will. Damn, Kimball, you know Hagan is a bad ass, so is Julia. Beth is tough and smart as hell, and they have Billy and Warren with them. That's not a bad team at all," Len said.

"Why don't they answer?"

"I dunno, Kim, but we'll find out. We have no reason to think they aren't okay. Give the girl some credit for being smart and tough."

Chauncey came running back with the rope.

"That was fast."

"They relayed the rope to me." Chauncey grinned.

They kept guns and lights on Kim as he went down first. "Not bad...about twelve feet," he called back.

It was a dark space about ten by ten with a body to the side.

Big Bill squatted next to Billy, who was dead. "Damn. Went through him like shit through a goose."

A sharp pipe had gone through Billy's lower back and up through his stomach, washing him with crimson gore. It looked as if Billy had been skewered when they fell to the floor.

"Blood here, too. Someone else is hurt." Johnny pointed to the ground. "Then it stops. Must have bandaged the wound." Metal poked out close to the blood.

"Doesn't look too bad, either," Len said. He jumped up, almost falling over as they scrambled to one side. Moans echoed from a dark crack in the wall, and a hand reached out, searching.

"Is it stuck in the crack? God, that's creepy," Johnny said.

"They fell, and Billy was killed. They heard the moans and saw the hand. Those gals never carry a light, so I am guessing Hagan may have had one. Billy's was broken. Warren wouldn't have had one. So there was only one light down here with that moaning from there," Kim said. "Shut it up; I can't think."

Big Bill grinned, took a pipe, and began jabbing it into the crack until something crackled and the thing stopped making noise.

"Thanks," Kim said. "With little light and their having lost Billy's, there was big stress. They were being quiet 'cause they couldn't determine how big the crack was, if anyone could get to them, or even how many there were."

"This is why he's a private investigator." Johnny patted Kim's back. "So little light, scared, zeds after them, and more could have come along and fallen in with them in here."

"They were literally backed against a wall," Len said.

"Right. So what did they do?"

Len darted forward, lifted Billy's head a little, and looked closely. "Hagan. He is a real zombie movie buff, I know…weird, but what he did was this; he used his knife and cut the brain stem."

"Wicked! Why?" Chauncey looked at the make shift surgery.

"Cause they didn't want the zed in the crack to get out and turn Billy into one of those things. But they couldn't wait 'til he bled out; he was hurting something awful."

"They could have." Johnny made a bashing motion with her rifle.

"Warren or the girls wouldn't be ready for that yet. Hagan watched the movies; he told me about the brain stem; he was smart and had finesse; he did it this way."

Kim was impatient. "Okay. So where?" He went to the small area again. "There." He showed them some hand and foot holds on a wall with a hole above.

"Makes sense. But they're going farther away from us."

"Hagan did it before. And they didn't have a choice, they thought. Besides, they knew we'd come for them. They are looking to hole-up," Len said.

"But Hagan isn't the one hurt," Kim muttered. "He's the one helping them climb; they'd need his muscle to do that." He took hold of a pipe, tested it, and began climbing. It was difficult.

Despite both being strong, Chauncey and Johnny both needed a hand up, making everyone feel Kim was right in his guess.

Once they had climbed up, they were in a long, but low-ceilinged area. Rewarded with a more open space, they breathed hard, falling back onto the floor, next to a circle of trash someone had left as a sign.

Kim grabbed part of a bandana from the circle. "Hagan is claustrophobic," Kim told them as they rested.

Len cast his flashlight over the area, a large area that they'd be able to walk in. He wondered if again they would find other rooms and lobbies full of the monsters. They didn't have the manpower to handle a horde. He told them they all needed to be very quiet.

One way out was a fairly tight crawl on a downward slope. The only other way they could go was up, again through sludgy water

Len stood, and then dropped back as a volley of bullets pinged around his head. "Shit fire, Hagan. Julia, it's us. Stop shooting."

Chauncey swore as he dropped back down.

"He's a live one," someone said.

"He's got a gun."

Len silently made a series of intricate, complicated motions to his team, each nodded, understandingly.

"Hey, asshole, you shot me," Chauncey yelled; unfortunately he was serious, muttering as Len tied bandanas around his upper arm.

"You have guns."

"But I didn't shoot you," Chauncey yelled back.

"How many with you?"

Len yelled now, "Two. How many with you?"

"More than that, so stay where you are," voices whispered. "You're gonna slide those rifles and your handguns out to us."

"Can't do that."

"Really? You know some gals named Beth and Julia? Wanna hear them scream?"

Len shot Kim a warning look and made more intricate gestures and motions.

"Maybe I wanna take a shot at you and hear you scream, bitch." Len was angry.

"Ummm, Len, he's holding me in front of him," Beth yelled back.

Len cursed; then, he and Chauncey tossed the guns out, unloaded. Len was betting they wouldn't check.

They were ordered out, with their hands raised, and Len told Chauncey to thread his fingers together with both hands and not just to raise his hands, but place them on his head and not give them a reason to feel nervous

"Keep your eyes on the chin of whoever is talking; walk slowly; be calm."

Len made last minute silent motions and hoped they all understood. He and Chauncey did as they had been ordered.

"On your knees," the man with the ball cap ordered.

"No problem," Len agreed; both he and Chauncey sank to their knees.

"What're you doing here? Where're you from?"

"We're a rescue team; we came from outside and found a way in, been climbing around in here."

"Rescue my ass." There were five men and a woman. One man stood with a pistol to Beth's side; he looked burned.

"Hey, Beth."

"Hey, Len."

"We found your friends here creeping around, thought they were zombies at first, so we hit one." Ball Cap chuckled. "That would have been the nigger with your group, sorry, the other nigger." He laughed at Chauncey.

"Is Hagan okay?"

"For now. He's tied up. Big ole buck, ain't he?"

"Why do you hate the black folks?" Chauncey grumbled.

"'Cause we don't like anyone but the white folks." Ball Cap laughed.

Len hummed a few bar of the *"Dueling Banjoes."* Long live interbreeding of the chosen. "What say we go on our way with our friends?" Len asked.

"What say we tell you what we want? Your buddy, Ward, sang like a bird once we encouraged him a little." Another man coughed wetly. He looked sick.

"He means Warren," Beth said. "They tortured him until he talked."

"Well, the Spic chick didn't wanna talk, even with encouragement…bitch kicked Billy Ray in the balls," one of the men laughed, "didn't appreciate him twistin' her tittie."

The man who must have been Billy Ray shrugged, "Won't stop me from screwin' her."

Julia cursed in Spanish from the shadows.

"Warren told the team how he and the other three came from below, close to the pharmacy; they got in here from the outside, didn't know how to get to the pharmacy." Beth looked at Len, trying to will him to understand her message.

He did. "So now what do you want with us? We just have the six of us who came from there."

"We want the drugs, man. Are you stupid? And we have the guns, so it looks as if we have a plan. We are in charge, see? We have the control, Boy."

"Okay. After we show you the drugs, we walk away? Go our own way?"

"Sure, but Ward…Warren said you had more guns; we want them," Ball Cap said, "and we keep the women."

"I dunno, they're mean bitches, might better let me keep 'em." Len shrugged. "Hey, what's wrong with him? Sick, Dude?"

"He's bitten," Julia called out; then, she let out a croak as someone obviously kicked her. The kicker walked out, grinning, his arm wrapped in a bandage, leaking with blood and green-yellow pus.

"Got two bitten, huh? Sick Dude and Dead Dude. You're dead, buddy and don't know it yet." Len chuckled. "Dumb ass."

"I wanna kill him," Dead Dude said.

"Just hang on; we want to get the drugs first."

"So we get guns and drugs and keep the chicks…you two go get them and bring them back. If I'm in a good mood, I'll let you and the niggers go," Ball Cap sneered.

"And Warren," Len stared hard at Beth now, willing her to know his plan, "we want Warren back; we can probably find better women than those two; they're kind of frigid."

The men laughed.

"Jerk," Beth said to Len, letting him know she understood.

"Oh, well, fuckin' problem. I mean, if you want what's left of him, see we didn't hurt him ourselves; we just had this little friend we let have a few of his fingers," Burned Man giggled, slapping the woman on her butt. She giggled back.

"They have a zed, Len. Tied up. They…they grabbed Warren and forced his fingers to the zed's mouth; it bit them off one at a time until he told them what they wanted to know. He's really sick."

"That fast? On fingers?" Len let his curiosity run wild for an instant.

"Ah, no, might have been when Freddie Zed was hungry for nose and lips."

Chauncey moaned, leaning over so his head touched the ground.

Len felt an intense hatred for the group, wondering why they had been immune to Red and so many others had died. How had such trash survived? People such as that were a waste of oxygen and were the kinds who could not be rehabilitated.

"That's pretty brutal, Sick Dude. Hey…speaking of, you know you and Dead Dude and Warren are gonna change? You're gonna be a zed, soon," Len taunted. "But that's cool by me. You're righteously some bad-ass dudes. "

"We had shots, dumb ass. We won't get sick."

"Shots?" Len asked; Chauncey looked up.

"Vaccines. Elwood's cousin works at a dog clinic, yanno; so we got the treatment before this shit hit here in the US."

"Yup," Elwood, aka Sick Dude, said, "got the rabies shots."

"Blow me runnin' backwards," Len said with a whistle. "Ya hear that,

Chauncey?" Chauncey nodded.

"We are immune now."

"They got shots. Hey, I gotta idea. If you hook me up with that rabies shot, I'll show you the drugs and the guns, hand ya the women with my best wishes, and show you some more stuff you might want. Those gals can't shoot worth shit anyway."

"Didn't want them for shootin'…'cept what I wanna shoot in 'em," Ball Cap laughed.

Len laughed, too. "So that's the idea?" Len said that worked for him.

"You got more good stuff?"

"Yep. And we can find people who can actually shoot a gun."

"I can shoot, Len," Beth interrupted.

"You can't either. How many times I tell you to get a target, and you

then take ten or twelve shots?" Len slowly rolled to his butt. "Knees killing me.

Chauncey…he don't care though."

"Twelve? Like hell," she yelled back.

"Shut up, and why can't we keep the women?" Chauncey whined. "I

wanna keep the women."

"Don't be arguing about who can have me; I'll have your balls, too,

Pendejo," Julia yelled.

Beth yelled over to her, "What do you mean twelve shots? Asshole. Julia

takes twelve shots, but I don't."

Julia rattled back in Spanish to Beth, calling her names.

Beth yelled back at Julia, turning her head to do so, and trying to get

space between her and the man who was holding her beside his knife.

Len and the men laughed as both women snarled at each other.

"*Cabron*," Julia yelled at Beth.

"That is it, you bitch," Beth jerked to the side, screaming, lunging towards Julia, falling as she went. She rolled.

A hole appeared in the center of Ball Cap's forehead, brains and blood shot backwards, spraying Dead Dude in his face.

Len and Chauncey lay on their stomachs, not moving, not presenting as dangerous, so the raiders swung guns up and to the side where Johnny, Kim, and Big Bill were hidden. Dead Dude went down, along with Sick Dude. Billy Ray and Burned Man shot back but dropped in a volley of rounds.

"Don't move," Kim yelled to the women, "is that all?"

"Yes." Beth crawled to Julia and Hagan to untie them. She worked the knots furiously, patting Hagan's face to get him awake.

"Who got Ball Cap?"

"Me."

"Good shot, Kim. Good for all you guys," Len said, getting to his feet and helping Chauncey to his feet. "Damned fine work, Johnny; you and Big Bill, rock." Len and Chauncey grabbed their weapons to reload.

"He's alive." Big Bill kicked at Burned Dude.

Len asked for help getting him and the woman tied.

Warren was barely conscious. "Sorry, I told, Len."

Julia patted his arm, trying to avoid looking at his ruined face, a hole where his nose had been, teeth were where the lips had been torn away.

He cried with the pain and had gone feverish, was becoming infected as the wounds turned colors and seeped fluids.

"Hey, I can't blame you; bastards didn't play fair." Len smiled at Warren. "You stayed brave and did a good job."

"Thanks. I tried." But it sounded like, "*Tanks, Eh tied.*"

"Hurting pretty bad, I know."

Warren nodded with a whine.

"I'd take you back if I could. But, Warren, you're awful sick."

"Just put me down. It hurts so bad." "*Dus ut ee own. Eh huts so ad.*" He gurgled, and his words were hard to understand, but they did understand what he wanted.

"I'll do right by you, 'George's terms', friend. But I'm a cold son of a bitch, and first, I'm gonna give you and the rest some retribution and justice, maybe some kind of peace. It'll make me feel a little better anyway."

Len had them help him gently get Warren into a better spot.

"Look, I don't even have a gun," the woman whined.

"That didn't stop you from suggesting that they use the zed to get information out of Warren, did it? And it didn't stop you from kicking Jules when she was tied up." Beth drew back, slapped the woman across the face as hard as she could, and then with fury, spat in the woman's face.

"I didn't shoot at anyone or do anything; I just hung around them. What else was I gonna do, all alone? What did I do so wrong?"

"And you don't hurt people to save your own skin. That's a coward." Kim glared. "And you called my friends some pretty nasty names; you held them at gun point; you shot Chauncey. Anyone of these would have risked his life to help you if you hadn't been part of this trash."

Johnny was now holding up Hagan, who smiled to show he was a bit better. "I can abide most anything but a cowardly whore. You went along with them, and that damned you," he said quietly.

Len faced his friends. "I've already said I was a cold son of a bitch. I have a mean streak maybe…maybe I am just sick and tired of seeing shit like this when things are bad all over, people hurting others for no reason. I have a strange sense of justice, and I won't say I'm a good man. But I live with what I do."

"What's wrong, Len?" Beth touched his arm, worried.

"I'm about to do something pretty bad. No, really bad. Those two," he motioned to the woman and Burned Man, "are about to get what they dished out to Warren while he and I sit here and watch the justice."

Beth paled and Julia muttered, "*Madre Dios.*"

"Oh, Len," Beth muttered.

"Now the screams won't go on long; go on over there, don't look, cover your ears, and hum, and I'll be along soon. None of you need watch this."

"Oh, Jesus and God," Johnny said.

Len walked over, and to his shock, Big Bill joined him, moving the woman and man close to the zed who moaned a little.

The woman and man stepped back close to Warren, where Len and Big Bill also stood. Kim stepped forward next to Len without a word, dreading this, but supporting his friend.

The zed grabbed the woman, and she shrieked as it pulled her close.

Chauncey walked over to Big Bill next, his head down, eyes on the ground, but standing in support; he shivered. Beth took Julia's hand, and they moved forward, with Kim draping his arms around both their shoulders. Big Bill, Len, and Chauncey added their arms. Johnny and Hagen came abreast of the team and added to the group. Hagan prayed under his breath.

In less than a minute, they had been bitten several times as they screamed for mercy; Len put them both down. Then he shot the zed. Len was dry-eyed, with pain set deep in his face, keeping it at bay by sheer will.

Johnny stayed Len's hand and took care of Warren who passed with a look of peace. He had neither condoned nor accepted the punishment Len had set forth.

Julia, Beth, and Johnny had tears on their faces.

They all carefully climbed down the rubble, helping Hagan, Julia, and Chauncey, who were in pain and exhausted; Chauncey was pale with pain.

Before Kim climbed down last, he looked over the nightmare where they had lost a friend and seen horrors. The stupidity and evilness of the raider group made him feel sick and angry. He called out to the empty area, "Rabies shots didn't do shit for ya, did it?"

21
CONNECTIONS

It was difficult returning with two fewer people, but when Hagan, Julia, and Beth saw the condition of the lobby and heard what had happened, they were shocked that anyone had survived. It was no less than a bloody war zone.

"Gotta teach Misty to stop chasing after Mark, who is too old for her, and teach you all to carry flashlights," Len said.

"Is he? Too old? Does it matter?" Kim asked.

"Would if she were my daughter."

"We were following your lead, Len, causing chaos back there, but we already have had that same discussion…about women being prizes," Beth said. "That was unnerving to hear them say what Bryan and you had just warned us about."

"Prizes?" Johnny asked.

"I'll have to catch you up on that; you have won, Len," Beth grimaced with the memory of what the men had intended to do to her and Julia.

"Julia, teach me something fast in Mexican to call Beth," Len begged.

She laughed quietly at him, "No way. But Beth is right; hearing what they said back there made me sick. Hang on." She paused to lean over and breathe deeply.

"What's wrong?"

"Nothing. Fine."

Beth felt unsettled and asked for someone to hand her a flashlight. She turned it on Julia. "Oh my, God. Why didn't you say anything?"

Julia, white faced, smiled. "I'm fine." And promptly passed out.

Getting her to the floor, they found her pants leg soaked in scarlet. She was the one injured in the original fall, and she had begun bleeding badly after being kicked; her bloody footprints were behind them. Len and Johnny tied padding and Len's belt around her thigh.

"I can carry Little Girl. She don't weigh a thing." Big Bill scooped her up into his arms.

"Lobby coming up. Go silent."

To their surprise, it looked like a battle zone, the glass doors shattered outward, the screens tossed to the side, and blood and gore were everywhere.

Len and Kim ducked and ran over to the lobby, looked inside, guns ready. Bodies were neatly stacked inside, heads crushed, a few sporting headshots. There had to be over a dozen.

Back on the basement level, they walked quietly.

"Identify yourselves."

"Len, Kim, Beth, Julia, Chauncey, and Big Bill," Len called out. "You?"

"Hi, guys; it's Mark." He came out to greet them. "What happened?"

"Nothing too serious; we need Sally though."

Sally joined them, directing where to put Julia and quickly cutting off Julia's pants. Julia had a deep gash that needed stitches and to be disinfected. The rest went to wash and then joined the group in the cafeteria to get drinks and trade stories.

"They broke out of the lobby right through the glass as if it was paper, and we had a fight," Roy said. "We took them out with a melee, all but a few."

"Sounds good. Glad you took care of them."

"We'll get bodies out later. And we didn't sustain a single injury." He grinned, taking pride in that.

"Glad the good guys did well."

Len told their story with a bare outline of the raiders, omitting the end and saying all were killed in the gunfight.

"We lost that girl, Theresa, who was cut up so badly and the Hispanic girl who had the burns and torn up feet." Sally took it pretty hard. The rest...some are in bad shape; some are gonna be okay if they don't get bad infections and can manage the pain with what we have," George told them.

They had missed eating, so they ate as if they were starving. Benny and Thurman got plates to take to Chauncey, Julia, and Hagan. They reported that Doc and Sally had said all three had taken serious injuries but should be fine with rest, medications, and time.

After everyone had gone to do other things, George, Benny, Tink, Thurman, Mark, and Misty gathered with the rest and asked what Len had not shared. They knew he had held back. To Len's surprise, not one judged him.

George shrugged, "We have 'George's Terms.' And now, when it is an eye-for-an-eye justice, we have 'Len's Terms'."

"I owed Warren. And to be honest, the way they treated and talked about Hagan and Chauncey and Julia....racist like...for no reason...and the way they talked about women, I was pissed off. They would have hurt other people in the future."

George and the older men asked Len to walk with them; Len was building his fury, and it would ruin him if he let it.

Beth and Kim went to check on the patients. Maryanne and Toni smiled and said hello. Toni was describing everyone to Maryanne.

"She said Beth is pretty with dark hair, and Julia, too, with her hair all chopped off so the zeds can't get her," Maryanne said.

Beth laughed, "Jules and me don't do much for the hairdressing profession."

"Kim is handsome, and so are Bryan and Len, but they are so old...like Hagan." Toni chirped. Everyone laughed. "Mark is dreamy."

"Why, thank you, Miss Toni." Mark chuckled, feeling Misty nervously nudging his hand. He finally took her hand in his, butterflies in his stomach. Johnny told them to move along. "Sally said you both need rest; you all go on now. And, Beth, I wanna hear about this 'women as prizes' thing later and how I won, Len. I wanna know what I'm supposed to do with his ass?"

Toni giggled.

They checked on Julia and Hagan; both were asleep. Chauncey complained that he wanted out and back to the action and that Sally was way too wicked for him. They laughed.

Beth changed into scrubs, ready to sleep. But Mark knocked on her door. "Come in, Mark."

"Can we talk?"

"Sure. Julia is in the clinic area, dunno where Misty is; the other spot is Johnny's, but she's helping Sally and Doc, so we are alone. What can I help you with?"

"Misty."

"Oh? What's wrong?"

He blushed. "Beth, I like her. And she likes me."

"I see. Well, I knew she had a crush on you."

"You know she's just turned sixteen."

"Yep."

"I'm twenty-six," Mark said.

"Does that worry you? Does the age thing bother you or her?"

He chuckled, "She doesn't care a bit. I feel a bit strange about it 'cause, well, a man my age can't date a sixteen year old unless he wants to get in legal trouble."

"Not that there is a legal system now," Beth said.

"I wanted to ask your permission, I guess. To be with her."

"Mine?"

"I trust you, and she admires you."

"When I was twenty-five, I went to this AA sponsored dance…where the alcoholics gathered and drank a bunch of soda and danced and didn't worry about being tempted. I went with my friend, Bobbi, whose friend was on the twelve-step. I was bored and tagged along.

Anyway, I met this cowboy there. He was younger than I, only nineteen, cute and fresh faced as could be, blond and blue-eyed. We danced the two-step, then a waltz. I found myself dancing every song with him." She smiled, remembering. "When we danced, he felt so nice, so strong, and he smelled good; I was just like jelly.

"We talked some. But to be honest, he was just the most handsome thing I had ever seen and was a year sober. As the night went on, I gave him my number but wondered if he'd really call or if I would really go out with him. I wondered about the age thing.

When the dance ended, I walked out with him to go home with my girl friends, but he wanted to show me his truck. He kissed me there beside his truck, and I about melted."

Beth smiled. "I wasn't a virgin, but I was a good girl; I told my friends to go on without me, and I let him drive me home. We spent the rest of the weekend, all Saturday and Sunday together.

Three months later, he gave me what he could afford, a small engagement ring with a little diamond.

A month after that, Cody was killed in a rodeo accident. A horse threw him."

"I'm sorry, Beth."

"I told you this because of a few things. First, love or lust, which becomes love, can happen fast. Second, happiness and time together can be fleeting. Third, had I worried about the age thing, I would have missed out on four perfect months with Cody. You came to me 'cause I watch out for Misty. If she wants you and you want her, then so be it. I'll support you both. Don't hurt her."

"I won't hurt her."

"She's young, and she may fall out of infatuation with you; I think she's pretty mature though, and she means it if she says it, but don't hurt her. If you sleep with her, then, you are a couple. You present as a couple, meaning you protect her, speak up for her, and put her first. And she needs to do the same. If you and she are ready to make love, then you are not gonna hide things such as a dirty secret, and you won't flaunt it, but you will treat her as your partner."

Mark blushed again. "I've just kissed her so far..."

"But you and she wanna do more than kiss."

"Well, yes, it's pretty intense, and I feel as if we're gonna be kissing and then...well, you know. So I wanted to ask you now. Before."

"I appreciate that. I'll make sure Len and Kim know I gave my blessings and to keep their noses out of your business."

"You do have a way with them."

She laughed. "We've seen enough of small-minded people; it's good to see anyone at peace or happy, now."

Mark hugged her and thanked her again.

"I guess I'll be sleeping in here alone tonight." She laughed, making him blush again. She would speak to Misty, too, reminding her to be loyal and a good partner to Mark. He was a real gentleman.

Chilled, she wrapped a blanket around her shoulders and went out to find Len and Kim. Pulling them aside, she yawned. "Look, I'm tired, so this is gonna be short. Mark and Misty have a thing going, and I gave my blessings, so butt out and leave them alone."

"She's sixteen."

"Len, had it been you asking for my blessing with her at your age, I would have given it. Life is way too short and tenuous to worry about the things that really don't matter. If you find happiness, then be happy. There. The end."

Beth walked away, leaving them baffled.

"Cute scrubs."

"Shut up, Bryan." He followed her. "Aren't you on guard duty? Go guard something."

He laughed. "You're rude and sarcastic to me 'cause you're hiding your deep feelings of attraction."

"Oh, is that it? Here I thought your getting on my nerves was why I was rude."

"Len told me what really went on with the raiders. God, that must have been awful. Are you okay? Do you feel shaky?"

Beth groaned, "What...you think I'm having another delayed shock? Do you have to be told everything?"

"They told me the other day...told Sally, and I was there. It was all of two sentences about your having had a bad reaction. Then Len told me that you watched what he did to the raiders."

"So did the rest. We all saw it."

"And I was worried about you, is all."

Beth sighed, "Sorry, I'm being a bitch. The last few days, I have seen the worst things of my life. I've had to do some rough things, yet I find myself laughing at times, and then like earlier, you'd think watching all of that would have sent me into shock, but it didn't. I cried a little, for Warren. But I didn't care about the raiders and what they got. So that makes me wonder what the hell is wrong with me. Yanno?"

"You're normal, Beth. I was puking when we had to bash in the first heads; then, in the lobby, I could hardly stop; I wanted to keep doing it; I wanted them to keep coming so I could split their skulls, and I didn't even care. I liked it."

"So what's wrong with us?"

"Not a thing. Remember stories about Vietnam and what our men went through? They burned villages and slaughtered women and children and were called names. But they were not bad people. They saw their friends killed over and over again; they went into this survival mode that told them to destroy and massacre with extreme prejudice. They went brutal."

"Oh."

"It's the deepest part of us that tells us just to destroy and kill...no flight...just fight to the ultimate. Annihilate. Only one can come out alive, and we want it to be us."

"The virus was a very sudden thing, and it caused a massive event...like when the meteor hit the dinosaurs," Beth said. "Those who could adapt had to instantly. The rest died out. It was a lightning-quick evolution, survival of the fittest."

Bryan nodded. "That's right."

"It still feels weird to get used to anything so...vicious."

"To be honest, I suspect we have just seen the tip of the iceberg, Beth. I think we are getting used to this horror because in time, we are going to be faced with much worse."

"Thanks. I do feel better after talking about this."

"I'm not a bad guy."

"You're okay. Sometimes."

Bryan stepped forward, and before Beth could think, he was kissing her.

To her surprise, she kissed him back.

"Beth," he mumbled.

She pulled away. Going to the door, she stood, pointing. "Out. Now." She felt confused and angry. Why couldn't he have left things on a good note?

He laughed as he walked out; she was so furious that she threw a boot at him as he stood in the hallway, "Stop laughing, you asshole."

Alex had come in with the Reverend and Doc as survivors. He scooped up her boot and handed it back to her with a puzzled look. "Man trouble?"

"Yep. They're all trouble. I hate men right about now."

"Oh, me, too, Honey. Me, too. I have some snoring up a storm in my room, and I could just smother them all."

She couldn't help laughing. He fussed about her room, picking things up and looking at things, and he was so unexpected that she forgot her anger at Bryan.

Uninvited, Alex grabbed her brush and pulled her to a chair. "Sit. Tell me about that hot man." He began brushing her hair.

"Bryan?"

"Yes...he is very hot. In a brutish way."

Beth was so astounded now that she just sat and let him brush her hair, glad she hadn't done like Julia and cut it off.

"He's hot, yes, but he is so very full of himself; he thinks all women just want him."

"And they don't?"

"No."

'I would have thought they'd be chasing him."

"He kissed me." She sputtered.

"Aw, you lucky thing. Was it heavenly?"

"I dunno, not exactly. It was a good kiss, but he isn't the one for me...like my heart didn't race, or I didn't go weak-kneed. He makes me mad most of the time." She fumed.

"They all do that; he likes you, but he's too macho to really be himself and show it.

That Len is another macho one, but bless his heart; he has a world of pain in his eyes. He will find a lady to take away the pain, but he isn't ready for real love. He doesn't love himself right now."

Beth began to relax with every stroke of the brush going through her long hair. Her scalp tingled. "Tell me more."

"That Mark...he is crazy for that girl, Missy."

"Misty."

"Ah. Okay. Now he's a goodhearted one...true hearted, and he is already in love with her. She is smitten with him, too. She may be a teen, but she's an old soul, and she loves him. He's her hero."

Beth grinned. "Good."

"Your pal, Julia, is it? She's a pistol. I bet she liked a lot of men...if you catch my meaning, but I like her. She's very real."

"Yes, she is."

"I like Johnny. She'll make a loyal, loving companion, and I bet she's a beast in bed." Alex chuckled. "I always had girl friends, never males as friends, but I acted tougher, masking my feminine side.

Then, the summer I graduated, I was with my parents at a beach house, and right there on the beach away from the water, I saw a god appear, bronzed with white-blond hair and pale blue eyes. I knew then I was gay," he laughed.

"Not until then?"

"I wasn't a hundred percent until then, but when I saw Todd, I was in lust. He taught me to smoke grass and make love. It was a glorious summer, and we kept in touch; he died of AIDS. I'm HIV negative, though."

"I'm sorry for your loss." For the second time that night, Beth told about losing Cody.

"Poor thing, you need a good man. Don't we all?" Alex suggested. "And now, with all this, what are the chances I'll find another gay man? It's even more impossible that if I find one, he'll be cute, or we'd hit it off. One in ten, my cute ass; there aren't five gay men in this group."

"None here at the hospital?"

"None. And all these hot men with guns, oh, it's a shame that Kimball is hot, you think so?"

"I guess." Beth blushed.

"Aw, you do! Those long legs, wow. He's a good guy but is used to being alone."

"You watch people." Beth noted.

"My favorite hobby. Now don't you feel better with your hair neatly brushed?"

"Actually I do. I could sleep now."

"I could but for the snoring."

"Go get your stuff, and move in here. Misty is going to be shacking up with Mark, I think, and right now, I'm alone in here."

"Okay." Alex beamed with pleasure, got his things, and settled in.

Beth slept like the dead.

22
DIVISIONS AND GAMES

Another day, another bunch of drama.

Donna hated being trapped more than anything else. She hadn't wanted to be at the hospital at all, but Paul's mother had been there, and there was really no way to get out of it.

At least, they had been down in the cafeteria for the blast, and his mother had been up there where it all collapsed. Had the woman been down stairs, trapped with them, Donna would have chewed through to her own veins. Now, they were stuck here with people, expecting her to work for them like a slave. She did kitchen detail to stay away from the burned and injured people.

She was bored out of her skull.

Surreptitiously, she watched Bryan and Len, Kim and Mark, and Hagan. Why didn't Paul want to be in the camp with the attractive men? Instead, he followed Roy, who was just a grumbling pest. The more she thought about it, the less she wanted to be in that camp or with Paul.

What were the new rules of divorce?

She smiled and joined the crowd as they gathered after a breakfast of cereal, baked apples, orange juice, coffee, *and powdered eggs*, yuk!

Most of them were reviewing how to clean the weapons; they chattered as they learned how to clean each one; smells were odd but pleasant enough.

"Half my team is down," Len complained, "But I want to raid the vending machines in the lobby where you put down the zeds. And those bodies have got to be moved out; they're too close to us here."

"We can handle it," Bryan said.

"We'll help if we're included more. I still want to know where Theresa, Mark, and Tom are," Chad said. He was one who had joined them the day before, after the battle in the lobby.

The fourteen of them had hidden in back rooms with snacks and water, waiting on rescue. Unfortunately, they had gotten too excited and run into the lobby where many had been killed.

Of the seven whom they had found, Bryan was able to bring back only four. Chad had complained since the minute he was rescued.

"Chad, I told you they were infected and didn't make it."

"Well, we were all standing there, waiting to come back here...seven of us. They made it. We saw them."

Roy said, "Like I said, Chad, they made it, but they didn't make it here. No one infected gets in. Bryan handled it."

"Handled it? He isn't a doctor."

Sally was taking a needed break and sighed, "But I am. I have fifteen patients right now, though Maryanne and Toni are about to be released from my care.

Of those thirteen, Hagan, Julia, and Chauncey will be released next, and that means they were the least injured, which is substantial when you think that

Julia's thigh was stabbed, cut to the bone and she could have easily bled out.

And Chauncey was shot. Those are the least serious; can you grasp how serious the rest are?"

"So you can't take any more wounded?" Chad didn't let it go. "We'd all help with them."

Bryan snapped back, "She means she can't and won't treat those who are infected. None of us will let the infected come in. Do you wanna get infected?"

"So if we get bitten on these work details, we get shot?" someone asked.

"It's not like that." George stood. "A bite means you aren't dead, aren't alive; your soul gets trapped. What kind of hell is that? I'd prefer someone set me free as for me having to walk around like that."

Roy shrugged, "What do you think, Padre?"

Bob thought before he spoke. "I saw those things we fought off when we were trying to get here. I won't call them demons, as they are infected people, but the disease is certainly as evil as I've ever seen. In some ways, it is as if they were taken over by demons, and we set them free."

"Amen." George sat back down.

"I won't say go on killing people with cruelty and causing them fear, but to release them in a kind way; I don't know. It's hard to say when they are still human, as we know them. I don't have an easy answer. But that's the best way I can understand and explain it," Bob finished.

"And we don't know...not at a hundred percent...if people might be immune to a bite. Right? Or if a virus could hibernate for years like rabies?"

"It isn't rabies," Kim said, remembering the ones who had thought themselves safe after taking rabies shots. Getting looks of disbelief, he told the group how they had taken the shots. "That's what they said they did."

"We don't know a hundred percent," Sally admitted. "But I won't sit beside someone infected, waiting for him to turn and rip my throat out."

Roy chuckled, "She still says some were dead and walking around."

"They were."

"Right," he said sarcastically, "walking dead, now."

"Call 'em what ya want."

"Can some of the rest of us learn to shoot?" Donna jumped in with a topic change. "May I?"

Mark slid her a pistol, empty; he had been cleaning it.

"It's so big," she purred, stroking it suggestively.

"Donna...what are you doing?" Paul demanded.

"Holding a big gun." She handed it back and watched Mark and Misty go off together. "Cute couple."

"We don't need guns," Paul snapped.

"We might," his wife argued.

"Beth, you told Donna about the lottery for the men you all have going?"

Beth glared at Bryan. "Lottery?"

"Sure. Winner gets Len. Bryan, we have you down for the booby prize." Johnny laughed as they lit cigarettes.

"As long as I am in it, I'm good," he said, grinning.

Alex slipped into the chair with Beth, sharing the chair as he got comfortable. She frowned, stood, let him settle, and then plopped down in his lap. He mock-groaned, making them all laugh again.

Roy narrowed his eyes. He didn't like queers, or rather he was a little scared they all wanted him. He didn't like Beth either for the company she kept, queers, blacks, Spics, and tough boys.

He had endured years of hell in high school when he was smaller and the target of teasing.

He wouldn't have tortured Warren, but he did understand some of the views of the little raider group they had run into the day before. He knew he could have reasoned with them in a way that would have kept them from getting killed. He might have joined them, but he didn't like the idea of torturing people. That was extreme. He wished he could have worked it out for everyone.

He also didn't like that Paul's wife was getting chummy with everyone. A woman had a place, and she was stepping outside her God-given place. Paul needed to get her back into her rightful place. He had grown up a certain way and wanted that standard kept.

For now, he would try to get along the best he could, and he did his part, no one could deny that, working just as hard as everyone else. He followed Len's orders like a good little monkey, too. But there would be a time when he and those with like minds broke off to go their own way.

Everyone kind of waited to see what would happen that day.

Len had thought to take off the day for rest, but his team was restless. They had kept so busy the last few days that now they could hardly stay still.

After listening to them, Len knew he couldn't sit and not train his team. They were too eager. He made sure each had a pack with light supplies and took Kim and Beth, Johnnie, Mark and Misty, Tink and Thurman, Alex, Roy, and Big Bill. Bryan, George, Benny, and a few others would stay on security detail.

In the lobby, Alex wrinkled his nose.

"Yes, they smell pretty bad." Len thought of the second lobby where the remains of survivors and zeds lay amid the rubble and grimaced.

"Misty and Alex, you are here with Tink to learn gun safety and how to guard properly. Thurman and Roy will not be watching you so much. But they may have advice as you go," Len said.

"Alex, you know how to use a melee, and Misty needs to get comfortable with it. The other teams will be coming in and moving bodies out in bags. Keep your eyes open for potential danger, and watch your team to make sure they stay safe."

"As we grow, you'll need your own team, Kim," Len said, "maybe Hagan, Beth, Julia; I'll take Mark and Misty. We can see how the rest want to divide up as we go; we will have two teams of six. Then when we grow, we will break off again into new teams."

"Len doesn't want Julia and me on his team 'cause we take twelve shots to hit a target." Beth laughed.

"I heard that," Kim said.

"What was with Donna flirting with you guys?"

"Was she?"

"Yes, with her husband sitting right there, she was batting her eyes at all of you guys. That's why Misty kicked Mark under the table and they left."

Mark laughed.

"Hmm," Len mused.

The area around the vending machines was clear, and they reported it was okay to loot them. Chocolate bars and candy, chips and crackers, cookies, pretzels, all were there to be added to their supplies.

A dark crack lined a wall behind that area; they were able to turn sideways and slip into it where it went, cave-like for a few yards, opened to the outside, then continued. They pushed a door open and found themselves in a stairwell that was largely intact.

"It looks, different."

Johnny agreed with Kim. The stairs and the walls were in a different style and different color than what they were accustomed to. Len grabbed his compass and began to mutter, thinking, trying to recall where the hospital stood and where they might be now.

"Look." Mark showed them the broken window that led out of the stairway onto a floor. "Hallways."

"Hotel?"

"There was one right beside the hospital. Is that where we are?" Beth looked in. "Oh great, I see movement!"

"Moaner?"

"Looks as if the movement might be one of them."

Mark grinned, "There will be a fire axe. Hot damn."

"Sick pup." Beth laughed at him. "We gonna check it, Len?"

"Speaking of violent people. A few days ago, you all shivered in your boots, and now you wanna go looking for zeds to beat with axes. You're all violent now," Len chuckled. "What did I create?"

"Let's play military; you give orders like that, 'kay?"

This time Len almost rolled on the floor, wiping tears from his eyes as he tried to stop laughing. "'Play' military, Beth?"

He tried the radios they had pulled from the supplies, wanting to learn to use them effectively. "Alpha calling base. Over."

"Alpha, this is base. Over."

"Base, we are going into the hotel, location through crack in the wall and stairwell. Request Bryan and Thurman for back up. Over."

"I like the radios," Johnny said, "they make it easier to 'play', huh, Beth?"

"Roger, Alpha. 5x5. Sending Bryan and Thurman. Out," Benny responded.

They waited for the two to join them, and Len went over the plan. "Even if no zeds were confirmed, we would be doing this the same, never a safe time; be on alert, and stay smart. Beth, call base, and tell them we are Oscar Mike."

"Umm. Alpha team calling base. Over."

"This is Base. Reading you 5x5, Alpha. Over."

"Base, we are Oscar Mike."

"Say, Over."

"Over."

"Affirmative on Oscar Mike, Alpha Team. Be safe. Over."

"Alpha Team out." Beth giggled. "That's fun. What is Oscar Mike?"

"Means we are on the move," Bryan told her.

Len laughed, "Bryan, they think 'playing military' is fun and hunting zeds and talking on the radio is awesome; what have we created?"

"I like when you do the Three Stooges thing," Beth told Len.

"You do what?"

"Huh?" Len asked, shrugging at Bryan. "What does she mean?"

"Three Stooges?" Kim asked her, "What does Len do?"

With a sigh, Beth showed them, pointing her first two fingers at her eyes, as if she were poking them.

This time, laughing, Len slid down the wall with Bryan, crying since he was howling so hard.

Mark and Kim started mimicking her motions, rolling with laughter.

Beth looked to Big Bill who turned his face, tears rolling down his cheeks as he joined in.

Thurman leaned down, hands on knees, laughing.

Johnny tried to keep a straight face, "It means watch me."

"I know what it means, but what'd you call it? A Three Stooges thing?" She made the eye-poking sounds from the show and began laughing with them.

Len pointed out the fire axe to Mark, telling him to get it fast because he wanted to use it since the zeds were moaning and walking their way, now. They moved forward through the door and into a hallway.

Mark ran over, broke the glass, and got the axe while everyone kept a close watch. Easily, he swung, lobbing off the zed man's head, following it, and smashing it with the blade, using his boot to hold the head and pull the axe free. Gore from the body was all over the carpets, painting a pattern with red streaks and pools.

"Sick fucks." Len laughed at Mark's big grin.

"Next time we see one, I want an axe," Kim said. Big Bill, Bryan and Johnny did as well. Beth, Thurman, and Len shook their heads in mock disgust.

The halls looked clear but for the one Mark trashed, so they looked at Len to ask what was next.

Since they had heard random noises behind doors and the zeds couldn't get out, he suggested clearing what halls they could and then checking rooms if they wanted. Survivors would hear them, hopefully, and call out, if there were any.

On the third floor, doors to rooms stood open, and there was a lot of movement. Zeds moved in and out of some of the rooms, all in a close group.

Johnny took a turn calling base and relaying the information.

"Funnel them. Mark and Kim can use melee if they want...guns on sides," Len said as Kim, with a grin, got his axe.

Beth and Johnny stood beside them; Big Bill and Len went down on their knees to shoot.

Once the sides were cleared a little, Kim and Mark used the axes to chop off heads and crush them. One of the heads rolled past them with its jaws still snapping viciously. With milky eyes, it stared with hatred, unable to moan.

"See how long it moves," Len said. They left it intact.

"Maggie's drawers, Johnny," Bryan called.

"Whose what's?"

"He means you missed a shot." Len laughed. "We're teaching you military terms." Len fell back so Bryan could replace him, then, tapped Beth to let him take her spot.

Kim threw the axe down and tapped Johnny to take her spot. Thurman moved to take Mark's place when he grew tired. In seconds, the hall was clear of zeds. Johnny smoothly used three shots to hit a zed who had come out of a room behind them.

"Good eye," Bryan said.

"Now that it's clear, we walk back and check all open doorways and clear the rooms. Big Bill, Thurman, and Johnny, front and back, watching the hallway. Mark, melee, and Kim, sidearm, to clear rooms. Beth, bathrooms, with sidearm. Bryan and I have your backs."

Inside the first room, they found a woman half under a bed, most of her legs eaten to the bone. They dispatched her quickly. "Clear," Beth called.

"Clear," Mark said after they checked the room.

Bryan slammed the door and marked it. "That's how it's done."

The second and third rooms were clear.

In the fourth, as soon as they were in, Beth fired. She couldn't hear because of the echo of the blast, but she yelled it was clear and stepped back.

After Kim and Mark finished looking around and finding the room empty, they glanced in the bathroom to see an old man on the toilet, slumped over with a hole in his face.

"Bravo Zulu means well done," Len told Beth, "and you are a Jane Wayne."

He then teamed them up so Beth kept bathrooms, Kim had rooms with Big Bill on gun, and Bryan stood in doorway to watch the hall and room. The other team was Johnny on bathroom, Len in the room with Mark on gun, and Thurman at the door.

Johnny got a kill, and the other rooms were empty, but it was good practice.

Mark smashed the moving head since it had not died. "Bastards are still trying to bite," he said. "How can it keep going without the body?" In curiosity, he looked down at the head, poking it with a boot.

"The virus must keep the brain active. That is like what the preacher said, as if they were possessed by demons. That's pretty sick."

"If it could, it would bite and infect someone, yuk!"

The fourth floor was filled with debris, but they covered it all the same, after taking out a horde that wandered the hallway. Most of the hall was so covered with concrete and twisted metal that they couldn't get through.

Len kept testing everyone and saying he thought they'd have three teams soon. "Maybe Bryan will take the third...or Hagan...not sure, and Roy can take one for security there at base. I like Benny on radio, though."

Fifth floor.

"Look at that," Bryan pointed.

A white flag was being held out from a doorway. It waved. "Hello?"

"Hello. We came to help any who need us," Len called. "We can get you to safety, food, and supplies if you need, including medical treatment."

"Are you military?"

"Yes. Just a second."

Len and Bryan looked at each other, whispering. Bryan shrugged and called back, "The US military is no longer serving this country, as it took too many casualties and had no orders. However, those remaining are trying to regain control for the citizens of this country. We are the US Militia, Colonel Len Barnhart and Major Bryan Collins with Major Kimball Decker."

"Major?" Len whispered.

"I got promoted. So did Kim."

"I'm not in the military."

"You are now," Len said to Kim. "I promoted both of you. This is going too fast. I wanted to think first, but we need this anyway...structure. US Militia? Hells Bells, this is CATFUed."

"Cat kung fu? Huh?"

"Beth, CATFUed...completely and totally fucked up." Len and Bryan laughed again at her.

"Gotcha, Major," she snapped back to Bryan.

"Mark, you are a captain."

"Wow, thanks." He suppressed a grin while Len glared at all of them. "That was a fast promotion."

"Colonel, thank God, you're here. Conner Pate, Lieutenant, US Army." A man stepped out and saluted. Len and Bryan and then Kim returned the salute.

"How many do you have?"

"Eight adults, Sir. Five children."

"Injured? Bitten?"

"Cuts, scrapes, few minor burns, no bites."

"See here," a man stepped out around Conner, "we're hungry and about tired of being bossed around by men in uniform. This dickhead left several people down on the first floor, and we need to get them. They are hurt."

"Identify yourself." Len felt his back straighten and the hair on the back of his neck stand up.

"I'm Steve," he smiled, coming forward.

Len didn't greet him but stood, gun pointed at the ground, still ready. He motioned for the man to step back. Others began to peek around Conner Pate, looking at the team.

"We have survivors, about a hundred, and food, water, supplies, and doctors," Len repeated

"We need food," Steve said.

"*Dios.*" A large, handsome, Hispanic man walked over, his hand held out to shake. "I'm Juan. We're glad you're here." In jeans, a checkered shirt, and boots, he looked strong and smiled broadly.

They greeted him with smiles and handshakes. Relaxing.

Diane was blonde and pretty, and she came over with her sixteen-year-old son, Mike, and five small children, holding hands and staring wide-eyed at the rescuers.

Rae was a young woman who carried her bag close to her side. She didn't speak but nodded to them and met their eyes.

Conner joined them, smiling broadly.

The three stood close to the open door; Steve was one of them.

"They are very unhappy with me," Conner said. "I made two leave us who were bitten. Then, a third earlier today, I refused to take any infected, and they thought that was wrong."

"You saved their lives by doing that."

"I thought it was the right thing to do, no matter how difficult."

"We've been out there and all over. Anyone who is bitten turns into a moaning zed. All Reds turn into zeds. If you don't crush the skull or cut the brain stem properly, they will be violent, trying to bite to spread the infection and consuming the flesh. Those dead…or mostly dead…will be zeds. There is no vaccine or cure."

Len told the three, "We don't allow infected to join us, and we take precautions with all who are exposed to the limited radiation outside. We have two doctors who have done research on the virus."

"Doctors and food, that sounds amazing," Diane said.

"Hot shower sounds better?" Beth asked.

"Wow! Yes," she said.

"He sent them down to a room, and the downstairs is full of those things," Steve said. "Is that protocol all over now?"

"Yes, it is."

"That sucks."

"I guess it does."

"Is your group all military?"

"The remains of the US military, holding up the US Constitution, have gathered as best we can, recruiting some civilians as they wish, to guard and rescue American citizens," Len explained. They had not said this, but it was what they had been doing. "We have civilians who do other jobs such as medical, food service, clean-up, and supplies, and we have a teacher who is planning to begin helping the children."

"I'd like to join. US Militia, Sir," Conner said, "glad to hear we still have a place to serve."

"Good to have you, Soldier." Len shook his hand again. "We are waiting out the radiation which is not as bad as we feared, and we have been carrying out search and rescue operations. We have tight security and beds; we have a good thing going." Len felt proud as he went over all they had. "As far as medical, we can do first aid, of course, and light surgeries. We don't have a lot, but we have good people. We have a preacher, too."

"Can you use the linens we found in a closet? Tons of white sheets."

Beth thanked Diane and said, "Yes." They needed to pack up all they could.

"Okay, we're in. We'll work," Steve said. He introduced his girlfriend, Pat, and the other man who was a rough-looking fellow with muscles, jeans, and a tight tee shirt. He was Richie. "We just don't like having to push injured people away."

"No, none of us like that, but one infected could kill everyone else. The virus only lives to spread itself."

Len suggested they bag all the sheets to be carried back with the survivors from this floor and the ones below. They would bash in the locks and loot them.

"Can we come back with a team and loot the rooms? We may get clothing that way for the civilians?" Johnny asked. "We need clothing."

Len, holding back a laugh at her use of the word, 'civilian', agreed it was a good plan. "Base, come in Base. This is Alpha Actual. Over"

"Base Actual here. Go ahead, Alpha Actual. Over."

"Base, we are bringing in eight adult survivors and five children. They are not infected. Do you copy? Over."

"Alpha, we copy. Eight adults and five children coming back with you. Not infected. Roger that. Over."

"Our ETA is thirty minutes. Over."

"Copy that, Alpha. ETA thirty minutes. Will be ready to do an intake. Over."

"Alpha Out." Len hoped he had impressed the newcomers. They all needed to be professional now.

"You sound organized," Juan said, "and take civilians for rescue missions?"

Bryan nodded, "We do. We provide training, experience, and gear...all in very quick time. Search and rescue. Whatever we're needed for."

"I may wanna be part of that."

"Me, too," Mike said, impressed.

"You're only sixteen," his mother, Diane, reminded him.

"And that's old enough, Mom. Things have changed."

"I know," she admitted, sadly.

"It's much worse out there, worse than what we've seen in here in the bomb ruins. Under siege, we have faced over a hundred of those things. You all may not want to go on search-and-rescue missions as they are very dangerous. We have lost a few along the way; they went out as heroes, but I'm saying some training might be good for the long haul when we all have to face the outside world."

"I don't think anyone untrained would last out there now," Beth said, "I wouldn't last."

"It's really that bad?"

"You have the zeds, and they are hunting in hordes; the sheer number of them can keep them coming back without feeling pain or damage, deadly.

Then we have seen raiders, and they are vicious in their own right," Beth told them. "When we ran into raiders and if Len and Bryan had not trained most of us, we all would have been killed; it took a lot of team work."

On the lower floors, they kept most of the survivors back while looting the linens.

"Did you all do this?" Conner pointed to the bodies. "We heard the shots."

"Yep. And we secured several rooms."

"We raided the vending machines, but those things almost got us; that's how two of the people were bitten. Three were killed in raids; I mean, they were torn to pieces; they became one of those things," Conner said. "I'm really amazed at how well your teams work."

"They work well together or die being torn to pieces, alone."

Len heard a moan from behind a door. They had planned to come back to go through all the rooms, but he wanted to seal a deal.

"Beth, bathroom; Kim, the room with Mark. Mark, may Conner borrow your gun? Conner, you watch the door so nothing gets past you."

"Yes, Sir, Colonel." Conner took the gun, and the others took their places.

"Go."

Kim kicked the door in, and he and Mark moved in. Mark carried his axe this time. Inside, Kim shot a teen and a child zed in the head while Mark swung and decapitated a heavy man. He then smashed the head. Kim kicked in the bathroom door, and Beth, without hesitation, placed a bullet in the center of a woman's head. "Clear," she called.

"Clear," Mark yelled out. They grabbed the suitcases full of clothing and closed the door, marking it.

"Balls to the walls," Conner said, shocked. "That was intense."

"That was amazing," Mike said. "Did you see that, Mom?"

"Impressive. Sick and scary, but impressive."

"We've seen enough." Steve glared, holding his wife close to him.

Len shrugged. "Good work, Conner. You'll fit in fine. We'll get you a gun and gear. We'll take you, too, Juan, and if you want, we'll train you. That's exactly what we do. Sometimes we find survivors like you guys."

"Sounds fine. I hunt, so I'm good with guns," Juan said.

Len led them out, a team in front, and Thurman, Big Bill, Bryan, and Johnny covering the back. Through the crack, and finally, they were in the lobby, now free of bodies. Roy and Benny, Misty, Alex, and Tink stood ready. Sally moved forward. "May I check for bites, please?"

Each came to her; she checked each one, sending them back to the rest. "All clear."

"Misty and Tink, provide escort, please."

Both looked serious as they followed Len's formality. They led the survivors out with the rest following. Sally wanted to check each and provide some first aid; she called to get them some food and drinks. They were added to the list and assigned rooms.

"Are the children not yours?" Wanda asked. She was a schoolteacher and had wanted to teach the children in the group, to give them structure.

"We were at the hotel, and a mob of zeds came up," Conner said. "I guess a half dozen, then a dozen; about that time, here came a bus full of people, maybe twenty children and ten adults.

They crashed into a car and saw us coming out, so they, already infected, ran to us; the driver was in bad shape; a few were trying to help, but we had no weapons or anything, and the zeds went after them. My God, Sir, they tore them to pieces. We lost three right there, trying to get the children to safety."

"Thirty people?"

"Like I said, someone was already turned and biting those on the bus, tearing them up even as they tried to get to us. Zeds were coming from all over, and then the bomb hit as we were getting inside; the timing was unreal.

The hospital started falling, but it still sheltered us a great deal; some of the hotel fell in, but it held fairly well. We ducked into the lobby with those who had made it, but the zeds didn't stop even with everything falling and people being burned; five children made it and four adults. Two were attacked in the lobby.

We gathered food, got quite a bit, started climbing, but the only floor that was empty was the fifth where we were; that was Diane's room, and then we broke into two more rooms that we could tell were empty."

"Then what?"

"One of the adults from the bus killed herself that night. Another one just vanished; she was gone the next day, and we never saw a sign of her, again. Her kid was the one who died in the parking lot."

Wanda took to the children at once, giving them plenty of food. Everyone ate as if he were starving. The teams also ate since they had missed lunch. Most were wide-eyed at all the food and drinks they had, their fresh Band-Aids and bandages, clean and white, and everyone welcoming them, as if they had been truly saved.

Julia cursed when they checked on her and told her what all she had missed. She wanted to see the cute Hispanic man they told her about. She swore she'd be up and back in action the next day, despite Sally's saying Julia needed a week of rest.

Hagan was scheduled for release and was ready to get busy again; his release made Julia curse and howl even louder.

Chauncey declared he was going to be up and working, too, and that he would be livid if Julia were up before he was. They all had a big laugh.

"If we can have security, we can strip the hotel, think soap, sheets on beds, toilet paper, towels, pillows, and the luggage with clothing," Conner said.

"Make me a list with that. We will do that today and tomorrow." Len thought that since they had cleared some of the hotel and had a system; it would be perfect for training his teams.

He spoke to Roy who was snide, but agreeable to a lot. They decided that Roy would get a few to train with guns and be the security for the hospital so teams could go out. Roy enjoyed being a leader and puffed his chest out. Leaving Roy and his team there wasn't the best, but it was a place where they would do the least damage.

Len asked Benny to be Base Actual long term and for Jeri to train with Benny so she could fill in if needed. Len stressed about the teams but finally got them sorted.

"Len, umm, I hear you are Colonel now," George laughed. "I never thought a bunch of 'old men' would be doing this kind of thing."

"You 'old men' are valuable to us. And you're my eyes when I can't see it all. I trust you guys."

"I won't say my joints feel good, but to be helping and feeling as if we were needed to do men's work, feels good, Len," George said. "I hate to be dancing on the death of the world, but I feel more useful than I have in ten years."

Rae had still not said a word. She came over, cleaned up, and dressed in military gear. She looked as if she were in her twenties, with a plain-faced and dark, short hair.

Without a word, she held her hand out to Len to take his gun. Eyes narrowed; he handed it to her.

Deftly, she locked the bolt to the rear, went through her steps, and removed the bolt assembly; then, in a second, she removed the cam pin, thirteen steps. Next, she reassembled the M16. "One minute, five seconds," was all she said.

"Can you shoot?"

She nodded once.

Len made a change on his paper. "Okay. I have your teams. You may be missing a person a few days, but he will come back. If we get more, we add to the teams. If you don't like the teams, I don't care; they are 'damned fine with cherries on top' who need some training and are at least two people each leader can depend on, no matter what."

He didn't tell them yet that he had asked some of the women who could sew to make them patches with their team's name and 'US Militia' on them.

Beth had said they 'played military', and people were demanding missions to kill zeds, so it felt, in a way, like a joke. Made-up ranks. Made up names. But they were doing what was right by the country. They were Americans, upholding the values and ideals that made the country great. Somehow, Len believed in this.

"Okay, we'll be training this mission. We will serve floors two, three, four, and five with four teams. Clear rooms, and mark with an x.

We will not, I repeat, not be on the ground floor. I want this lobby as Base where Benny and Rita will be Base Actual.

Roy, I want your team patrolling the cafeteria and camp. The volunteers you gathered will go into marked rooms and loot from the list I gave you. We want those items. While one team clears a room, the other will provide security. Then rotate sides of the hall. Questions?"

"Comment?"

"Go."

"When you clean a bathroom and room, say 'clear' for each," Kim said.

"Right. Okay. We go to floor five, first, Bravo and Charlie. Alpha and Delta will take floor four.

Roy, are you ready to relay the loot?"

"Sure am. We've got security and the supply crews pulled, everyone to help so we can move fast. Even the kids are going to stack the lighter things," Roy said.

"Alpha under me…Mark: Captain; Tink, Misty, and Rae: Lieutenant. Bravo will be Bryan: Major; Johnny: Lieutenant; Julia: Lieutenant but in medical; and Diane and Mike: in training, providing security and training only."

"If placement and no civvies are allowed, practice fire. Charlie will be Kim: Major; Beth: Lieutenant; George: Lieutenant; Big Bill and Chauncey are in medical. You clear every room, Delta." He paused, knowing this was a big deal and people would question this choice if anything happened. "Delta is Conner: Captain; Hagan: Lieutenant; Thurman: Lieutenant; Juan and Alex in training."

Hagan walked in, grinning. "Sally released me, and Julia and Chauncey are mad and cursing a blue streak. I love it." He got some laughs.

"Welcome back."

"You all look good. Stay alert."

They walked out, feeling a part of something big. The world might be dying, but each felt he was doing something that mattered. The organization and camaraderie raised morale.

On the fifth floor, Kim's team, Charlie, began the routine, making it crisp and clear to Bravo team, who watched.

In the hall, Bryan and Johnny showed Diane and Mike how to hold security, two facing forwards, and two to the back of the hall. They had a lesson on safety as the rooms were cleared. They heard shots on the floor below.

A fourth of the way done, sixteen rooms, and they had killed a dozen zeds. One made a lucky grab, catching Kim sideways, and Big Bill calmly took it out, splattering brains all over the room. He was trying the fire axe and with his huge size, and he was doing damage.

Beth had found two. George stood ready each time, watching his team. The way they worked was like a well-oiled machine. Even Bryan and Johnny were impressed with the teamwork.

At the halfway point, another fifteen down, Bryan stopped and let Diane and Mike try the guns. Diane showed promise; she was steady and calm. Excited, Mike missed his targets a lot but was enthusiastic and listened to instructions well, asking questions when he was unsure.

"George, Charlie, team, can Diane and then Mike stand in for George if he stands with them?" Bryan asked. "Unfortunately, they need to see and smell what combat is really like so that they know it's much scarier than target practice."

"I think that is a good idea," Kim said, "Be ready, it is fast, stinky, and violent."

The next room was already empty.

At the next one, a zed stood next to the window. Kim motioned Big Bill to handle it, might as well show them the worst part. Big Bill lifted the axe back and swung. It hit the woman in the ear area, crushing part of her skull, her brains oozing out in a grey jelly. Her blood splashed against the wall behind her, with her skin and ear smashed into a thick pudding. The smell wafted out. She was a Red, so they got the smell of vomit and feces as well.

Big Bill pushed the woman down, Kim held her head with his foot as she snapped at him with broken, filthy teeth, and Bill got out the axe. He lifted, Kim moved, and Big Bill slammed it into her face. The skull cracked in half with a thud.

Diane turned and vomited up everything she had just eaten. Mike looked pale but big-eyed and shocked.

"You okay?" Bryan asked. "I puked, too, the first time we did a melee."

"Wow. That is bad."

"Some are much easier, I promise. Clean shots are. But there is worse than that, too. Much, much worse."

"One of our friends was caught by a raider and fed slowly to a zed; that was hell. I have seen my friends torn apart, too. It can be worse, but sometimes such as when we found all of you, it was very worth it. We are saving everyone we can and trying to make things better," Beth told them.

"Can you handle it?" Bryan asked.

Diane nodded. "I think so. Mike did better than I did."

"Just know you do it for many. Beth has been through hell, seeing friends killed, kidnapped by raiders; she's a hero and you can be, too." Bryan did his pep talk.

"Okay, next zeds...let's take out the legs and let them try shooting," Kim said.

Three rooms were cleared before the zeds had a chance. Diane had good accuracy and was able to finish the two in one room.

"Don't shoot," someone called from the bathroom as a zed lurched towards him. The zed was nude, both feet in thigh-high stilettos which had been turned over and broken, her body had high, firm breasts that were beginning to sag and go mushy with decomposition. Her make-up made her look clownish. Kim finished the woman while she was shambling, and then they waited.

"Porn zed," Kim whispered.

"Do you have food?" the man called.

"What's your name?"

"Eddie. I'm starving, man."

"Who was the zed?"

"The what? Oh, that was...shit...it was a hooker, okay? So sue me." His voice was wavering, slurred, and wet sounding. "Look, I'm hungry."

"Are you injured?"

"Listen, do you have food; damn it, yes, I am just sick; that is all. And I have a bite, but it's better."

"Open the door slowly, please."

Eddie opened it. Beth recognized the nasty smell of the bite on his arm. His bandage, a formerly white towel, was soaked through with green and yellow, thick pus and blood. He was sweat soaked, pale. His shirt was off, and they could see his shoulder and chest were discolored as the flesh rotted on his body. Beth took a big step away, shuddering. He reeked.

Kim motioned the team out. He said that they needed a second and asked if Eddie would sit down, facing the other way for a minute.

Bryan stood in the doorway on guard, and in a few seconds, the others heard one gun shot. Kim walked out and vomited.

"That's when it gets bad, like I said," Beth told Diane and Mike.

"But as bad as it is, those aren't the people they were before; that is the virus in them, using them like puppets. He is set free now to go on wherever he is supposed to go. To be trapped in a rotting body and used by an evil disease, that is wrong. It hurts us to do that, but it is the right thing. Would you want a loved one or yourself to be like one of those things?"

"No," Diane said. "I see what you mean. And I see why you do this. My God, someone has to clean up the world."

Johnny sighed, "Welcome to the US Militia clean up crew."

"More than that. You saved our lives. I may not be as strong as you all, but yes, Mike and I need to learn to protect ourselves, and we can do this."

"Even if we puke," Mike said and then looked ashamed he had smiled.

The rest laughed a little and showed him it was okay. The hallway was cleared without further problems, and they found fewer zeds.

Finally, with all rooms marked, they radioed in a 'clear', and one team helped the supply team gather items while the other stood guard; they stripped the rooms of everything they could use.

Len met with Conner, Kim, and Bryan. "Sitrep?"

Kim told them about Eddie. Len and his team had had no problems like that but had found quite a few zeds.

Kim reported: Misty was trained; she needed practice but was ready for more responsibility. Juan was a natural and took to everything as if he had been trained long before. Alex was doing well, and Rae, who never spoke, moved like a deadly panther. Len was very curious about her story, but she wasn't telling.

Rooms were stripped of every item on Conner's list unless zeds had been in the room with the items.

The supply teams were excited about all of the usable items. Even shower curtains would have some use, they knew. They liked the more comfortable chairs as well, to replace the plain ones in the cafeteria. Fluffy comforters were better to keep warm them, too. With so many sheets, Sally could have people roll bandages from them and use them for many other things. The towels, tons of them, were a great find.

Clearing the fifth and fourth floors was enough; they had enough to sort until midnight now, and they were hungry. Using a lot of soap and then alcohol satisfied Sally, and they called it a day to eat and catch up with the others. Most ate a second serving of dinner.

Doc sat down, weary. "The girl, Tina, is going to lose the foot; the ankle is too shattered, and the lawyer Bart who came in with the crushed hand, he's gonna lose it."

"Can you do that surgery?"

"Well, we can do it. But can we do it without an anesthetist?"

"Oh, God," Len groaned.

"Sally and I plan to tell each one the bottom line. We'll let you know what we decide, but it will be tomorrow morning if we do this."

"Wanda has the children settled, and they are starting school tomorrow. Some of us have moved to the other hallway to give more room," Roy said.

"Okay." Len knew the ones who had moved were those who always had their heads close to Roy, planning and watching. So far, they all did their part, but the division was still clear in military-type and Roy-type.

Beth spent time with Katie and the others she was friends with.

Conner gave Len a lay out of the ground floor of the hotel. He was interested in the restaurant that served the hotel, one that Conner wished he had the right people to get there and loot. "I suspect they have a lot of food there."

"I hate the sound of dealing with so many zeds, but the food is needed to hold us over here longer."

Thinking about a dozen to a hundred zeds were daunting, but they had good teams, and with the location so near the hospital, it was a matter of time before they faced the walking dead anyway.

Len saw Paul and Donna walk by, arguing as usual. He had a lot to think about.

Near his room, he saw Bridget, she of the heavy make-up, perfumes, and fancy hair. They had exchanged maybe a dozen words since she was most often hanging around Roy. He wondered what she wanted.

Bridget smiled and slipped into his arms. Closing his door, he had his answer.

23
BATTLES

"Shhh, don't tell Jules I'm here. Sally released me, but I have to take it easy, and I promised to watch more than taking part." Chauncey grinned as he joined his team. "Sore and all, but I can do this."

"Same orders I got." Julia popped up from the floor where she was checking her backpack. She waved at Chauncey.

He laughed and 'high-fived' her.

"Both of you hang back, and don't get anyone killed while you are trying to do more than you can," Len ordered.

"Alpha and Delta will go in to the left where the doors are and where it should be heavy in zeds. Charlie, you take forward, and Bravo watches our ass and takes right."

They all slid through the cracked wall to the stairwell, then down to the ground floor, exploding out in teams.

The teams moved into place and began firing as soon as they were through the doors; the smell hit them as several dozen zeds began moaning and moving towards them.

It escaped no one that if he were not armed and shooting, the creatures would easily pin him, ripping him to shreds. Several, despite being busy themselves, turned to glance back as they heard unfamiliar shouts and gunfire from the side of the hotel. Len motioned Charlie team to check it out.

Down the way seemed to be where the restaurant was, plus conference rooms and a hotel bar. Charlie team began clearing out the zeds that approached, with Chauncey covering the back, if needed.

Without warning, they were in the middle of the moaning and infected already inside and a group of people being over-taken by zeds, coming in from a side entrance.

"Stay on targets," Kim ordered. As much as they needed backup, the other three teams were neck deep in their own hordes.

The smell was enough almost to knock them over, but the Reds and shambling dead, bodies torn, infected with nasty, thick pus, covered in dried blood, urine, vomit, and trailing open intestines, came at them. They hissed, moaned, and groaned with ropey, slimy saliva dripping from their filthy chins.

The group, who shot back and used baseball bats for melee weapons, was losing. It looked as if they were out of bullets now.

A woman screamed as she slapped hands away, but the creatures tore at her arms, pinning her down and darting forward to rip at her neck and face. Her eyes and cheeks, then nose and lips disappeared into filthy maws, painting them all in fresh crimson. She gurgled. Fingers cracked off, torn from her hands.

A man, trying to help her, fell to a half dozen zeds that ripped at his neck and shoulders. He beat at them, smashing brains to a pulp, spewing gore into his own wounds.

The five remaining on their feet used bats and pipes to bash those between their group and Charlie team. Two were wounded and splashing blood all over.

Kim, Big Bill, George, and Beth, kept firing but the close quarters and lurching moaners were backing them against the wall quickly. The newcomers made it harder to take clean shots.

"Bar, behind you," Kim yelled to them. As soon as they ducked into the bar, he and Big Bill covered the rest while they ran into the darkness and then followed, slamming the doors. Quickly, they shoved furniture into place to block the doors. Chauncey got lamps and candles lit in seconds, so they had a warm glow to assess damages.

"My. God, how many followed you?"

"Maybe fifty." They introduced themselves, thanking Charlie team for the help. "We'd be dead but for you guys."

"You looked as if you were in trouble."

"Bad trouble."

"You all alone?"

"We had ten then; we would have all died if Jeff hadn't gotten us here."

Jeff, filthy in faded jeans and a shirt covered in dried blood, looked a bit under twenty, but he was obviously the leader, with long, lean muscles and glasses that made him look to be a smart jock. "Ran out of ammo."

"Jeff taught us to fight. He kept us together as we found food and other items. He kept us moving forward."

"I just did what I had seen in the movies and in my video games," he said shyly. "I always played zombie-killing games."

"Guess it came in handy."

Kim turned back to the group. "Base and other teams have been advised we are okay here. We need to clear the room."

In seconds, they did a quick search and found themselves safe and alone in the bar. One of the women was bitten, her arm torn to the bone, already deep purple and dripping blood with red and greenish streaks running down her hand and up to her shoulder. She grimaced and moaned with the pain, wrapping it in a bar towel. Johnny handed her a strip of duct tape to hold the towel in place.

The other victim was her husband, and he was bitten on the hand, his pinky stump bleeding. They wrapped his wound in a towel and taped it in place.

"Jeez, this is bad," Jeff looked at their wounds, catching Kim's eye, "looks as if you guys are well outfitted."

"US Militia. We are the remains of the US military. We can offer you a stopping place, or you may join us as 'civvies' or part of the militia. Our new jobs are doing rescue mission," Kim said. "Kimball Decker, US Militia," he hardly stumbled on his new title.

"I wish we had met a bit sooner then," the wounded man said sadly, "but glad you guys are still trying to protect our Country."

"So are we. Wish we had found you sooner. We have supplies, food, doctors, but…"

The man nodded. "I don't suspect you suddenly found a miracle cure, huh?" he hugged his wife.

"Awe, man," the second man said. Earl, in his thirties, tall and lean, was in jeans, a wife-beater shirt, boots, and a ball cap. "Isn't there something you can do with doctors?"

"Afraid not. We understand there is no cure for Reds or for anyone once he has been bitten. Everyone turns into a zed. Sorry...I really am sorry," Kim said, looking to George.

"A bite or scratch that is infected with the saliva will infect whoever has the bite or scratch. Unfortunately, we've seen it personally and not just heard gossip...lost a few friends that way. We sure wish we could have found you sooner and helped so you wouldn't have gotten bitten or have lost your friends."

"This is really bad for us," Jeff said, "we've been on the run, and now this. What can we do for them?"

"I wish we could do something, but there isn't anything that will help. I'm sorry," George said. "But I've sat with some who were bad sick; you'll start feeling numb and feverish. I imagine you're in a lot of pain."

"Already feeling that," the man said, his wife nodding and crying as well. "We don't have long, do we?"

"No. Again, I'm awful sorry. You can wait and...well...you know, but I understand it gets painful and all. Or you can use what I call my terms...'George's Terms'...you can go out your own way."

Beth and Johnny sat several bottles up on the bar with shot glasses. Beth poured for each, pouring into a larger glass for the man and woman who were injured. Big Bill claimed he never drank alcohol, but with his eyes on the couple, he took one shot of rum. Then a second shot.

Outside, the moaners beat on the doors occasionally, shambling around, looking for a way in. From the other areas, shots were heard. Len had reported that all teams were fine and uninjured.

Chauncey told them he had found an empty storage room; he looked pointedly at the couple. In a bit, the man stood and shook hands with his friends, and they patted the woman on her back. "I think it's time we went to sleep, honey," the man said. They had children at college who had called a few days before, saying they had Red and were really ill. They had lost heart, knowing their children were gone.

With an apologetic shrug, the man explained to them that they were Catholic, and Kim nodded.

Kim felt like an angel of death.

George shook their hand, "My terms say we help friends 'go *gently* into the good night'," he misquoted, smiling kindly.

The other woman, Angie, wept into her hands. Johnny pulled her aside to talk to her quietly.

"You guys be safe and give 'em hell," the man said. "Earl, you learn some new jokes and stop being such a redneck." They laughed. "Jeff...like I said...you're young but a smart dude and a born leader. Help these good folks all you can. Angie, it's been an honor; you're a good one for sure." He was bleeding heavily now, and his face flushed with fever. Already the bites were pus-filled and going green, smelling like evil.

He saluted. He and his wife, along with George and Kim, walked into the room, closing the door behind them. No one envied Kim and George the task.

"Can I pour a drink for you all again?" Beth offered. "I hate this."

"Not as much as we do." Jeff sighed. He upended a shot. "Do you have a large group? I mean the radio thing..."

"Over a hundred. We are one of four teams who do search and rescue."

"Impressive. We really would have all died if not for you guys."

Beth nodded. "What you don't know, is that if *you* had made it past that hall and if *we* had not, and if *they* had kept coming, *you* would have run into at least a hundred on the other side."

"A hundred more?" Jeff gulped.

"Give or take a few; our friends are clearing them out and will be over here to get us all out."

"Are you sure? I mean...a hundred?"

"Piece of cake," Beth said, "they can handle it."

"I don't know. If this had happened without you guys showing up, well, I'm out of bullets, and I can't hit them in the head; damn, I'm glad we found you all."

"Seems as if we could take the alcohol out of here, too." Chauncey said, looking over the bar. It was decorated in burgundy and shades of blue with an ocean theme: pictures and nets, shells, oars, and other sea-related pieces.

"Maybe keep it in a locked room; we don't need a bunch of drunks around guns," Johnny noted, "or give it all to Sally and Doc as medicine."

"That's smart," Beth agreed. Her eyes darted again to the closed closet door. She got her radio, "Base, This is Charlie team. Over."

"Base here, Charlie. Go ahead. Over."

"We will be bringing in three survivors, adults, all uninjured. We'll need intake. Over."

"Copy three adult survivors coming in with you. We'll have Doc or Sally standing by when we have an ETA. Over."

"Charlie out."

"What's your base camp like?" Jeff wanted to talk.

Beth shrugged, "We're in the hospital area...basement. We have a cafeteria with food and water, military supplies, a teacher for the kids, teams and a base for missions, and two doctors."

"That sounds like paradise right now," Jeff said.

"Were you military, too?" Earl asked Beth.

"I wasn't. I was recruited. We have some who are, and they train teams to do this. So far, we've done pretty well finding survivors," Beth said. "If I weren't doing this, I would go crazy sitting around, knowing those things were out there."

"We were in a house a while, but we got hungry, and those things kept coming around, making a crowd around us," Earl said.

They jumped as two shots went off at almost the same time.

Kim and George came back and accepted shots of rum.

Kim took a call from Len, and they sat, waiting. Their friends were headed that way.

In the hallway was a barrage of shots for several minutes. "You all okay?" Len beat on the doors. They moved everything that was piled up to let them in.

In a few minutes, the far doors were well blocked, and nothing could get into the hotel. Several accepted a shot of whiskey or rum.

"Hairy out there?"

Len said it was. He met the three survivors and gave condolences on the losses. "While you all relaxed in here with the booze, I thought those bastards would never stop coming; they just poured in."

"That's how it was here, too," Kim said. "But if we had fifty thousand in the area, ten thousand with Red, maybe ten still okay, thirty thousand are where?"

"Out there, maybe twenty with Red, so thirty left, and we have seen less than five hundred healthy and unturned, so we have maybe what? Maybe a quarter are okay and hiding still; eight thousand, the rest are zeds who are gathering in hordes, or people who are dead or walking dead from the blast."

"You think we have eight thousand out there? Alive?"

"Maybe," George said, "no meds, accidents, age...old and too young...and you have less, seven thousand, maybe. Out on farms, in houses and buildings, some in groups in places where there is food; maybe that is right now."

"In a month, the zeds and disease, accidents and other bad situations, will take all but maybe five hundred. I'm guessing. Of those...raiders...people who are unarmed...in two months, I'm saying maybe fifty at best."

"We have more than that," Kim said.

"We may do better while other places will have none; make it out of fifty thousand. It evens out. But I think we are out-numbered."

Bryan took a second shot, savoring the burn of the rum. "Fifty against forty-nine hundred. Wow, gotta love those odds."

"That's why when we can, we ditch the city and go out to the country to find a place," Len said. "I didn't say it was easy."

"They said you're the man to see about this military," Earl said. "I wanna be part and not a victim waiting. I can shoot, just don't gotta gun."

"You will have one." Len shook his hand. "Jeff?"

"Count me in."

"Good, we can use someone who's survived out there and led people." Len shook his hand, too.

"This is Angie." Johnny brought her over. "She's pretty blue about losing two good friends; they lost quite a few."

"I'll do whatever you need me to do to help out," Angie promised. "I have shot a gun before, but I'm no expert, don't love guns, but I can swing a bat and kill those bastards that way, if you want."

"We like anyone who can use a melee weapon, and at times, we fire axes and pipes, whatever works. We'd love to add you and the rest to teams. We need a few more to get eight to a team," Len told her.

He turned to the radio. "Base, this is Alpha Actual. Over."

"Alpha Actual, we read you. Over."

"Base, we request supply teams for the food and alcohol. We will be guarding with two teams and helping with the other two. We, also, will be sending three survivors to you for intake. Over."

"Alpha Actual, we copy: you are sending supply teams, and we will be in-taking three survivors. Over."

"Base. Alcohol needs to go to Sally and Doc. Over."

"Copy that. Alcohol to doctors, over," Dallas barked in the background.

"Alpha Actual out."

Jeff grinned for the first time. "You have a dog?"

"Yep, he belongs to Benny, the radio operator, at Base Actual."

"Food, beds, safety, and a dog." Earl sighed.

"Alpha and Charlie on guard duty, we'll take the other side; you take this side. Other teams help with supplies; Julia and Johnny, please escort Earl, Jeff, and Angie to Base Camp for Sally and Doc."

"On the way, Colonel," Julia said as she and Johnny led the way for the new comers. From the bar, the others began to box the alcohol and cheered as they found huge boxes of bagged peanuts and fresh fruit.

Beth inhaled a lime as she packed it up. In another few days, fresh fruit and veggies would be just a memory.

It was late when all the food was stripped from the restaurant's kitchen and the bar was emptied. They also found that the hotel had served breakfast, so they found cereal, coffee, and much more. The kitchen detail made a party-like meal to celebrate the newcomers of the last few days, and Len okayed some of the alcohol being served as well.

They ate creamy chicken pasta, beans and corn, cheesy rice with vegetables, and a variety of pies for dessert. To everyone's surprise, the children had made colorful paper chains and paper Chinese lanterns which were hung as party decorations. Cheering, they all made a big to-do over what the children had done, and all the little ones grinned. Sally slid into her seat and gratefully downed a glass of spiked fruit punch. "I had the worst day."

"What's up?"

"John, the guy who was flash burned and blinded, died. I think he just gave up and didn't want to live; he was bad off emotionally. Bart, the lawyer, his hand was so crushed; the wrist was shattered, and both were getting infected. I gave him local shots, and then we loaded him up. Doc removed the hand above the wrist, and Bart woke up a few times, crying out and fighting us. We had to get help to hold him down."

"How is he?"

"Dunno. He needs blood, and we have no way to give it to him. I don't know if he'll make it because of that, but I think...maybe...he is beginning to respond a little to the antibiotics. Could be my wishful thinking, but he might be."

"And the girl with the smashed foot?"

"Tina. Her whole foot is mangled. I don't think emotionally she can survive our removing her foot. She's sick, too, drank bad water. I tried to set the bones, you know, today; I removed the bad tissue, but she needs grafts. If she survives and the foot stays, it will be little more than a locked up stub...and painful at that."

"Will the liquor help?"

"Ah, it helps very much." She sipped more punch and smiled thinly.

Len laughed. "I meant, will it help *patients*?"

"It may, thanks."

Benny came over. "Rita is getting the hang of the radio, too; she'll be able to spell me when needed."

"That's good news."

"Did you know Roy and his group are in the other hallway now?"

"Yeah, Benny. I can't say I like the division, but he's good so far on supply teams. I don't know what to think."

"Me either. That man Paul and his wife keep fighting; she doesn't wanna be there, I guess."

They turned to the couple arguing who stood close by. It was escalating. Bryan walked over, "Everything okay?"

"None of your business," Paul snapped.

"It is if you two are upsetting the children and everyone else by screaming."

"We're working it out."

"We are not," Donna yelled back, "I don't like you deciding everything for me; I'm sick of it."

"Everyone here has a voice in the group," Bryan stated.

"Then my voice says I don't want to be down that other hallway. I want to be with the rest," Donna said.

Roy shrugged, "Donna, it doesn't matter; we all work together. Doesn't matter where we sleep. We just aren't part of the pseudo military."

"You have a gun, but we don't. I get nervous," Donna said. "I don't like being ordered to sleep somewhere; I want to decide where I am and what I do in the group; and maybe I want to be in the military search and rescue."

"Hell no. You're my wife, and you're not toting a gun and playing soldier."

"Just like that? I have a right to decide. I am not *owned*." Dramatically, she jerked away from his hand.

Julia, Alex, and Beth were watching, trading knowing glances.

Bryan reached out, and Paul violently moved back. "Don't touch me, you son of a bitch."

"Newcomers' seeing this isn't good," Beth whispered.

"Hey." Len stood, and around the room, Hagan, Kim, Mark, and a few others began to stand.

"Donna, I'm trying my best to take care of you; now come on, or I'm finished," Paul said.

"I'm staying. Please, Paul, stop fighting me on this."

"It's her choice," Bryan said.

"Damn it."

Donna cringed behind Bryan.

Johnny went to her feet, "Let's all knock this shit off. Enough, personal shit needs to go behind doors, not out here, making people nervous."

"Damned right, Johnny," Julia whispered.

"Just let me go, Paul," Donna whined, making Paul tense again and making Bryan react with an offensive posture.

"Just get your stuff, Donna, and stop the scene; it's over," Beth called.

She had seen too many women cause dramatic issues when they should have handled things, simply and easily. It looked as if Donna liked an audience and was pulling Bryan's strings for attention. Donna glared at Beth and Johnny, confirming Beth's opinion.

"My, God, what are you doing, Donna? Are you fucking him yet?" Paul yelled at her.

Roy chuckled.

Bryan was in Paul's face now. Len and several others walked over to keep Bryan from fighting. Hagan suggested that he cool off.

"You have something to say about me?" Bryan demanded.

Paul narrowed his eyes, "Just wondering if my wife were whoring."

"She isn't with me."

"I find that hard to believe; she goes for smart ass dicks like you."

"Maybe she just misses a dick, period," Bryan snapped.

With a curse, Paul swung wildly; Bryan neatly grabbed his wrist, twisting him around so his arm was against his own back. He howled.

Len shouted, and he and Hagan grabbed Bryan while Kim pushed Paul back towards Roy. Roy stroked his gun nervously but didn't raise it.

"This is over," Len stated. "If you can't work as a team, then get out."

Beth watched Donna watch them with spider-cold eyes.

"You can have her," Paul spat at Bryan. Cursing, Roy, Paul, and a few others moved towards their hallway but still close to the rest. Donna moved over to cry against Bryan; he patted her back absently watching the others.

Paul wasn't finished. He looked at Beth, "She'll screw anything in pants; you're losing your boyfriend."

"Funny. I don't have a boyfriend," Beth said as Julia laughed.

"I think that's enough," George added.

"Didn't ask you, old man."

"They all stick together, don't ya'll? Queers, Spic chick, lesbo." He pointed to Beth.

"Hey," Alex protested.

Juan stood up. "Knock off racial remarks."

"I'm not a lesbian; you just said Bryan was my boyfriend; you just name-called like Roy...like some stupid parrot." Beth fumed. She was angry with Donna for starting this drama-fest in front of everyone.

"He can have you both then," Paul muttered, "carry guns, all of you, like some bullies on a playground. Stealing men's wives and shooting injured, sick people; what the hell is wrong with you?"

Steve the man they saved the day before walked over by Paul, "We wanted to go help our friends on the ground floor."

"Your friends were zeds," George told him.

"Shot two more today, I heard," Steve added. Paul shook his head in disgust.

"Infected who asked to be saved from turning into one of those things," Julia said to them.

Conner looked at Pat and Richie who had walked over with Paul, "That how it is? These people save our lives, and you turn on them like this?"

"Not turning on people, just picking my side. I don't like the military shit," Steve said.

Paul and some others agreed.

"Military shit saved our lives," Jeff stated. He was echoed by Conner, Diane, Mike, Angie, and Earl.

"Bitch," Paul said to Beth, "couldn't you keep your big mouth out of this?"

"What did you call her?" Kim came over, face flushed with anger. Beth put her hand out and told him it was okay. She wasn't sure why Paul was blaming her now.

"I called her a fucking bitch," Paul screamed, moving right up into Beth's face, she tripped backwards, barely catching herself.

Kim swung, cold-cocking Paul on the side of his jaw. Paul snapped around and hit Kim, who dodged and landed a blow to Paul's stomach.

Len and Hagan came flying across the room with Mark and Julia right behind them.

Hagan grabbed Paul, Mark grabbed Roy who was going in to fight, Len grabbed Kim, and Julia and Johnny stepped close to Steve. Len yelled, "Okay, everyone, knock it the fuck off. Now."

Both sides stepped back.

"We'll police our own area and come over to help with meals and to eat," Roy stated. "We're done with supply runs until this blows over. There's too much bad blood now."

"Then you better hope you don't need anything but food and water. If you don't help, you don't get the profits," Len said.

"Fine. We don't need you," Paul spat.

"You get attacked; don't look for my help," Len added, "show's over."

Roy took his people and left the cafeteria, going to the far lobby and hallways; he looked unsure if he were glad this had happened. Len told Kim and Bryan to cool off.

"We had 'em." Julia grinned.

Kim looked at Beth. He was normally very dependable, calm, sure of himself, but he was still angry now, and Beth wasn't sure he looked fully stable with fury in his eyes. "Oh, it's okay for now, but it's a matter of time before I kill that bastard." He walked away, leaving Beth stunned.

"Holy shit," Julia said. Alex hugged her.

"I think he's a bit pissed off."

"It isn't normally like this," Alex told the three newcomers. They chuckled.

Earl whistled, "Beats television, huh?"

"They're assholes," Angie declared.

Len motioned everyone to continue on as if the argument hadn't happened. He noted that Rae had been stroking the trigger on her gun the whole time as she watched Roy and his crew with cold eyes.

He really needed to hear her story now.

24
VICTIMS

Deanna watched the bomb hit, fear gripping her. She had used all of her energy caring for the sick family, finally burying Karen and Nelwyn in the garden as best she could. In her short life, she had seen hell in the prostitution and porn business, only being freed when she was fourteen.

How many times had she wished Ed would have taken her home so she could have been in his family? But, now, he was dead of a gunshot. She had tried to honor how good he had been to her, treating her like a human and not a sex toy for hire, by going to her family and helping them. His kind eyes and smile had changed her life.

She had nursed Karen and daughter, Nelwyn, who was Deanna's age. Emptying bedpans and vomit bowls, changing sheets and washing them, and cleaning blood from faces had all been part of her new job. During all that, she also had taken care of Karen and Ed's youngest child. She had read the Bible to Polly.

Nelwyn had gone into a Red coma first, and then Karen had slipped away. Deanna had cracked each in the head before they could come back as monsters, crying as she had done it.

Worrying about the state of things, Deanna filled jugs with water and left the home to shop or scrounge for food. When the earth shook and things fell, Deanna put everyone in the bedroom, then had begun pulling supplies to them in a basket, dumping load after load, carrying everything at a dead run. She put the family cat, Mr. Doody, inside the bedroom with Polly. Her muscles screamed, but she continued making trips with the supplies. Luckily, she moved most before the bomb hit.

A mattress from another room was put over the window, and Deanna had moved the dresser and more furniture over to block it. She closed the door, and never had she been so exhausted before.

"What is that?" Polly asked.

"I guess a bomb of some kind."

"That's bad."

"Yes, it is, but we're safe here. I don't know about this stuff, but I think we have to hide in here for a little while until the poison from the bomb goes away in the rain. I think that's how it works, like in Japan."

"It's poison?"

"Yes, it causes cancer, I think."

Polly hugged her stuffed bear, "My Granny died of that."

"We won't die, but we have to stay inside a while."

"Mr. Doody and I don't like dark."

"Well, we have to stand it 'cause we can't open up the window and we don't have that many candles. We'll figure it out as we go." She slid to the floor to rest, "We're okay; just let me rest a bit, and then we can get organized if I can ever move again."

They slept a lot; Deanna slipped a part of a sleeping pill into Polly's drinks so she would sleep instead of crying for her mother and sister. Deanna cried when she had a few minutes alone.

The bucket for waste smelled bad.

One morning, when Deanna had awakened, stretching her arms and legs and then going cold, she found that was alone with Mr. Doody; Polly wasn't there, but she never had gotten up alone before. So Deanna did a quick search and found that her charge had left the rooms.

Deanna searched all the rooms downstairs, and then ran upstairs to look under beds and in cabinets. Nothing. With dread, she went to the back door, opened it, and found Polly sitting on her swing.

Back and forth, she went in the dirty grey rain and cold. Trees were shriveled, some lying on the ground. The grass was brown. Around them, a few houses were partially rubble, but the damage was less than Deanna had feared. "Hey. How long have you been out here?"

Polly shrugged. "Don't be mad. I had to see."

"But how long?"

"Dunno. The trees look ugly."

"Yes, they do."

"People look ugly, too."

"What people?" Deanna felt scared again.

Polly shrugged again, "Monster people were bloodied and going, 'Grrr' like that. I hid from them, and they went away." She looked at Deanna finally and said, "One man chased a *nekid* woman."

"That's horrible. You shouldn't be out here."

"I know, but I had to see."

"Those people are like the ones on TV. They are all crazy; they will try to take our food; they will try to take you away and eat Mr. Doody."

Polly's eyes filled with tears, "Nooooo."

"Then you do not come out here at all." She stood, and the two headed back into the house. At the door, she paused while sending Polly inside.

Suddenly a huge weight knocked her to the dirty ground; a hand slammed over her mouth. Fear for herself and Polly filled her as she hit at the hand, fighting like a pissed-off cat.

"Shut up, and don't scream, or you'll alert the zeds," a voice whispered. "If I move my hand, will you stay quiet?"

She nodded and sat up.

He looked like the most popular boy in tenth grade, handsome and smart, witty and charismatic. A jock. He was the one all the girls would swoon over. Deanna hated him at first glance.

They heard moaning.

"Let's get inside."

"You're not coming with us," she whispered angrily.

"Yes I am. I am exhausted, and I don't wanna be their next meal."

Deanna could have killed him. "Then go to another house and hide."

"It's only until I can rest a little bit. Then I'll gladly go," he snapped.

"You promise?"

"Yes," he said, as the moaning got closer. She motioned him to follow her as they ran inside, locking the door. Then, once into the big bedroom suite, she locked that door. Polly stared with big eyes.

"He's just here until the monster people go away." She glared at him, "If they find us, it's your fault, asshole."

"Bad-word jar, Nanna. You owe a dollar."

"She's the one who was out there swinging; it would be her fault," the boy said. "You're Nanna?"

"Deanna. That's Polly."

"I'm Josh." He sat. "Thanks for letting me in. It's bad out there."

"Like what?"

He told them, skimming over parts, spelling some words, or just looking at Deanna so she understood and Polly didn't.

Polly went to play, and Josh was able to speak. He had watched his family ill with Red, then comas. They vanished one day, leaving bloody footprints and nothing else. In his search for them, he was chased by zeds. From then on, he hid and ran a lot from the creatures but never saw his parents and brother again.

"Why are you alone?"

"Well, our father, Ed, was killed a while back. He was a policeman, and a teenaged hooker caused him to get shot and killed 'cause she distracted him while he was doing his job," she said, remembering. It was her story, and she could make it up anyway she pleased. "Mom, Karen, died, and so did our sister, Nelwyn. I buried them."

"How did they die?"

"Red."

"Did they," he shrugged, "umm…turn?"

"No." That part was true anyway.

"They all turned," he said.

"They didn't turn."

"Sorry. I may be paranoid, but I feel as if they're all after me, those outside. I've been running for hours."

Deanna wasn't sure what the word 'paranoid' meant, but she nodded anyway. She hated his good education, too. "Just go, soon."

"Most people would want to find others."

"I'm not most people. I'm fine alone with Polly."

When Polly awoke from a nap, later, she was feverish. She showed Deanna the blisters in her mouth. Deanna looked to Josh.

"I don't know; she should be okay unless she drank the rain water; it has some radiation."

Polly smacked her lips, "It was yummy water in the bird bath. When I used to lap it like a puppy, mommy always laughed."

"Oh, my God, Polly, did you lap water from the bird bath?"

"Yes." She pouted.

In a bit, the little girl was racked with stomach cramps that caused diarrhea and vomiting. Deanna stopped asking Josh to leave and sat with Polly, praying, and cleaning her.

While Polly slept, they traded life stories, and Deanna made things up she had seen on television about how she had been a cheerleader and had been in a contest with mean cheerleaders who cheated in the competition. How she had given her friends makeovers so they could win the most popular boys in school, and about her best friends, Rosalie, Emmitt, Alice, and about the truck Deanna owned. How her school had banned dancing, but had won it back by Deanna and friends fighting the school board. She wove deep webs of fantasy, and Josh listened, asking what Edward thought of such and such and how did Jake react, and he laughed at Bella's antics as Deanna wove tales.

In a few days, Polly was no better and no worse.

"I think we should try the hospital, maybe find a way in. Maybe there's someone who can help."

Deanna dreaded the thought of being around new people. She looked at Polly and shivered. Josh always said 'we', and he talked as if they were a team; it was enough to make her panic. She was used to him now.

But Deanna decided they would try, for Polly.

25
VISIONS

Kim gathered a few people together that Maryanne had requested, Beth, Hagan, Len, Mark, and Bryan. He said Maryanne wanted to see only those in her room for something important. Julia and Misty were already waiting for them.

"Hi, Maryanne, how're you feeling?"

"Good, now. I wanted to speak to all of you, but this is really difficult."

"Take your time, then," Len said.

"When all this had happened, Maryanne had a real bad feeling about things. The bomb had been a shock, but not a huge surprise," Misty explained.

"And Sally said that with Maryanne being blind, there was just no way she could have made it through all that rubble and gotten here safely; it had been near impossible, but she did it," Julia pointed out.

"Okay," Len admitted, "Maryanne, you are pretty amazing."

"You'll think I'm crazy when I start talking, but things are bothering me. I have some strong feelings about things, and I feel I should tell you."

"Well, give it a try."

"The last few weeks, I've seen...in my head I mean...this huge light. It made me feel really scared, and I didn't know what it could be. I think it was the bomb going off. There was nothing I could do, and I didn't know when it would happen, but I think that I saw the bomb before it happened."

"Okay," Len let her talk.

"Toni described all of you to me; some of you heard that." They laughed. "But when you are around, I focus on your voice, where you are standing, the heat of your bodies, and scents."

She went around the room, pointing out where each sat or stood. "See? But in my head, you are all lights and colors to me. I see you not as people and bodies, but as lights and colors; it sounds weird, but it's how I can keep up with many people and how I perceive them."

"That kind of makes sense," Beth said.

Maryanne smiled, "You are a deep green, Beth."

"Oh, is that good or bad?"

"Good. Green is earthy and strong, no fakeness, like an emerald." She turned to Kim, "And you are a deep sapphire blue. You walk alone mostly, but you have a true heart and are a searcher. Bryan is yellow-green."

"A coward?" he groaned.

"No." Maryanne laughed again. "Hagan is blue but with purple; that is his spiritual side, and Misty is blue with some green in there; she's changing and becoming bluer, like Mark, matching his color. Len, you are yellow-gold. A leader, but with pain deep inside and you have an important role to play one day."

"What about Roy?" Kim asked what they all were curious about. Beth wondered about Donna, too, but didn't ask in front of everyone.

"Dirty brown and not much light, all his people have that."

"Sounds right to me," Mark said.

"Maryanne, your other senses are stronger, right? To make up for your lack of sight?" Len asked.

"Yes. Sometimes I get other pictures in my head such as snapshots of people, things I wouldn't normally know."

"Is that like ESP?" Misty asked.

"No. I don't know. It's little pictures…snips of ideas…things I know about all of you."

"That's hard to believe."

Maryanne turned to Hagan, "Like your mom wanting you to be a doctor? She was a nanny." He flopped back in his chair, jaw open.

"Thunderhead? Thunder something…he took something away from you," she said to Beth.

Beth went pale. "Thunderheart. The horse that threw my fiancée."

"Misty, your sister had a terrible surgery right before Red. Len, a friend, no…fellow worker…military friend…someone died of a brain problem."

Misty nodded, thinking about her sister's abortion. Len sat back, and he nodded as well. "Brain aneurism in boot camp."

"Okay, I believe," Kim said, and the rest agreed. It wasn't something that they could understand, but Maryanne knew things she could never have known, and they had no choice but to take her seriously.

"I don't peek around in people's heads. There are just flashes I get," Maryanne told them, "and I can't tell fortunes or predict the future or do party tricks."

"If you don't mind, I'd rather believe in magic; it gives me hope," Beth said.

Julia agreed, "Me, too, magic sounds nice."

"I have the feeling Roy won't let things go," Maryanne said.

Len chuckled, "I'm not psychic, and I feel the same."

"Just be aware, and if I tell you something, please don't doubt me, but trust I know something?" Maryanne asked. They said they would believe her. Katie and Toni came running into the room for her attention now.

26
MORE STRUGGLES

"Len," Conner came barreling in, "we have a problem."

"We always do," Len mused.

Close to the sealed lobby doors, the black man whom they had seen drinking beer from his bottle in the paper bag days before, was holding Bridget close to his body, poking at her side with a pocket knife as he giggled madly.

She looked scared to death.

"He won't tell us his name or what he's doing," Conner said.

"Let me go." Bridget squirmed.

"Stay still. We have this," Len said. Roy and his people stood watching. The strange man had grabbed her as they had walked by in a group. Len approached him and said, "Why don't you let Bridget go? You're scaring her."

He cackled, eyes far away and mind gone. The man motioned them back as he fumbled to open the doors to the pharmacy, despite everyone's yelling for him not to go outside.

Bridget cried, screaming for help and begging him to let her go.

As he slipped through the opening, pulling Bridget with him, Juan tackled Bridget, yanking her to safety. They went down in a lump.

Burned, torn and chewed, bleeding and infected hands reached inside as the zeds began to moan and hiss. Although the black man batted back at them, he fell into the arms of the zeds. They tore at his skinny arms with their teeth, scraping his bones as they crunched; one ripped off his ear, sucking at the gristle. He was lost as two zeds fell on him, dragging him to the ground, chewing and ripping wildly.

Juan kept rolling, pulling Bridget further away as Roy reached to grab her.

Len, Mark, and Kim shot at the creatures that kept pushing at the doors, widening the gap. Bryan, Conner, Beth, Julia, and the rest, moved into place to hold them back.

Len gagged as the heads popped open with wet slops of partially cooked brains and chunks of jellied black blood. The zeds always smelled horrible, but these had been burned when the bomb hit, and the under-scent of burned flesh and burned decomposition was ten times as bad.

So that they would have better shots, they kicked at the zeds with their boots, causing them to tumble down, one over another. They shot the man in his head as he got up, eyes milky, torn to the bone in places, drooling, as he joined their ranks. It was the fastest turn they had ever witnessed.

Roy was yelling, "Close the doors."

"Not with them out there," Julia screamed at him, "get out of the way, useless *hijo de perro*."

She moved in as Alpha team began to move out into the pharmacy, instinctually working as a team. Julia and Bravo team held at the doorway, then moved to the left to help. Charlie and Delta stood in the doorway. No one would get past them.

Len's team suddenly lunged forward into the midst, kicking back zeds and blowing them apart. Bravo rushed into place, and body parts and fluids flew. Len and Mark walked backwards, with something behind them, towards the door, yelling for Sally. "Intake, Intake, intake," he yelled back, continuing to fire.

A lucky zed, coming too close, grabbed for Diane, snagging her shirt. Her son, Mike, and Jeff fired simultaneously into its head, seeing teeth and flesh flying backwards.

Johnny pulled Julia to the side to take out a zed whose skin was eaten away to the bone on its skull; she fired point blank. Earl came by, making a head shot each time, pulverizing them as he went, cursing them in anger.

"About clear here," Bryan finally yelled. His nerves were jumping from the terrible smell of the burned walking dead and the sheer number that kept coming, their infernal moans and slobbering noises sickening. His team seemed especially angry, shooting the zeds and then with fury, destroying their head, even stomping on some and kicking at them.

To one side, Big Bill roared and then swung his machete that he grabbed from his back, aiming it right at the hand he held against a wall. *Crack*. His finger flew off in a bloody stream, and he grimaced. Beth yanked her bandana out and wrapped his hand, pointing to the door.

"He's bit; he's not coming in?" Paul sputtered.

"Scratched. But I have their blood on me," Big Bill stated.

"That's a no go," Roy said madly.

Juan pulled Big Bill by him, "He lopped his own finger off; give it a rest, and see if it works."

"I agree," Sally said as she and three other figures in dark clothing, plus Big Bill, went down to medical.

"Different rules for different people," Paul said bitterly.

Thurman glared, "That's about enough. Save it."

"Clear," Len yelled.

Kim and Bryan called the same back.

The area was littered with bodies, intestines snaking in grey-blues, open and stinking while blood pooled in black puddles and brains and flesh oozed. The stink of pus and burned flesh surrounded them. Soon several had vomited.

They came back and closed the doors.

Beth told Len about Big Bill. Len was glad they had saved Bridget, even if he had told Roy they wouldn't help him or his crew. Doc came out and said Sally was still checking people over. "Anyone hurt out here?"

No one was injured.

"How about our newcomers and Big Bill?"

Sally is getting him cleaned up and stitched right now. The three are uninjured: a sixteen-year-old, a fourteen-year-old, and her sister, a seven-year- old. Male, female, and female."

"Those things may have been following them, but we already have a horde at the door, it seems," Kim said, "glad we got the kids…and Bridget."

"Does anyone really know that man?"

"Don't think so; he kept to himself and never spoke."

"Maybe he was crazy; that's horrible," Beth said.

George looked sad, "More and more are going to go crazy; the world doesn't make sense anymore."

"Like the raiders?"

"Them, too. Some are just evil people and are dancing on the graveyard of the world, enjoying the spoils. Some are neutral or were good people, but they lost their minds with all this…a constant nightmare they can't awaken from."

"I feel crazy half the time," Hagan said.

"Yes, I know what you mean," George agreed.

Beth, Johnny, Julia, and Alex were ready to sleep. In their room, Julia snapped off the light and asked, "Do you think we're all going crazy?"

"Yep. I know I am," Johnny told them.

"Maryanne told me earlier, the strangest thing; she said my brother was still alive. He's a doctor. How would she know he's a doctor when I never even talked about him? That is crazy."

"Do you believe it, Beth?"

"Yes, I do, Alex. That is crazy, isn't it?"

"No crazier than anything I've seen or done lately," Julie said.

"Hangin' on by a thread." Alex turned over to sleep.

27
EVIL

For the last few days, everything had been almost peaceful. Len's teams and Base had done admirably, clearing out the rest of the hotel floors to add supplies and searching more places.

Before it was over run, they cleared out the pharmacy area a few times as well, and without incident. From what she heard, the militia teams were doing well, especially with the new additions that had been trained.

Maryanne awoke.

She had been sleeping deeply but now was wide awake; listening to Toni's slight snoring. Had she had a nightmare? She tried to remember but was blank. The dark was heavy. Cloying. Trying to relax, she felt her legs quiver, her heart pound, and her breath go ragged. She was like a child scaring herself with a boogieman in the closet.

Her hands were in tight fists as she shivered; was she getting sick? Sleepiness gnawed at her, and she knew, if she fell asleep, something terrible would happen.

It's coming.

She sat up. Oh, God, it was terrible, and it was almost there. Limbs like ice, she got to her feet, knowing she shouldn't wake Toni, but unsure of where the door was. *Think,* she ordered herself. She had to get to Roy's hallway. It was coming, and it was *death*.

In the side lobby, many couldn't sleep that night and didn't know why.

Kim relaxed, listening to Hagan and Benny debate politics. Diane, her son, Mike, along with Bryan, and all of Bravo were on guard duty. Jeff traded off with Chauncey. They walked the halls.

Beth had gotten up, unable to sleep but a few hours and was braiding Misty's hair while Mark watched. After a peaceful week, they were somehow nervous and jumpy again. Maybe they had drunk too much coffee; she felt wired.

Some of them went toward where Roy's group was to check things.

"Time to walk Roy's hall," Bryan said, "should be fast and easy, and before anyone warns me, I'll keep my mouth shut and temper checked."

"I'll come along and make sure." Beth joined them. "Mike's been doing better lately, and I wanna see him in action doing his guard duty."

"Mark is with us; I'll behave."

"You think I feel better knowing that?"

Bryan laughed, "I heard Big Bill skunked you on target practice today." He stopped walking and looked at Beth.

"He did," Beth admitted. She was still amazed and thankful the man had shown no symptoms of being ill. She said she would be along soon and stopped to check on Sally.

"I'll wait," he said, lighting a cigarette.

Then they heard the yelling. "See, it wasn't my fault," Bryan said.

"I see that."

"Go get Hagan and Len and whomever else you can find," Bryan yelled as Beth took off the way they had come. Her boots thumped as she ran.

Maryanne?

She finally found the door, slipped out, and managed the hall towards where she knew Roy's group was.

The area was laid out in a box formation. Maryanne walked in a door, falling on her rear, but getting up, and trying again as panic rose. Trying to save time, she cut across an open area, slamming her knee into a low table; she stumbled backwards, falling, ripping two of her nails to the quick, and rolling to her back in pain.

It was easier to give up. But 'it' was almost there. Minutes. And she didn't know what 'it' was, just that whatever 'it' was, 'it' was evil, and if she didn't get there in time, death would win. She was seeing horrible images, and she was already too late to help some.

She sobbed.

'It' was here.

In the hall, Bryan ran toward the fight where he saw someone on the floor and Paul swinging a board over him like a bat. Had the zeds gotten in? Johnny was to one side, holding her arm, trying to help Diane who was down with Steve kicking her; Mike lunged for Paul. It wasn't a zed on the ground by Johnny, but was Mark being pounded.

What the hell was happening?

Paul brought the board up to swing at Johnny, and she kicked at him, getting his shin. He side stepped, groaning, and hit Mike, making Diane and the boy yell. "Leave my son alone," Diane screamed. She hit back.

Kim flew out of nowhere, rushing in to protect Mike, but Paul got lucky again with a swipe, cracking it into Kim's rib and arm. A man slammed a pipe into the same spot, driving Kim to the ground.

Bryan tackled Paul.

Roy and a man named Danny, kicked at Mark, who rolled to one side. Roy grabbed another board and hit Mark to keep him down.

"Put it down," Kim yelled. Someone hit Bryan in the back of the head, and he slumped. They were losing this fist fight, and it was about to go to the guns.

"Check fire," Bryan shouted as dizziness and blackness threatened to suck him down.

Johnny reached for her gun but was kicked again; she curled up and turned turtle to protect herself. Cheap bastards had made a surprise attack, and without guns, the militia wasn't shit. She moaned.

Beth saw Maryanne as she ran back with Hagan and Len. "Oh, my God. Are you okay?"

"It's here. He's here," Maryanne said.

"What?"

"Bryan." Maryanne was shouting now, confusing Beth who was trying to get to the rest and help. She winced as if she had been struck, clutching her head and ribs with a bloody hand.

"You want Bryan?

"No. We have to help, or he'll die."

"Bryan?"

"No." Maryanne stomped her foot. "Kim. He'll die. Hurry."

There was a wild fist fight, people on the floor being kicked, injured people crawling, people darting in to kick or use boards to do damage, and people rolling around, throwing punches. Beth tried to make sense of the chaos and saw only random people hitting each other in the dim light. Roy's crew had used pipes and boards to fight with, and it wasn't a fair fight.

A gunshot almost deafened her.

Three men stood, grinning and showing tattoos, dressed in jeans and flannel shirts, holding assault rifles and sporting narrowed, cold eyes. No one moved.

"Well, hello there," one drawled, "I knew that trail led somewhere interesting." They had come from the direction of the lobbies and where the team had met the raiders.

"Where did you come from?"

"My mama's womb, originally, but lately, we followed a blood trail from out there. Someone hurt my buddies; shot them and threw them to the zombies."

"You're with them?"

"Not now, seeing as they're dead," he said it like, *Day-id*, "I'm Frank."

"They did it...killed your friends." Paul pointed.

"Did they? The ones all of you are kicking the shit out of?"

"It was a cheap attack," Bryan said, "using boards and pipes, not wanting to fight like a man fist to fist, cowardly fuckers."

"We came over here and split off of that group, so we aren't with the military," Paul said, wiping his bloody nose.

"That so?"

Roy nodded, "That's true. We broke away from them." He didn't like this at all, but it was done. The situation had gotten way out of hand after some insults, and his crew had used weapons and not fought fairly, but it was much too late for regrets.

"'Cause they're chicken shits," Mike bellowed back, despite his mother's warning looks.

"Well, I ain't," Frank fired at the boy hitting the floor. Mike, inexperienced, went for his gun, and Frank dropped him with a shot to the chest. The other two men with him, Hank and Dave, had guns on the rest. If they moved, they would be shot. Diane screamed, throwing herself over her son.

"Not Mike, no," she wailed hysterically.

Beth and Maryanne stood at the doorway. Hagan was behind them.

"You bastard." Diane flew at Frank, and he stepped to the side, shooting her in the face, taking her beauty. Several cried out. Even Roy blanched, regrets almost smothering him.

Dave jerked Julia to her feet with his gun at her head. "She one of them?"

She didn't curse for once, but stood, dark eyes full of fear and dread.

"Yes," Paul said. "All those wearing army clothes." Steve and Bridget, Wanda the schoolteacher, Chad and Roy, and Richie and Danny stood together now. Roy moved closer to them. Unfortunately, he was in this crew. If he could do it again...

Richie threw the board at Bryan, and his gun went sliding away, "Sneaky son of a bitch," he sneered. "Don't try anything, smartassed."

"Good aim." Frank laughed. "You ain't so smart, are ya?" he asked Bryan.

"Guess not." Bryan waited to be shot, locking eyes with Len; when Bryan was shot, Len needed to act and use the distraction.

"Come here," Frank ordered Beth.

"No."

Dave ground the barrel of the gun into Julia's temple. "Do you think we're joking, bitch?"

"No." Beth stepped closer to them. It was like being right back with the original raiders only this time, Kim, Johnny, and Big Bill weren't hiding, waiting to take them out. "Your friends shot first and took hostages. They tortured our friend."

"I don't care," Frank said. "You care, Hank?"

"Naw."

"Hank don't care." Frank waved the gun around, pointing at each person he saw.

"There's no need for this; we can work together like Roy did with us," Len tried.

"You, Roy?"

"Yeah."

"You in charge of this group here that ain't military?"

"I guess so." He shrugged.

"They're trying to run things?"

"Yeah," Steve said. He didn't like the killing, but he thought it best to be on the winning side now. The sight of Mike bleeding out and Diane's face a mess of skull shards, broken teeth, and bloody skin made him sick. They had survived together. But he was scared for himself and Pat. The others had beaten them pretty badly, despite not using weapons. He felt three loose teeth and a broken nose, lips shredded, and a broken rib.

"He, her boyfriend?" Frank asked Steve about Beth and Kim.

"Don't know, they all chase each other."

"What's your name?" he asked her.

"Beth."

"And who is that?"

"Julia."

"Okay, Beth, you wanna behave so Julia and your boyfriend don't get shot, m-kay?" Frank was deadly; he had done a dime and a nickel for killing. Had the world not offered this beautiful chance to raise hell and for him to enjoy himself, he would have eventually been charged with the beating death of his girlfriend, a meth whore, when the police finally found her remains in a garbage dump.

"Sure," she said, "I can behave."

"You ever want a real man, Beth?"

"Maybe."

"Maybe?" Frank laughed. "I bet you do. You like things dangerous and dirty?"

"I don't know. Never tried that." Beth shivered.

"Maybe we should try it; you'd love it. I'd give it to you like a real man."

"I bet so," she said, "I do know I'd be more fun if you didn't kill all my friends."

"Come over here, and get on your knees."

Walking closer, Beth dropped to her knees. Her legs were so weak it was easy. She could feel her friends worrying, but her fear was fading as she accepted what was going to happen. In this new world, men wanted to rape her and her girlfriends, and they wanted to torture and kill the others. She hated that they were watching her humiliation.

"Beg me not to kill your boyfriend."

"Please, don't kill Kimball."

"Say, 'please Frank'."

"Please, Frank, don't kill Kimball." Despite herself, tears rolled down her cheeks. She wasn't sad, but angry. Furious. If he did as she thought he would, she would die, but she would die only after biting his dick off.

Frank teased, pointing his gun at Kim.

A gunshot exploded beside Frank's head.

Kim rolled as Bryan flopped down to fire. It was unexpected, but they took advantage. They both moved for cover. Dave's head popped open, spraying fine mist all over Julia as she dove to the ground. "Gotcha," Bryan yelled.

Hagan fired, catching Danny as he skittered to safety, and the man's arm was blown in half. He missed Steve and Paul as they zigged and zagged to their own cover. Len shot at Frank, missing as Mark crawled over and tackled Beth to the ground, his body covering her.

Chauncey fell back as Hank fired at them, using Frank's gunshots to try to get the upper hand again. Moaning, Chauncey clutched at his stomach, his face showing confusion, as Johnny fell across him, trying to stop the blood flow. He was hit right above his waistband.

Bryan and Kim both shot a man who was with Roy, one of the quiet ones who had not gotten to safety, two bullets spinning him around, dead. Len aimed at Hank, taking him down with a shot to the chest. He added a few more hits, angry with them all.

The rest were gone, vanished into the hallway and through the lobby where they had fought zeds. Some must be hurt because they left blood spots.

"*Dios,*" whispered Julia.

"What's happening now?" Maryanne cried, dropping the pistol she had grabbed from the floor. It was Bryan's and was the one he dropped when he had been hit with the board.

"Hang on. We're checking," Hagan said, taking the gun and putting his arm around Maryanne.

Sally and Doc came running in as the others gathered to watch.

Kim had bruises on his arm and ribs but was okay, as was Bryan who, Sally said, had a concussion. Johnny had deep bruises all over and maybe a hairline fracture of her arm. Julia and Beth sat, hugging each other for a minute. Misty fell into Mark's arms, but he winced, bruised, and beaten. Doc sadly shook his head as he checked Chauncey; he had bled out, and Johnny had not been able to save him.

Mike and his mother, Diane, were both dead. Angie, whom they had spent time with in the bar and had rescued, caught a bullet from a ricochet. Doc and Sally got her to the medical bay, but the bullet was in her head, and they weren't equipped for that kind of injury. They had three dead and one critical; the enemy had three dead and an unknown amount injured.

"Who shot?" Len asked, as they began to move the bodies.

"Hagan?"

"It wasn't me," he said. "I wish I could have, but they were watching me."

"It was from your direction," Bryan said, "who was it then?" He stopped working, puzzled.

"Maryanne," Beth whispered.

Len dropped Dave's feet as he spun. "What? No f-ing way."

"I just shot. Did I do right?" Maryanne asked, crying.

"You saved us."

"Not some though," she said.

Julia hugged her, "Maryanne, Hon, many more would have died? You did great."

"How…how did…" Len looked to the rest.

"He means how did you do that?" Kim asked.

Maryanne sniffed, holding on to Hagan tightly. "I just could see in my head where to shoot. If I didn't, I saw Kim dying, too, and Mark and Beth, and Julia, Johnny, and Bryan. I saw you all dying."

"You are amazing," Bryan told her. How had a blind woman fired at just the right time and with accuracy?

Exhausted mentally, she leaned into Hagan and fainted. He scooped her into his arms and said he was headed to Doc and Sally with her. He didn't want to leave her side, despite Sally and Doc telling him to go.

"She's magic," Hagan said quietly.

"Well, let me take care of her now," Sally demanded, "Go."

He went back to where the bodies were. The raiders they threw out in the pharmacy with the other corpses. Their three friends went down to the morgue. People pitched in and sealed off the hallway so that they couldn't be reached through any of the other lobbies. The pharmacy doors were now the only way in and out.

Kim pulled Beth aside and sat with her, "Are you alright? God, you keep getting threatened, and I can't do a damned thing to save you."

"I'm fine. I was scared for you."

"You begged on your knees; it made me sick." Kim buried his head in her neck. Strangely, she felt an odd fluttering in her stomach. Beth gulped and tried to control her feelings. If she turned her head, would he kiss her?

She felt his lips against her neck and the fluttering became warmth all down her body.

"Kim, we need some help," Len called from far away.

The moment faded, and she looked at Kim in the eyes. There was a promise there that death had not taken.

28
FALLING APART

The night after the attack, Beth went to Kim to check his bruises as per Sally's orders. It was almost bedtime, and he was in his small room. For days, Beth had been more conscious of his eyes on her or how they always sat close together and walked guard duty together. So busy surviving, she had forgotten to notice the world around her was still turning.

With his shirt off, Kim grimaced a bit as she ran her hands over each discoloration. "Sorry it hurts." He was doing better, but they had taken a severe beating in the fight.

"Feels nice." He smiled.

"My hurting you feels nice? That's sad."

"Just your hands," he hung his head, embarrassed, "I like it."

Beth paused. "Me, too."

"I don't care if the world goes to hell. I met you." He looked at her again, watching her eyes, and then gently reached to pull her close, kissing her softly. She moaned, desire hitting her full force with so many feelings she hadn't wanted to admit. He began to kiss her more urgently, and she yanked her tee shirt off to feel his warm skin on hers. It should be just them; there wasn't room for anything else, but what they had released.

As Kim made love to her, he whispered, "It's always been you." Even joined like this, Kim didn't feel close enough to her; he wanted more.

"Always," She promised him.

"I love you, Beth." And he showed her over and over that night until they fell asleep, exhausted. He held her tightly against him to sleep.

She moved into his room.

Len insisted on heavier guard duty now, and they took in a few more survivors, despite the people's having to come in through a landscape of hell: the pharmacy. While they had moved most of the bodies, they were still close enough to reek; Benny was right in that fewer zeds came around now that the smell was so thick.

Without Wanda to teach the children, another woman took charge.

Angie, her head ruined by the stray bullet, died two days after being shot.

The inactivity might make them safer, but they were restless, and depression was thick in the air.

Dirty water, oily and grey, seeped in now, pouring and trickling everywhere from above, pooling around the rooms on the floor. A few ceilings came tumbling down, one tossing a rotting, severed arm out among the debris. With eyes on the above, they feared the whole thing would come plummeting down on top of them.

Some of the rooms, such as the cafeteria, were still stable as were many other parts, but the medical area was looking less safe.

One of Sally's patients was developing thick keloid scars from the burns and should have been doing better by now since she had been there over three weeks, but some of the burns looked infected in a way Sally was unsure about.

Doc said he wondered if the blast had thrown the Red infection into the air, and if it had, did it have a long incubation. If so, then this was what was happening, and if so, any injury might lead to becoming a zed.

She watched the infection closely and waited for it to take on the tell tale smell that would indicate Red.

Likewise, Bart the lawyer, whose hand she had removed after it was crushed, should have been doing better by now even though he had lost a lot of blood and had been very ill with normal infection, but he was still very sick. Sally almost cried as she saw a trickle of water soaking his bed. In disgust and pity, she began moving his bed away from the flow of water. She would have to get him dry, put on clean sheets, and change the bandages. To her horror, the trickle became a full flow, like that from a water hose. She yelled in frustration.

"Sally?" asked Bob who had been coming in to pray for the patients.

"We're getting soaked," she said.

Across the room, the other man was getting splashed as well. Some bricks, a few pieces of concrete, plaster, wet and gluey, and boards fell, sliding into the room with a deluge of water.

"I need to get them out of here," she yelled, pulling at Bart's bed.

Calvin's bed was on the other side of the room, and now debris was between her and him; it would be a bitch to get his bed moved with the trash in her way. Bob was calling for help. But Sally would soon have her patients back, clean and dry.

Conner and Juan rushed in to help. Conner grabbed Bob's wheelchair, and they both lifted it backwards and sent him rolling back down the hall, as Conner called for more help.

The men yelled to Sally to get out as chunks of debris fell, several pieces leaving bruises on the men. Sally was frozen, between her patients, her face terrified. "I have to get them out," she called as pebbles pinged down in a constant rain now. A chunk of concrete fell, slashing her head open, and she bled onto Bart's bed, the water turning it pinkish grey.

Conner tried to get into the room, but a barrage of snapped boards fell in front of him, causing him to back-step back out. "Sally, now, get out."

Sliding, roaring, like a landslide, the above debris fell into the medical area, burying everyone and everything to the top. Sally screamed once. Conner and Juan barely stumbled to safety, falling back into the hall beside Bob's wheelchair.

"Who? What?" Johnny yelled, running to them.

"Sally, Bart, and Calvin."

"Oh, hell." Doc and Tink saw the damage.

"Let's get them out." Johnny reached for a brick. "I need help."

Bob wheeled over. "Johnny, hey…"

George stepped in and took Johnny's arm, "They didn't make it, Hon; they're gone." The rubble was solid, compacted, and huge. No one could have survived, and it was best to let the dead rest."

"Oh, Sally." Johnny sat back.

"My father was a contractor," Len stated, "some of this place will stand for a hundred years and be perfectly safe; then, some of it is so weak; it's crazy."

"Is it all falling in?" Misty asked as she arrived with Mark.

"No. I don't think so. We should have moved her and the patients out."

Doc looked sick. "Too late for them."

Len said they would move the rest to a safer place with all the medical supplies they had gathered; it took all day to move everything and everyone. During, the next few days, they went over all the rooms, moving supplies and people if the ceilings looked unsafe.

The rain finally stopped, and everyone again grew restless with nothing meaningful to do.

"One day, it'll be time to go out," Bryan said.

"No way," Misty declared, "you wanna go out with the zeds that are out there hunting us and everything else?"

"We can't stay forever; the food will run out, and I bet the generator is very, very close to being empty of fuel," Kim said. "We're running out of time."

"There's nothing out there."

George nodded, "It seems that way, just monsters wanting to bite us, but there's more, there are people like us, and we'll see sunshine and find a safe place, grow fresh fruits and vegetables, gather animals to raise…rebuild."

"With no running water, electricity, or Internet?" Alex frowned. "How do we do that?"

"We have gasoline though," Hagan said.

"It ruins in a few months, so no, we won't have that either," Len said.

Alex sat back in his chair, "Then, how do we survive?"

George laughed, "Believe it or not, man has survived far longer without those things than with them."

"But those were the old days."

George patted Misty's hand, "And what was old is new again. We have to rebuild the world the old way."

"Without power tools," Kim added, sighing.

"How can we have shelter and gather food when things hunt us?"

"Misty, cavemen did it; we can if we relearn." Mark promised her, but she didn't look convinced as she looked at Alex.

"Maybe this is why the Red happened; we all got too dependent on technology and science and forgot the old ways."

"Like God did this?" Misty frowned at Bob who said it wasn't God that had sent Red.

Benny thought, "Not God...but nature. Nature corrects itself. Man is part of nature in a way. We got too dependent, and man or nature or both corrected it. We made a real mess of the world with red and the bombs but think of the messes before...over population...extinct animals and plants. We had used up most of the fuel sources and had been polluting water. As bad as what we did, maybe we rescued the planet from ourselves."

It was a lot to think about.

"Survival of the fittest," Beth said, "Bryan and Len talked about this: how the strongest pairs would survive and reproduce."

"Ah, the lottery," Len chuckled.

"I won you." Johnny poked him in the arm.

"Here we go again," Beth said.

"How are we supposed to rebuild and reproduce with those monsters chasing us and biting us?" Alex demanded.

"There lies the big question." Benny admitted. "I guess we also have to be smart and clever to survive this."

"Dumb people will die out? Good, there goes ignorant Roy and his camp then," Alex said.

"Drunks and the dumb always have some side luck going," Len reminded him.

Bryan said he was curious to go out.

Most said they weren't going until they had to.

"I'm thinking a big RV and a few SUVs for the road," Bryan said. "We could modify an RV if we had one; shoot from the top like a fort."

"That didn't work well in movies."

"We're smarter than the people in movies."

"I wanna look for my brother; Maryanne says he is alive and he's a doctor," Beth stated. No one argued now with anything that Maryanne said.

"I miss Sally," Misty said.

"Maybe two teams out and two staying here for guard duty, just a short look around to get an RV to modify, two nights out or so."

"Makes sense, Len," Kim said. "Maybe the women should stay here where it's safer."

"You so want an ass whoopin'." Julia threw an empty can at him. With a chuckle, he ducked.

"If Mark goes, I go. If he stays, I stay," Misty said.

Beth gave Kim a look that said the same; she could tell he would argue the issue with her later when she didn't have Julia to back her.

"We can't leave this place unguarded. I doubt Roy or Frank's group forgot us," Hagan said. Several glanced at Donna. She had tried to fit in now, but some still distrusted her.

In restlessness, people drifted around the area.

Misty drew Beth to the side, "I still haven't gotten my period. You don't think…" She pointed to her stomach.

"Sally and I talked about it; none of us have. It could be the stress, maybe the radiation, or like Benny said, nature correcting things."

"Oh."

"You might want Doc to look at you," Beth told her. "I guess some of us aren't using birth control; I didn't even think about it much."

"You love Kim?"

"Yes. I think I have since I first met him, just took me a while to realize it. He knew all along." She laughed. "But we don't need pregnancy adding to the problems. I think we all need to get with Doc."

"The other girls, are they not having periods?"

"Not Maryanne or Johnny."

"What if we're, ya no…"

"Sterile? Then Benny is both right and wrong in his theories."

"Is Maryanne magic?"

"Well, she's as close as we have to magic now. She didn't foresee what happened to Sally; she said she only sees a few things. When she gets those feelings, then those are things she can somehow, change, I guess. Like she did when she shot the gun."

"That was unreal. I get a weird feeling sometime…not like her…but…" Misty looked for the words, "as if some are bad…Roy's group and Frank…maybe we are good or trying to be good, and we have Maryanne."

"George and Benny said something like that." They said that if the theories were right, then maybe the world was re-set to good and bad, evil and honorable, and magic would be magic again."

Misty giggled, "I heard…I thought they meant like King Arthur and the Holy Grail and knights, the magic sword."

Beth looked at her in a strange way.

"What? I sound stupid, huh?"

Beth shook her head, "No, that suddenly made sense in a weird way. It fits in with what they said. Why not magic again, when we need it the most. I have read the Bible and a lot of that was magic. Noah used magic when he built the ark; maybe we use different words, but it all means powers of nature and our minds and maybe God or the devil."

"So we're all magic, maybe?"

"Maybe. I do know we're way too lucky most of the time, and that makes me feel we have a bit of the good magic or God on our side. Bob says we do, anyway."

"That's deep."

"Way too deep."

"Come in here." Misty found Alex and got him to join them with Johnny. "I have saved this all this time." She pulled out a home-rolled marijuana cigarette.

"No way!" Alex hooted. "Misty, you are so bad."

They shared it, giggling.

"Beth?" Kim knocked and came in seconds after the four had finished. They looked at him guiltily. "Umm…wow, I like the air freshener you guys have."

Johnny fell to the floor, laughing with Alex.

"I did it," Misty said.

"You did? Well, next time, why don't you selfish pigs share with Mark and Julia and Len and me?"

"I didn't think you would all approve."

"As if we would judge. When Julia comes in here, she's gonna be furious you left her out," he said.

"Next time," Misty said with a grin, patting her back pocket.

"Bryan thinks we will have to clear out Roy and Frank and not wait 'til they come back here trying to kill us for food. Several agreed."

"They killed friends of ours. Mike and Diana, Angie, and I liked Chauncey a lot," Johnny said.

"But zeds don't shoot back, or will they?" Alex pointed out.

They rejoined the others for the discussion.

"I know a way in to where they are; we go in, take them out, and then come back; if we don't, they'll come here for us," Bryan said.

"If we do this, we do it my way. I take a special team, and no one bitches. The rest stay and guard, and if we don't come back, well, Kim will be in charge."

"Guess that means I'm not going," Kim said. Beth relaxed a little.

"I go, Bryan, Conner, Juan, Earl, and Rae," Len said.

"That's it? You're crazy; I don't care if you did say not to bitch," Julia said angrily.

"We can move faster and more quietly this way. I'm leaving some who can defend well, if we don't make it back; it's what I feel is best."

"We can ask Maryanne," Misty said.

"No. She'll worry and not want any of us to go. This is my choice. If any doesn't want to go, tell me now."

No one said a word.

They gathered close to the radio that Benny manned and helped double check packs and weapons. Len wanted everything they might need, but still wanted to travel light. Julia gave Len a big kiss on his mouth that made everyone laugh.

"'Len's terms'. No prisoners," George whispered to Len.

"Damned right," Len said, "All of the time, I feel as if they're biding their time until they come over here to kill us."

"Nope, they won't let it go; they're bad men," George said simply.

Len said it was time to go.

The route Bryan had planned for them took some crawling through tight places and scrambling up and down rubble, but it didn't take very long. They were finally right outside the lobby which they had once used on supply runs for the radio and intake, where they had looted vending machines, and where the zeds had crashed through the glass, back what seemed years ago.

The weeks had gone by slowly and yet fast as well. They took a second to recall how well the operations from here had worked. In places, the above floors had fallen in with the rainwater.

The second lobby was still filled with broken zed bodies; they had to pull bandanas over their noses against the reek of decomposition. This was the place that had given them several nightmares since the battle.

More debris had settled in with water, making it more horrific to view. Skirting it, they went down the hall, then into the hole in the floor where the rest had fallen that day. Bobby's body was still there but covered. The smell of it and the zed that had been in the cracked wall, made a miasma of stench.

Next, they climbed upwards to where Len had faced the raiders the first time. The blood trail from those injured led there. He felt a wave of hatred for the men they had killed there and wished the situation had gone better for Warren, whom they also had left, covered.

"This is where you faced those nuts the other time?"

"Yeah, Chauncey was a hero then." Len missed the funny guy who had been so brave and loyal.

"They need to pay," Juan grumbled, "they had more chances than they deserved."

Bodies, wet from seeping rainwater, reeked, causing all of the team to shiver and wish they could be free of the smell; nothing smelled as bad as a decomposing human.

They went down the mostly cleared hallway, dodging debris and listening for the raiders as they went.

"What the hell?" Conner sniffed. There was a sickly scent of roasted meat that made their stomachs growl. Empty cans from food and the remains of the raiders and Warren made the stench bad, but the smells of cooked meat were strong. Bryan motioned them to follow him as he went down a hallway.

"How do they have fresh meat?" Juan complained, "A deer or something? Are they hunting?"

Eyes darting into every corner, they didn't see anyone or anything.

"Smells like pork," Conner agreed.

Len grabbed Bryan's shoulder and stopped, sinking to his haunches a moment, thinking. They looked at him quizzically as he sat there a second, his face greenish white. "It isn't pork unless you count long pork," he muttered sickly.

"Huh?" Earl asked.

"They may have cooked a person." Bryan gulped, giving Len a hand up. "Maybe it was a pig; maybe it wasn't a human."

"That's bad." Earl rubbed his mouth.

They came around the corner, and Juan vomited as he saw, thrown into a corner, a skeleton stripped to the bone. It was not disjointed, and the flaying tools were thrown behind, so they knew a zed had not done this to whoever it had been.

A second skeleton was close by. Both had been carefully stripped on the legs, arms, and buttocks, its chest and stomach opened, most likely the liver and other choice parts had been eaten, as well. They looked at each other with pale, furious faces. This was butchery.

"Shhhh," Bryan whispered as he darted to the side.

A blur flashed forwards, and Len slammed his gunstock neatly into the man's head. He took a few seconds to keep hitting until the head split open.

Paul vaulted at them with a snarl, looking more animal now than human as he was covered in dried blood, grease, and soot around feral eyes. He was human. Rae fired once, dropping him to the ground, but in anger, Juan added a second and third bullet to the man's head.

From a dark spot in the room, Wanda screeched at them, drawing an unsteady gun upwards, spinning wildly to scream at him as she tried to stead the gun.

Earl behind her, stepped in, pulled her back to his chest as he snaked his arm across her and neatly dragged his big knife across her throat, cutting her open and tossing her to the side so her blood didn't pollute him. With a frown, he wiped his knife on her pants. Len took shots and dropped targets as Bryan searched for more movement.

Finally it was quiet and still. The team hadn't even broken a sweat and was still looking for blood, so furious were they over the cannibalism.

Chad, on his back in dirty rags, lay watching them, his arm swollen like a tight black sausage, the skin splitting to leak pus. The skin was mottled yellow, black, green, and purple as it rotted. "Hi," he said cheerfully, eyes bright with fever.

"Anyone else hiding here?" Bryan nudged him with his gun barrel, wincing at the smell when Chad shifted, his arm gushing vile fluids.

"Naw. They were waiting for me to die. You seem to have gotten them all." There was no concern for his fallen partners.

"Doesn't look like that'll take long for you to die and find those flames waiting for you." Len glared. "I hear burning for eternity is a real bitch."

Chad grinned manically, "Can't be much worse than this."

"Oh, it can be," Juan promised.

Len looked around, "Pretty stupid for them to attack us like that."

"They were hungry again," Chad said, "I was next and taking too long to die, but when they got close, I chomped at them."

"You infected?"

"Naw, but they scare pretty easy."

"Where's Roy? And the others?"

"Out looking for food." He grinned grotesquely, "I guess you saw Steve and what's her name. His wife, Patty."

Juan heaved, "That's sick, Dude. I knew them. We hid together a few days."

"They were a bit out of their minds, but that is just wrong," Conner added. "Didn't have to be this way if they hadn't gotten in with you sick sons of bitches."

"You will find some more bones back down there if you look enough," he said. "We had to eat. They found survivors and brought them back here for food." He laughed hysterically for a few seconds. "I was starving, you try being that hungry and smelling roasted pork."

"It wasn't pork." Bryan spat on Chad in fury. "There's plenty of food out there, cans and cans of it for the taking."

"But not fresh meat."

Rae kicked his injured arm, sending him into screams of pain. It was a bit before he stopped howling and just cried quietly.

"Frank made us do it anyway; he's one bad mother fucker. If you had seen what Frank and Paul did to that girl first, you'd be glad they killed her finally, if you have any pity for anyone. It was enough to scare us all shitless; she was begging to die there at the end. Wanda was worried she was next, but I think Frank likes 'em pretty."

"You all should have stopped him."

"Well, should have, could have, too late now. Roy, and even Richie are scared of Frank. We all fear the bad-ass dude."

"Who's left?"

"Frank, Roy, Richie, and a girl. And hey, I got what I deserved, hurts bad. You should all be glad." He coughed wetly, "I bet they don't come back; they just left us here."

"Nothing here," Bryan reported to Len. "Looks like they did cut out and leave them. Why'd they leave Paul?"

"Check his hand; he got bit this morning, tip of a finger, and didn't cut it off; he was gonna turn, or maybe he turned when you got here. I don't know, don't care. They didn't leave us anything but that empty gun Wanda was toting." He laughed at the thought. "You got water?"

"I have *my* water; don't want your germs in it." Juan took a drink from his own canteen, showing off as he savored it, "That's good, cold water."

"You have no regrets, huh? For what you did?" Len asked him, curiously.

"Not so much. I regret I'm in pain."

"Not that you were part of killing some good, innocent people? You had it a lot better with us."

"Yes, I did, but I didn't have that good barbecued pork roast." Chad winked. "So, you wanna finish me off? Put me out of this pain?"

"I'm more prone to feeding you to a zed. Alive," Len sneered.

"You wouldn't do that."

Bryan snickered and gave Chad a wink. "Bet?"

"Awe, no, hey."

"We can hamstring him so he doesn't decide to follow us," Earl said, waving his knife happily at Chad.

"I have a sure-fire way," Bryan promised.

"Give the rest of the raiders our best when you get to hell, Chad," Bryan told him. Chad whined and begged them to finish him off, but they moved back down the hall, without looking back at him.

As they left the chamber of horrors, Bryan showed them what he had gotten from Billy and Bobby a while back. They had only a few, but these would seal that area and solve many problems.

"Good plan. Let them all be buried together so no one ever finds that place again," Len said.

Bryan tossed the grenade and yelled, "Fire in the hole," as they ducked.

They barely got through the little room that had fallen in, where Bobby still lay, before that too collapsed into a tomb. Bryan spared a second grenade to destroy most of the lobby where they had fought so bitterly. The entire area had felt dark with evil. They had let Bennie know before they did it, and now they radioed that it was finished.

"Base Actual says thank you," Benny said, "come on home. Out."

29
CHANGES

By the time the team members got back to the safe zone, everyone had heard the thunder of the explosion; the team members told everyone what was used to seal off the area. Conner told the others what they had seen, looking sick as he told parts of the story.

"Cannibals?" Hagan gagged. "What the hell?"

"I knew they were evil," Johnny said, "good riddance, but too bad all of you didn't get the other four of them."

Donna looked shocked, and tears filled her eyes; she ran from the room.

"I forgot Paul was her husband," Conner said.

"It makes me feel sick, but is anyone really shocked by what evil people can do?" Benny muttered.

"It's easier to be evil, maybe," Beth said.

"And have no doubt they will organize and work harder than we do."

"That's not so."

Benny cocked his head, "Really? The name Hitler ring a bell?"

Before they slept that night, Len thanked Rae for going with them. She paused. "My parents. They were members of the Israeli military. People here still fear and hate those from my home, so I don't speak; thus, they don't hear my accent and hate me."

"I think they'd still like and respect you, Rae."

"I would rather stay quiet with my own thoughts. But Len, I, too, am a good person even if my accent frightens people sometimes." She gave him a quick salute and left to be alone.

He knew her story now, and yet, it didn't explain a thing.

The atmosphere was different in the morning. "We have reacted a lot. We did reach and rescue, but it was a reaction, too. The last time I felt any type of real pro-action was back when we went to George's neighborhood."

"It was bad, and I could hardly shoot, but I felt more alive," Beth said.

"I'm tired of hiding."

Everyone looked around, holding one another's eyes, searching, asking what each should do. The best plan was to send a large team out that could split off as required and to leave a strong force behind. Len was determined to hunt down Frank and his crew and finish them.

Beth, Misty, Johnny, Katie, and Maryanne cried together that night.

George, Tink, Benny, and Thurman said their farewell, feeling the four would never again be together.

Bryan, Kim, Len, and Hagan shook hands and finally hugged each other with no embarrassment; two were staying.

Mark openly let tears fill his eyes, saying he knew he'd never see his friends again.

And in the morning, on the twenty-eighth day after the bombs, fifteen survivors said their last good-byes, readjusted heavy packs, and stepped out into hell. They didn't look back as they passed the point of no return on the horizon.

(Fort Worth)

ICE STATION ZOMBIE
JE GURLEY

For most of the long, cold winter, Antarctica is a frozen wasteland. Now, the ice is melting and the zombies are thawing. Arctic explorers Val Marino and Elliot Anson race against time and death to reach Australia, but the Demise has preceded them and zombies stalk the streets of Adelaide and Coober Pedy.

www.severedpress.com

The Coalition

When the dead rose to destroy the living, Ron Cutter learned to survive. While so many others died, he thrived. His life is a constant battle against the living dead. As he casts his own bullets and packs his shotgun shells, his humanity slowly melts away.

Then he encounters a lost boy and a woman searching for a place of refuge. Can they help him recover the emotions he set aside to live? And if he does recover them, will those feelings be an asset in his struggles, or a danger to him?

THE STATE OF EXTINCTION: the first installment in the **COALITON OF THE LIVING** trilogy of Mankind's battle against the plague of the Living Dead. As recounted by author **Robert Mathis Kurtz.**

www.severedpress.com

MACHINES OF THE DEAD

The dead are rising. The island of Manhattan is quarantined. Helicopters guard the airways while gunships patrol the waters. Bridges and tunnels are closed off. Anyone trying to leave is shot on sight.

For Jack Warren, survival is out of his hands when a group of armed military men kidnap him and his infected wife from their apartment and bring them to a bunker five stories below the city.

There, Jack learns a terrible truth and the reason why the dead have risen. With the help of a few others, he must find a way to escape the bunker and make it out of the city alive.

www.severedpress.com

JUDGMENT DAY

Dr. Jebediah Stone never believed in zombies until he had to shoot one. Now they're mutating into a new species, capable of reproducing, and the only defence is 'Blue Juice', a vaccine distilled from the blood of rare individuals immune to the zombie plague. Dr. Stone's missing wife is one of these unwilling 'munies', snatched by the military under the Judgment Day Protocol.It's a new, dangerous world filled with zombies, street gangs, and merciless Hunters desperate for a shot of blue juice. Has the world turned on mankind? Is Mortuus Venator the new ruler of earth?

www.severedpress.com

TIMOTHY
MARK TUFO

Timothy was not a good man in life and being undead did little to improve his disposition. Find out what a man trapped in his own mind will do to survive when he wakes up to find himself a zombie controlled by a self-aware virus

www.severedpress.com

NECROPHOBIA

An ordinary summer's day.
The grass is green, the flowers are blooming. All is right with the
world. Then the dead start rising. From cemetery and mortuary,
funeral home and morgue, they flood into the streets until every
town and city is infested with walking corpses, blank-eyed
eating machines that exist to take down the living.
The world is a graveyard.
And when you have a family to protect, it's more than survival.
It's war.